CROWN OF SHADOWS

A RELIC HUNTERS NOVEL

KERI ARTHUR

Cover Art by JMN Art—Covers By Julie

All characters and events in this book are fictitious. Any resemblance to
real people, alive or dead, is entirely coincidental.

ISBN: 978-0-6453031-0-0

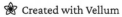 Created with Vellum

With thanks to:

The Lulus
Indigo Chick Designs
Hot Tree Editing
Debbie from DP+
Robyn E.
The lovely ladies from Central Vic Writers
JMN Art—Covers by Julie for the amazing cover

CHAPTER
ONE

I f you believed traditional folklore, pixies were short folk blessed with a love of dancing, a fondness for stealing, and a penchant for leading travelers astray. Some believed we had pointed ears and wings, while others declared we were green of skin and clothes.

Absolutely no one ever painted a pixie as a six-foot-six bear of a man with short but unruly red hair and eyes the color of frost-kissed grass.

"Bethany, my darling," he said as he stumbled down the tavern's old wooden entry steps and then staggered sideways into a table. Wood splintered under the impact, but he either didn't notice or didn't care. "It's been ages since we've seen each other."

"It's been a whole week." I crossed my arms and regarded my brother from behind the relative safety of the bar. "I thought you'd given up drinking?"

"I have." He lowered his voice and dramatically added, "Nary a drop has touched my lips since All Hallows' Eve."

Meaning he'd lasted nearly a month and a half. Which,

if I was being at all honest, was something of a record for him.

He crashed into another table and then tipped over several chairs. I briefly considered going out to help him— maybe directing him *onto* a chair rather than into them— but he was ten inches taller than me and twice my width. If he toppled, he'd not only take me with him, but damn near crush me.

"So if this"—I waved a hand at his unsteady progress forward—"is not drunk, then what the hell is it?"

"This is ... I don't know what this is."

I raised an eyebrow, absolutely not believing a word. My brother was capable of many things, but lying well wasn't one of them.

He slapped a hand on his chest, the sound echoing through the tavern's shadowed stillness. "I swear—on our sainted mother's soul—that I have not had a drink tonight."

Our mother had been no closer to sainthood than one of the shadow folk, but he'd never make such a declaration if it weren't true.

He crashed again, this time driving a table into one of five sturdy oak posts that basically held up the place. The table shattered, and he crashed to the floor in an ungainly heap.

"Up," he muttered, suddenly sounding a whole lot more sober and serious. "Help me up. I need to leave."

"When you've only just gotten here? This has to be a record for sibling visits, Lugh."

"It's not a visit. I was just taking a shortcut."

"To the lane? Why?"

"Easier to get lost."

"And why do you need to get lost? What have you done this time?"

He waved the question away and, with a low growl, rolled onto all fours and made a somewhat ungainly attempt to rise. He didn't succeed.

"Damn it, Lugh, will you just stay down? I'll get you some coffee to dilute whatever the hell this is—"

"It won't help."

A statement that said he at least suspected what was happening to him, despite his earlier disclaimer.

He slapped a hand against the oak post, and an odd sort of a shiver went through the building. I briefly raised my gaze, studying the old beams as dust rained down. It almost looked as if the smoke-stained floorboards above our heads were crying, and, in some respects, that wasn't far from the truth. It wasn't only the two branches of elves —light and dark—that had some form of rapport with nature. We pixies did as well, and for our particular branch, it was trees. Whether they were alive or dead, in the forest or in furniture, didn't matter; we could manipulate it all. That oak post—and indeed the entire structure of the building—had reacted to the unintended fierceness behind the blow.

"Up," he repeated. "I must get up."

I rolled my eyes and came out from behind the bar. Obviously, he wasn't in a sensible sort of mood tonight. If I didn't act, I might not have a tavern left in the morning. And this place—which Mom had renamed Ye Olde Pixie Boots when ownership had passed to her a hundred or so years ago—was not only right in the medieval heart of Deva's walled town and one of the oldest in Cheshire County, but part of the heritage listed Deva Rows. Its destruction would lead to all sorts of dramas with the local heritage council, and we were still in their bad books after Gran had made an illegal extension to the roof structure—one that had made the third floor livable for us taller folk—some one hundred and fifty years ago.

Lugh waved in my general direction. "A little help here, if you please."

I gripped his hand but didn't help him up. Instead, I stepped closer and pressed my fingertips into his shoulder. He might be ten inches taller and physically stronger than me, but pixie women had one advantage over our male counterparts: an ancient goddess had blessed us with the so-called six gifts of womanhood—beauty, a gentle voice, sweet words, wisdom, needlework, and chastity.

Of course, the women in *our* particular branch of the pixie tree had apparently gone into hiding when most of those womanly accomplishments were being handed out— especially the whole chastity thing. The only virtue we really could claim was a variation on the gentle voice and sweet words theme—we could calm people down with our voice and our touch.

It was a very handy gift to have when running a tavern that served all races, though it wasn't exactly a cure-all when it came to fights. Humans and shifters were easily swayed, as were the bulk of those who came under the fae umbrella—faerie, other pixies, dwarves, and most of the night folk—but it was a very different story when it came to the two branches of elves. For one, they had an intense dislike of each other and weren't easily distracted when things got inflamed; two, neither could truly hold their alcohol; and three, they were immune to our wiles. It made for some interesting evenings when things inevitably got heated.

Which was one of the reasons I usually wore my knives when working.

"Lugh, please stop trying to get up and just sit still." My voice was soft and melodic, filled with magic as powerful as it was old. "I'll go make you a coffee and then we'll sort out the problem, whatever the problem is this time."

"Damn it, Beth, don't you dare magic me."

"Too late, brother mine. Now sit back against that pole while I go get your coffee."

"Damn it," he repeated, even as he obeyed. "I hate it when you do this to me."

I smiled, but concern rose. His skin had gained a sheen that really didn't look healthy. He might not be drunk, but something was definitely wrong.

"I'd love to say I'm sorry," I said, keeping my voice even, "but I'm not."

"You are so like Mom sometimes, it's scary."

"Thanks for the compliment." I patted his shoulder lightly. "Tell me what happened tonight."

"What happened to the coffee?"

"Your skin is gray. I want to know why."

"Later. Go lock the front door. And then you'd better ring Darby."

Those slivers of concern deepened. Darby was a long-time friend of mine, an elf healer who specialized in poisons.

"Lugh—"

"Just do what I ask. Door first."

I spun on a heel and strode toward the front steps, the old floorboards bouncing lightly under each step. "Why is locking the door so vital? Shifters patrol the tourist quarter, not human cops. No sane thief or thug will be out looking for mischief."

"It's not the sane thieves and thugs I'm worried about."

A smile twitched my lips, despite the deepening concern. "Does that mean an insane one crossed your path tonight?"

"No. Just lock the damn door."

I raised my eyebrows at the edge in his voice but didn't say anything. But as I neared the heavy oak door, a shadow crossed the leaded glass windows to the right. I paused, unease prickling across my skin. There was something very odd about that shadow—something misshapen and grotesque.

"Lugh," I asked softly, "were you followed here?"

"For your sake, I hope not."

I glanced around. His gaze wasn't on me but rather the window, and the frosted green depths of his eyes ran deep with worry. It only reinforced the suspicion that he knew exactly what was happening.

"Hope?" I said, voice still deliberately light. "Since when does an antiquarian ever rely on hope?"

"Since things went ass up four nights ago. Lock the door."

I slid the old iron bolt into place, then dropped the wooden latch. Though the shadow had disappeared, I didn't feel any safer.

Whatever that thing was, I had a bad feeling it wasn't going to be stopped by the door's medieval hardware. Whether the strings of magic that protected the building from unauthorized out-of-hours entry would hold was a question I fervently hoped we didn't get an answer to.

"Now ring Darby."

The drunken lilt remained in his voice, but it was pretty obvious now that it had nothing to do with alcohol. I tugged my phone out of the rear pocket of my leather shorts—which, along with the leather-and-lace corset, thick woolen leggings, and pointed leather boots, were all part of the tavern's "gimmick" to attract tourists. The other part was the multitude of bright-colored "pixie" boots hanging from the ceiling's beams—some of which were real but most simply playing to tourist expectations.

Hey Darby, I sent, *are you able to come to The Boot and check Lugh for me? Now, I mean?*

Her reply was almost instant—*Sure, can be there in ten.*

A smile tugged at my lips. Darby had always fancied my brother, even if he generally considered her nothing more than another kid sister, and an annoying one at that.

Use the lane entrance, I sent. *There might be problems out front.*

Has Lugh stolen something he shouldn't have again?

Not sure. Maybe. Theft *was* an unwritten and unofficially approved part of his job at the National Fae Museum, after all, and a good third of the artifacts now held within the museum's hallowed halls hadn't been legally procured. Of course, said artifacts had often been initially stolen from the original owners—and from the old gods, in some cases —and then sold on to private collectors. To quote my brother, the thefts his small team indulged in were really nothing more than a righting of past wrongs. And when it came to the artifacts of the old gods? Well, many of them were simply too powerful or too dangerous to be in the hands of private collectors who had no clue as to what they were really dealing with.

Best put your knives on then, just in case his problems followed to your place, Darby sent. *I'll see you soon.*

My gaze returned to the window, and unease stirred again. I shoved the phone back into my pocket, then walked over to the bar. While we did have a proper coffee machine in the kitchen, I'd only just finished cleaning the thing, and there was no way I was going to fire everything up for a couple of black coffees. I grabbed the old kettle we kept under the bar for emergencies, topped it up with water, then plugged it in and turned it on.

"Darby on the way?" Lugh asked.

"Yes. Who poisoned you?"

"Don't know." He scraped a hand through his already unruly hair. "I really shouldn't stay here, Beth. It's dangerous."

"So is being poisoned. Who did it?"

"Don't know."

"Then where did it happen?"

"I was approaching The Cross from Watergate Street when I felt a shadow slip behind me, so it most likely happened then."

The Cross was a monument that stood at the center junction of the four main streets within medieval Deva. It wasn't an actual cross, but rather a red sandstone shaft topped by a crown, a finial, and a ball. The wide, three-stepped plinth was used as seating by tourists and pigeons alike.

"The problem with *that* statement is the fact shadow folk can't cross into our world when there's a full moon."

The shadow folk generally weren't the monsters or demons that many believed, but rather an offshoot of fae who lived in Annwfyn—the lands beyond, or Otherworld as some also called it. It was a place that existed alongside and yet apart from our world, with the two being joined by bridges of darkness. Humans often referred to Annwfyn as either the home of the gods or the dead, but in truth it was neither. It might be a world of permanent twilight, but it wasn't an incarnation of hell and, from what we could discern, really not all that different from our own world.

Of course, the Annwfyn were also fierce warrior hunters and considered human, elves, and the like something of a delicacy.

"So legend would have us believe," Lugh was saying, "but there have been multiple examples over the centuries speaking to the falseness of that."

"Even so, why would they be targeting you? They usually prefer easier game."

The kettle boiled, so I made our coffees, then grabbed my knives out of the still open safe. The old gods had gifted them to my family back in the days when we'd been their guardians and, as such, they could only be used by someone from our bloodline. They'd also been blessed by multiple goddesses, which made them a very effective counter to all sorts of magic—and maybe even certain gods, if the legends were to be believed.

Of course, in this day and age, old gods weren't such a problem, given most had left long ago, but the wickedly curved blades were made of silver, and *that* always made the most aggressive shifter or fae think twice about tackling me. No matter how clever their fabled healers were, not even elves could easily fix a wound made by blessed silver.

"Until recently, I would have agreed," he said heavily.

"Seriously, can you stop dribbling out bits of information and just get to the point? What the hell happened four nights ago, and what has it to do with you being poisoned tonight?"

I slammed the safe door closed with my foot and carried the two drinks over. He accepted his with a nod. The gray sheen, I noted, was worse.

"Nialle was murdered four nights ago. I think they're now after me, but in a more subtle manner."

I stared at him for a moment, then dropped hard onto a nearby chair. I'd known Nialle for most of my life—he'd gone through boarding school with Lugh and had often come here during school breaks rather than go home to his family's estate when his parents were either overseas or in London.

"How come you've not said anything until now?"

"I didn't want to get you involved."

"Then you shouldn't have taken a shortcut through my tavern. Besides, telling me he's dead doesn't get me involved."

He raised his eyebrows. "Doesn't it? So you're not already plotting ways and means of uncovering how he died and who's responsible?"

"Absolutely not—"

"But only because you haven't had the chance to as yet."

That was a truth I couldn't deny, and the amusement creasing the corners of Lugh's eyes said he was well aware of that fact. I took a sip of coffee and then said, "Was he also poisoned?"

"No. Beaten and then knifed."

I blinked, then scraped a hand across my eyes. My fingers came away wet. Poor Nialle. He'd been a gentle soul and certainly hadn't deserved such an ugly death. "Do you have any idea why?"

Lugh reached into the front pocket of his jeans and pulled out what looked to be a simple black stone. "It might have something to do with this."

I carefully plucked the stone from his fingertips. Power caressed my skin, and something within sparked to life.

Visions rose—visions that spoke of fire and darkness, bloody death, and deep deceit. Surprise hit, along with thick trepidation, and the urge to throw the stone away was so damn strong I actually half raised my hand before I stopped it.

While second sight *did* run in the family, it was something that had never truly plagued me. Mom used to get visions at annoyingly regular intervals, however, including one on the day she'd gone missing.

Had this stone somehow stirred that dormant ability to life? If so, how? And why did I get a bad feeling that this was just the beginning?

I rolled it around my fingers uneasily. "What is it?"

"Some sort of key, I think."

My gaze shot to his. "What sort of weird-ass lock uses a black stone as a key?"

"A lock made by the old gods."

Which might well explain the deep thrum of power evident within the stone's black heart, but not the images I'd seen.

"It's black, so if it was a key, it would have to belong to a god or goddess of night." Light ripped jaggedly through its heart as I spoke, its color a deep, dark purple. "So if you have this key, why was Nialle killed?"

"Because I think he stole it and then posted it to me for safekeeping while he made his way back to England."

"Think? You're not sure?"

"The address was typed rather than written, but who else could it have been from?"

I suspected *that* was a question we'd be seeking an answer to sooner rather than later. "Where was it posted?"

"Nialle was in France, so likely from there."

I raised my eyebrows. "Does that mean he didn't return

home immediately? He'd have gotten here quicker than the mail, otherwise."

"He did, and that's probably the only reason we still have the key. My place was ransacked the same night he was murdered."

I dropped my gaze to the stone. Power hummed deep in its heart, and it whispered of death and darkness. Some godly artifacts were cursed rather than blessed, and those who handled them were often dealt a swift death. If this was one of them, well ... maybe I'd better start getting my affairs in order.

"He obviously suspected he was being watched if he sent this to you," I said. "Was there a note with it? Something that might explain where it had come from or what it might lead to?"

"There was, though it was somewhat enigmatic." Lugh reached into his other pocket and handed me a small, crumpled envelope. "But the stone has to be connected. He's been working on a case for over six months now, and his trip to France was the first time in ages he'd pulled his nose from the parchments in the museum's crypts."

Which did *not* contain coffins or bodies, although there were some lovely religious relics in the crypts' older sections. What they *did* hold were all the precious artifacts that weren't currently on display, as well as those that were simply too dangerous to be placed in front of the general public.

I put my coffee on the floor, then opened the crumpled envelope and pulled out a small piece of parchment—the real stuff, made out of old skins. My gaze shot back to Lugh's. "Parchment? *Actual* vellum parchment? Did he make a habit of using it for notes?"

Lugh nodded. "He made the stuff in his spare time."

"He did? Not in his apartment, I hope, because eww."

Lugh smiled. "No, he owned an offsite factory."

"But ... why?"

"Because there's a demand for it, believe it or not."

"Huh."

I glanced down at the note. *That which seeks darkness also draws it,* it said. *Use the Eye only when it calls.*

"The Eye? Why would he call it that if it's a key?"

"I have no idea."

"But the writing *is* his? Because it looks a little too spidery to me."

"It can get that way when he's in a hurry."

He wasn't sure, in other words. I replaced the note and then smoothed the envelope out on my knee. "Lugh, this isn't addressed to either of us."

And it was sent to the tavern's post office box rather than his home address, which was odd.

"Yeah, but he could have done that to throw people off the scent."

People meaning his murderers, no doubt. "There isn't a postmark, either."

"Wouldn't be the first time mail has somehow skipped being postmarked properly. Besides, he was dead by the time this arrived, so it couldn't have been hand delivered."

"Why not? He could have given it to someone else to deliver if something happened to him. Someone he trusted."

"He didn't even talk to his parents about his research; he certainly wouldn't have trusted the delivery of something like this to a stranger."

I folded the envelope and handed it back. "So, no one else other than you knew what he was working on?"

"No."

"Don't you have to make progress reports to the higher-ups at the museum?"

"We run pretty autonomously these days. Makes it easier for the museum to disclaim any responsibility if things go ass up."

Which was one way of describing murder. I rolled the stone around my fingers, feeling the caress of its energy and the hint of deeper, darker secrets. "I take it you think the scrolls led him to the location of this stone?"

Lugh nodded and drank some coffee. His color did not improve. I pushed down the growing wash of fear and added, "What was he researching?"

"Agrona's Claws."

I raised my eyebrows. "There's a goddess called Agrona?"

He nodded again. "She's an ancient Celtic deity who was apparently responsible for eternal rest and warfare."

"The whole death and destruction field is definitely a crowded one when it comes to the old gods, isn't it? You'd think one or two of them would have branched out and done something different."

He smiled, but it was a pale echo of its usually robust self. "It's more a case of new civilizations rising from the ashes of the old renaming the various gods or goddesses to suit their own beliefs."

"A fact that doesn't make it any less confusing." I drank some coffee. "I take it Nialle's research notes are missing?"

"I'd presume so, but I haven't been able to get into his apartment to check yet."

I frowned. "You didn't find the body?"

"No, his girlfriend did. She did ask if I could go in and see what's missing, but at this point, I haven't been given permission."

"Why not? I'd have thought that would be a priority in any murder investigation. Who's leading it?"

"The Eldritch."

The Eldritch were a small but specialized offshoot of the Interspecies Investigation Team that were called in on murders resulting from a strange or magical means.

"But Nialle was knifed, so that should have put him beyond their purview."

"Yes, but his apartment wasn't broken into, and the security cameras outside showed no sign of anyone coming or going. There was no trace of magic or electronic manipulation on any of the door or window locks, and no indication the security cams had been accessed or tampered with."

Sweat now dribbled down the side of his face, and his breathing was becoming labored. I glanced at the old clock sitting on the wall behind the bar; three more minutes before Darby got here.

Fear strengthened, but once again I did my best to ignore it. Pixies—or at least our branch of them—were damnably hard to kill, thanks to the fact that the old gods had always favored us. No one had really been able to explain why we'd been so blessed, but Gran had always theorized it was because godly blood ran in both the Aodhán and Tàileach lines. It was the reason we were the two tallest branches of pixies, and also lay behind our being the guards of choice for gods and kings. Until, that is, an ill-advised theft by a Tàileach had cast both lines out of a job. They, of course, blamed us, and knowing my family tree I actually wouldn't have been at all surprised if that were true.

"Was there any sort of power failure? Were the street or apartment lights off?"

He shook his head. "Both were fully lit."

Which *should* have discounted the possibility of his murderer being someone from Annwfyn ... and yet it hadn't stopped the attack on Lugh tonight. *If* that's who'd crossed behind him. It was possible it had simply been someone using magic to conceal his or her presence. Fae folk might in general be sensitive to the presence of magic, but that sense was not infallible—especially if we were in a hurry or our minds were elsewhere. And Lugh's obviously had been. He'd been an antiquarian for a long time now; keeping alert during a hunt or a rehoming job was second nature.

A gentle tremor ran through the floorboards under my feet, an indication that someone walked across the rear veranda, heading for the security door. I tensed, but a heartbeat later heard the soft beeps of someone entering the code and relaxed. Only a handful of people knew that code, and only one person had any reason to be here at two in the morning.

Darby appeared a minute later. She was typically light elf in look—tall and slender, with long, pale-gold hair platted into a thick rope that ran down her spine and eyes the color of summer skies. Her features were sharp but ethereally beautiful, and she moved with a lightness and grace I could never hope to achieve.

She and I had been friends for a long time now, and it never ceased to amaze me that she and Lugh had never gotten together. Granted, the eleven-year difference in age between Lugh and I did mean it hadn't been practical when we were in our teens, but those years were well past us all. There was a very obvious attraction between them, and she'd certainly made it abundantly clear she'd happily participate in any sort of sexual encounter he desired.

For some reason, he just didn't desire, though I'd

recently caught him studying her speculatively when he thought no one was looking.

She flashed me a smile of greeting, then squatted down in front of my brother. "That gray tone you're running at the moment really isn't a good look on you, Lugh."

A smile tugged at his lips. "Not doing it willingly, I can assure you."

She slung her bag off her shoulder and dropped it near her knees. "So, what are we thinking the source is?"

"A shadow slipped behind me near The Cross. More than that, I can't say."

She grunted, opened her bag, and pulled out a pair of latex gloves. "If it *was* a shadow who administered this poison—if we are indeed dealing with a poison—then we'll have to work on the theory it was vapor administered through either the skin or breath." She glanced at me. "You've had no direct contact?"

"Not skin on skin. I did magic him through his clothes."

"Ha! Wondered why he was sitting here all calm and collected. It's generally not his style."

"I *am* sitting right in front of you both. No need to talk about me in the third person."

She snapped on her gloves and then patted his knee. "Sorry. Been dealing with cranky kids and their moms all day at the fae hospital. Talking to the adult in the room is force of habit." She leaned forward and pressed her fingertips against his temples. "Remain still while I do a scan."

Her gaze narrowed and her magic rose, a warm and bright caress of energy. It washed from the top of Lugh's head down the long length of his body, then returned at a slower pace.

After several minutes, she sighed and sat back on her heels. "It's definitely poison. The good news is, it's not sourced from Annwfyn and it's not transferable via skin contact. The bad news? It's Dahbree, which is basically a deadly truth serum. It's not a poison I've come across very often."

"But you *have* come across it and can cure it, can't you?" I asked, unable to keep the inner anxiety from my voice.

She gripped my hand and squeezed lightly. "He'll be fine, I promise. But we can't risk moving him too far and the cure will knock him for a six."

"There you go, talking like I'm not in the room again," he grumbled. "And you're surely aware that my frame and the accommodation portion of this damn building are *not* compatible, no matter how many feet Gran raised it."

"You're still supple enough to bend at the waist, old man. You'll be fine." Her voice was dry. "Beth, do you want to release him so I can get him upstairs?"

I leaned over and pressed my fingers against his shoulder. "Brother mine, follow Darby upstairs and do whatever she asks you to."

"Oh," she said, her voice suddenly holding a decidedly sultry note. "In any other circumstances, that's an order I could thoroughly abuse."

I laughed and rose. "Do you need a hand getting him up there? If not, I'll start cleaning the trail of destruction he left in his wake."

"I should be fine, but I'll shout if I do need anything." She picked up her bag and then stepped back. "Come along, ancient one. I've a warm bed and a warmer man waiting for me back home."

My lips twitched. If she'd had a man in her bed, she wouldn't have been so quick to respond. It had obviously been said solely to needle my brother.

He muttered something under his breath but nevertheless climbed slowly to his feet. The effort left him panting hard, and I glanced at Darby. She gave me a quick smile of reassurance, but I could see the concern in her eyes. This really wasn't going to be an easy fix.

I shoved the black stone in my pocket, picked up his mug and my unfinished coffee, then moved back to the bar and dumped them both into the sink. Aside from the fact I wasn't a fan of instant, it really was a little too late to be drinking much of it, especially if I wanted to grab a few hours of sleep before we had to get ready for the new day's trading.

I'd finished picking up the chairs and was in the process of sweeping away the remnants of table destruction when I felt the slight caress of ... not evil. Not exactly. But definitely something out of place and wrong. My gaze jumped to the windows; no shadow moved past the rippled old glass, and there was no indication that anyone or anything stood in the street beyond the reach of the lights lining the tavern's front.

And yet ... something or someone *was* out there.

I propped the broom against the nearby oak post and walked toward the door. But as I reached the steps, that sense of danger sharpened. I paused, my heart galloping and my breath caught somewhere in my throat. For several, seemingly over-long seconds, nothing happened. Then something fierce and bright smashed through the ancient glass and shattered all over the floor. The stink of petrol filled the air, and flames leapt, quickly catching hold as the pungent liquid flowed across the old floorboards.

I swore violently, reached for the nearest fire blanket, and quickly released it from the container. With the blanket held in front of me for protection, I raced over to the flames and carefully placed it across them. Thankfully, the fire hadn't yet managed to spread any wider than the blanket and it was smothered very—

The thought stalled as an odd sound snagged my attention. I quickly looked up.

The grotesque shadow I'd glimpsed earlier now stood at the window, and it was attempting to unravel the magic that protected this place.

I pulled my knives from their sheaths and raised them just enough for the tavern's dim lighting to catch the blades and make them burn a deep and deadly blue. "One more move to defuse that magic, and these knives will feast on your fucking blood."

The shadow's head snapped up. The veil that hid him from sight briefly shredded, revealing amber eyes and a rather grand-looking moustache under a sharp nose. Not one of the shadow folk, then, though that wasn't exactly any sort of relief.

He turned and fled.

"Darby," I shouted, "someone just attempted to firebomb the tavern. Keep sharp while I go after the bastard!"

"Beth, don't," came Lugh's response.

"Like hell I won't!"

I unlocked the door, ran out onto the street, and looked around. No immediate sign of him, but he surely wouldn't have gone down to The Cross. It was too bright for someone wrapped in shadows. Had he wrapped himself in a screen of light, it might have been a different story.

I pulled the door closed, then swept my fingers down the ancient oak to reengage the wooden latch. I couldn't do anything about the bolt, because I had no power over steel, but at least with the latch down, the protecting magic would reactivate.

I sprinted down the cobblestone street, away from The

Cross, and after a few seconds, caught sight of a malformed patch of darkness racing around the various pools of light. He was surprisingly fast and made absolutely no sound on the old cobblestones. Whether that meant he was elf or it was simply a by-product of the concealing spell, I couldn't say.

The night was clear but fiercely cold. Goose bumps raced across my bare arms and populated under the lace in my corset, but I wasn't about to go back and get a coat. The Boot had stood on Eastgate Street, basically unchanged, for hundreds of years. There was no way I was about to let some random firebomber get away with a destruction attempt—especially when I had no idea as to *why* someone might want to destroy it. Even if it *was* connected to the attack on Lugh, what was the point of burning the place down if they were actually after the Eye? It'd be rather difficult to find a small black stone amongst all the rubble, especially when they couldn't use any sort of magical means to find it. Not without raising undue attention to themselves, anyway.

The shadow jagged left and disappeared into Godstall Lane—a pedestrian walkway that ran between Eastgate and St Werburgh Streets. I raced up the half dozen steps a few seconds later, mighty glad the pretty shops that lined either side of the lane were closed and nothing more than moths fluttered around the warm puddles of light that protected the shop fronts and the walkway. My shadowed quarry was nowhere to be seen. Whoever he was, he was damned fast.

I slid to a halt at the end of the lane and quickly looked around. A thin woman with a nest of red hair walked toward me, her face pinched with cold, and her hands shoved deep into the pockets of her oversized overcoat, but no one else was visible. There was no traffic on the street, and the church grounds directly opposite appeared empty. If it *had* been one of the shadow folk I was chasing, I'd have been able to wipe that area off the list of possible directions, as they had something of an aversion to holy ground. Few others did, though, and the cathedral had certainly been a refuge for all manner of folk in times past.

For no particular reason other than gut instinct, I went right, heading for the lane that ran down to the old bell tower. The coach lights lining the lane didn't really do all that much to lift the shadows haunting the ivy-wrapped hedge that divided it from the church grounds, so I kept to the right, close to the wall and the brighter edges of the light. It was less likely anyone would jump out at me there.

Halfway down the lane, a dark glint on an ivy leaf caught my attention. I hesitated then walked over, knives held at the ready should it be some sort of magical snare.

It wasn't magic. It was blood.

Had my quarry somehow injured himself?

I studied the area and spotted another gleaming droplet down the far end of the lane.

Deliberate?

I didn't think so, but I was well aware that I didn't know enough about the man I was chasing to be absolutely certain.

I moved on cautiously. The slip of darkness was nowhere to be seen, but the intermittent blood spots led past the bell tower and up onto the City Walls walk. I paused again and looked right. The beautifully ornate Eastgate Clock—which stood atop one of the four still-standing original gates into Old Deva—gleamed in solitary magnificence. While it was no surprise the area was empty given the hour, if my quarry was a darksider—the term used for the various night-loving fae and other magical beings—it would have been the more logical route to take, as it led down toward the River Dee and the main encampment that lay in one of the river's deep meanders.

But the blood spots led left.

I flexed my fingers on the hilt of my knives in a vague effort to ease the tension and then resolutely followed the droplets. They were all I had.

My footsteps echoed lightly on the old stone, but nothing stirred the darkness ahead. Yet I had a vague feeling that something ... or someone ... was close.

I glanced around uneasily. The cathedral's grounds to my left were empty and silent, and the barren branches of the old oaks that lined the outer wall glowed cool silver thanks to the spotlights surrounding their trunks.

Everything was still. There was no breeze and very little sound. And yet air whispered across the back of my neck.

Someone was behind me.

Someone who intended to kill.

CHAPTER

TWO

I swore and dropped low; the metal pipe that would have caved in my skull soared over it instead, the air whistling under its deadly force.

I twisted around and slashed with a knife; a shudder ran through the blade as it tore through my attacker's protecting magic, then ripped through flesh and muscle. Blood spurted, and a roar that was both agony and anger shattered the night. But my attacker didn't back off. He simply swung the metal pipe around for another hit.

I quickly shifted position and then kicked at the leg I'd torn open; the force of the blow sent him staggering backward. He flailed his arms in an obvious effort to keep his balance but fell hard onto his butt. The metal pipe clattered loudly onto the stone and rolled away from his hand. He swore and lunged after it, but I kicked him again. This time, the heel of my boot smacked into his chin, knocking him back yet again. His head hit stone with a sickening crack, and he didn't move.

I swore, scrambled up beside him, and quickly felt for a pulse. It was there—fast and thready, but nevertheless there. Relief stirred. The bastard might have tried to kill me, and he might well deserve such a fate himself, but the last thing I needed was blood on my hands. That never went down well for us pixies—not since we'd left the service of the old gods, anyway.

Besides, I could hardly get answers from a dead man.

He wasn't the firebomber, because he didn't have a moustache, but I nevertheless pried open an eye just to be doubly sure, given the moustache had almost been too glorious to be real. Blue eyes rather than amber. Which led to the next question—was he connected to the firebomber, or was it a random attack? I guess we'd find out once he was conscious.

I sat back on my heels. There was still nothing to see other than those damn blood spots, and it was possible they were unrelated to either attack. And yet, curiosity wouldn't let me leave them be.

Of course, we all know what curiosity did to the cat.

I sheathed one knife then pulled out my phone and made a call to Sgott Bruyn—who wasn't only the man in charge of the IIT's evening branch but also a longtime family friend. Frustratingly, it was rerouted to the Force Control Room, meaning he was either off duty or on another call. I quickly detailed the two attacks, gave the location of my mugger, and asked the operator to send an officer over. I made a second call to the medics, though whether my attacker would still be here when either party arrived was another matter entirely.

I rose and continued on. Beyond the trees lining the outer wall were empty parking areas and lonely-looking warehouses. Lights surrounded the latter, but there were still plenty of shadowed areas in which to hide. It was highly unlikely my firebomber was, though, if only because he had no real need to do so. All he had to do was remove the veil of darkness and pretend to be just another drunk trying to get home.

There were a number of stairs interspaced along the wall that led down to a lower walkway, but the blood dripper appeared to be heading toward Guinne's Tower. Smugglers had once been a major problem around these parts, and the tower was one of four sentry points set up along the canal section of the wall. I had no doubt ill-gotten goods were still being transported on the waterway, even if these days it was mostly used by tourists in narrow boats.

This particular tower had fallen into such a state of disrepair in recent years that the heritage council had ordered it sealed. Which was a shame, because the view over the main city center from the sentry room was quite amazing.

Of course, it was possible that neither the tower nor the canal was the final goal of the blood dripper, but rather the towpath that ran between the base of the wall and the water. One that happened to go right past a bridge of darkness. Few knew what it was, of course, as it was little more than an unremarkable fissure in the moss-covered red and gray bedrock. Deva's council had marked its location with an unadorned black metal plaque, but there was little else anyone could do. Magic couldn't be attached to something that didn't fully exist in our world, and lights—and even light spells—strung across its entry point had proven too easily destroyed.

Guinne's Tower soon came into sight. The metal gate that gave entry onto the external red-stone stairs leading up to the sentry room was padlocked, but the oak door into the main stairwell was open. The lock lay on the ground, whole rather than broken. Whoever had entered this place had a key, and that at least meant I wasn't following one of the Annwfyn.

Unsurprisingly, the blood spots led right into the tower's deeper darkness.

I stopped at the door, torn between the need to uncover what was going on and the knowledge I might be walking into a trap. Curiosity was always going to win, of course, but I nevertheless pulled out my phone and sent the IIT another quick message. Whoever they dispatched to investigate the mugging would be seriously annoyed that I hadn't hung around, but at least someone would know where I was and what I was doing.

I turned on the phone's flashlight app and shone the light into the tower's round interior. No shadows slithered from the brightness, and the air was filled with the smell of damp and rot but little else. My bleeder obviously wasn't wearing any sort of perfume or aftershave, because both would have lingered in a closed environment like this.

I shone the light up to examine the watchtower's wooden flooring and beams, seeing decay and hoping like hell nothing triggered the whole thing to come down while I was underneath it. I couldn't see any sign of magic, and the old oak wasn't giving any audible indications of imminent collapse, but still ...

I quickly checked behind the door to ensure there were no waiting muggers, and then aimed the light down the winding stairwell. Nothing to see, nothing to hear.

Which didn't mean there was nothing waiting.

I drew in a deep breath that did little to ease the growing inner tension, then slowly made my way down the steps, keeping my back pressed against the wall and a knife gripped tight in my free hand.

I was halfway down when a slight breeze teased my skin. The bottom door was open.

I continued on warily and eventually reached the tower's base. The padlock on this door had been positioned on the outside rather than inside—a fact I knew only because a U-shaped section still hung off the shackle; the rest lay in shattered pieces on the ground. Either my bleeder had outside help or was magic capable.

Neither was a particularly calming option.

I turned off the light, edged toward the door, and listened to the outside world for several seconds. Again, there was absolutely nothing to indicate anyone was close.

With my finger hovering over the flashlight app, ready to switch it back on at even the slightest hint of a shadow, I cautiously moved out.

Light pooled gently along the steps that led down to the towpath, though the area wasn't as well-lit as it should have been. The lights to the immediate left and right were out. Thankfully, the lights atop the wall were bright enough to not only chase away the immediate threat of shadows but gleam off the water's dark and gentle waves ... and the body floating facedown in them.

I swore, flicked on the flashlight app, and raced down the steps to the canal's edge. After a quick sweep of the light to ensure that nothing and no one hid nearby, I placed my phone on the ground, then knelt and leaned out. It was possible he was still alive, but even if he wasn't, the ellul— eel-like beings with human faces—haunted these waters, and they had a taste for flesh. The stranger was bleeding profusely from a wound on the back of his head and another on his arm, and all that blood would draw them in.

The wounds also meant he was probably the bleeder I'd been following, but how in the hell had he ended up in the water? His coloring and the pointed tip of his ears suggested he was a dark elf, and they weren't easy to bring down. Had blood loss finally caught up with him? Or had the invisible firebomber made a brief but deadly return?

I snagged the end of the stranger's long black coat and dragged him toward the edge. I briefly wondered what the best way to get him out without further damage was and then smacked that stupid thought aside. He was facedown in the water; if I didn't get him out and breathing, no number of subsequent injuries would matter.

I rolled him onto his back, then shoved my hands under his armpits and hoisted him up. Water sluiced off his body, but it didn't really make him any lighter.

With a grunt of effort, I hauled him up and over the canal's edge. Once most of him was out, I laid him down on the path, then quickly grabbed his legs and pulled them out of the water. Several sinuous forms briefly rose, and dagger-like teeth flashed.

Ellul.

I grabbed my phone and shone it onto the waves. The ellul quickly dived, but I had an uneasy feeling they hadn't gone too far. The bastards were capable of surviving in air for a good few minutes, and it wasn't unknown for them to jump out and drag prey back into the water.

Although, as strong as ellul were, I doubted even they would be able to move the dark elf's dead weight.

I called for a fae medic, then checked the stranger for breathing and a pulse. He had neither. I swore and began CPR, alternating between chest compressions and two quick breaths.

It seemed to take forever before the wail of distant sirens broke the silence. A few minutes later came the sound of running steps. I didn't stop or look up—whoever approached was doing so from the top of the wall, and I suspected that meant it was either Sgott or one of his men.

The stranger coughed, then water spewed from his mouth. I rolled him into the recovery position and watched to ensure he kept on breathing.

Which he did.

I sighed in relief and thrust a hand through my hair—which was just as short and unruly as Lugh's—then finally took the time to study the man I'd rescued.

Unlike their golden kin, dark elves were neither slender nor delicate, and this man's powerful body was nothing short of magnificent. His chiseled features were sublime, but it suddenly struck me that his ebony skin was paler than it should have been. Whether that was a side effect of the near drowning, a result of blood loss, or something else entirely, I couldn't say. But it was worrying.

His eyelids fluttered, and he muttered something I couldn't quite catch. Then he tried to get up, though the movements were weak and uncoordinated.

I pressed a hand against his arm to keep him down. I could have been gripping iron. *Heated* iron. "I've called in the medics, but until they arrive, you'd better remain still."

"Can't," he said. "Meeting to attend."

His voice, though faint, was deep, velvety smoke, and the urge to lean down, press my lips against his, and kiss him senseless was so fierce I was halfway there before I caught myself. Which was annoying, as I knew it had nothing to do with his voice or his overall gorgeousness, but rather the flaring of his inbuilt magnetism as consciousness returned. The fair folk might be divinely beautiful but dark elves were sex on legs. They could make the iciest of maidens weak with wanting without the slightest bit of effort.

And no one would ever call *me* an ice maiden.

"I think we both know the whole meeting story is a lie," I said evenly. "You were out here hunting someone, and it nearly cost you your life. You'll remain exactly where you are until the medics get here."

He shifted a fraction, and suddenly I was falling into twin pools of smoky silver and drowning in heat and promises—the "let's tear off our clothes and have hot and sweaty sex" kind.

If he hadn't been broken, I may well have taken him up on those unspoken promises.

"And," he said, amusement evident despite the pain that haunted the corners of his lush mouth and glorious eyes, "you really think you can stop me if I wish to move?"

Gods, *that voice*. I bet he could read the blandest, most boring book in the world and still make you come.

"Yes, I do." I calmly drew one of my knives. "Because I have a couple of stingers I'm not afraid to use."

He blinked and then laughed. The warm, rich sound ran over my skin as sweetly as a caress, and only added fuel to the fire of wanting. "So you save my life only to threaten it again?"

"If that's what it takes to keep you still until the medics get here, yes."

"Interesting." He looked amused rather than threatened. But then, a man his size was unlikely to really be threatened by a pixie, even if I was one of the larger varieties. "Do you have a name? Or shall I just call you Red?"

Sweat rather than river water now dotted his forehead, and when combined with the paleness of his dark skin, it reminded me a little too much of Lugh's symptoms. I hoped I was wrong. Hoped like hell the medics got here soon.

"If you call me Red, I might be tempted to gut you anyway. My name is Bethany. You?"

"Cynwrig. Friends call me Cyn."

I didn't make the obvious comment, but I certainly thought it. And I'd definitely be happy to participate in it ...

The sharp tattoo of approaching footsteps had my gaze leaping past him. Sgott approached, and with him was a first-responder medic. The latter was a light elf, though his broader than normal shoulders and shadowed eyes suggested mixed blood. It did happen, despite the overall animosity that existed between the two.

"What the fuck are you playing at, lass?" Sgott growled the minute he was in hearing distance. He was a big bear of a man, with thick, wiry brown hair, brown skin, and a fierce, untamable beard. "Your mother would have my hide if anything happened to you."

A smile twitched my lips. Despite the censure in his voice, there was deep concern in his brown eyes. He'd been my mother's lover for over sixty years and was the closest thing to a father I'd ever known, as he'd come into Mom's life when I was little more than two. Though they'd never had children—bear shifters, like most of the various shifter subgroups, weren't fertile with those outside their own race—he'd always treated me as one of his own. And he'd had five before he and Mom hooked up.

"I think we both know that if Mom were here, she'd be gently reminding you that I'm totally capable of looking after myself."

"She said the same thing about herself, and look where it got her."

Though his voice was even, frustration and pain flitted across his expression. Six months had passed since she'd disappeared, but it remained raw for all of us. I think Sgott felt it all the more keenly because, even with all the resources he had at his fingertips, he'd never been able to uncover what had happened to her. She was simply gone, and while her last vision undoubtedly could have given us some sort of lead, for the first time in her life, she'd left without telling one of us where she was going or why.

But I'd glimpsed the deep fear in her frost-green eyes as she'd run out the door. Whatever she'd seen, it had been *bad*.

Sgott's gaze dropped to my patient, and his demeanor became more formal. "Lord Lùtair, the medic will now examine you, and then we'll move you to the waiting ambulance. I'll need to get a statement, but that can be done after you've been given the all clear."

Lord Lùtair? That meant he wasn't any old dark elf, but the oldest son of their king, Eanruig. And while he *was* heir, he didn't hold that position alone. Unlike their golden kin, heirs to the dark elf crown could be either male or female, and, the last I'd heard, Cynwrig and his twin sister jointly held that position.

Of course, the only "official" royal line in England these days was the Windsors. The fae had never expected to lose the Great War to humans and those shifters who'd sided with them, and it had cost them both sovereign lands *and* rights. That, unfortunately, included the right to royalty.

Humans might not be as powerful or as long-lived as fae or even shifters, but they'd always bred like goddamn rabbits and were sneaky, clever bastards besides. Speed, strength, and the ability to manipulate forests and earth were of little use when your opponents could obliterate whole areas from a very great distance.

And they certainly had. It had taken the elves and we pixies centuries to heal the scars on our lands and forests.

These days, the various fae kings bore the official titles of dukes and were members of both the House of Lords and the High Council of Other Races, which was based in London and acted as an advisory body to the government. There were also "ruling councils" in the various counties that held large populations of fae, shifters, and night folk, and these took care of everyday administrative requirements. But there were few who saw that as any sort of recompense for the loss of being completely autonomous.

"I assure you, Inspector," Cynwrig was saying, "there's no need for me to be taken to hospital—"

"There's every need," I cut in, my gaze rising to the medic standing beside Sgott. "I believe Lord Lùtair might have been given Dahbree."

The medic sucked in a breath, horror briefly evident before he got his emotions under control. "That's an extremely rare poison—"

"Yes, but my brother was given it tonight—"

"Lugh?" Sgott cut in. "Is he all right?"

"According to Darby, yes."

"Ah. Good."

Hopefully, it would be. "Unfortunately, Lord Lùtair is showing the same symptoms, and I don't think we dare take any risk." My gaze met shadowed silver. "I didn't save your magnificent butt from the ellul, my lord, only to see it lost to an old but deadly poison."

A dark eyebrow winged upward, and devilment danced in his eyes. "That's the first time my butt has ever been described as magnificent."

"Oh, I doubt that, especially when you're laying on the charm."

He chuckled again, but it ended in a racking cough. He did *not* sound well.

The medic muttered something under his breath and then said, "Inspector, I need to get Lord Lùtair to the waiting ambulance. Immediately."

"And the head wound?"

"Is the least of his worries if he *has* been administered Dahbree."

Sgott stepped forward and scooped Cynwrig up in one smooth motion. Cynwrig might be a big man, but you'd have thought he was little heavier than a child.

"Lead the way, Jepson," he said. "And Beth? You'd best follow. We need to chat about the mugging once Lord Lùtair is safe."

The medic took off at a fast clip, keeping to the towpath but heading away from the tower. Sgott and I followed.

"Mugging?" Cynwrig said, voice suddenly sharper. His gaze found mine. "Were you also attacked?"

"These things do come in threes," I said lightly. "And you'd best stop talking and conserve your strength, my lord."

"Or what? You'll stick me with those knives of yours?"

"Trust me," Sgott said heavily. "She has something of a temper, and it would not be the first time."

I grinned. "I did give them warning. Not my fault they didn't take me seriously."

"If you were wearing that outfit, I'm not entirely surprised," Cynwrig commented.

I raised an eyebrow. "What's wrong with the outfit?"

"Nothing. Absolutely nothing."

I harrumphed, despite the amusement bubbling through me. "Giving the customers exactly what they expect is never a bad business decision."

"And do you always give people what they expect?" There was a subtle but undeniable deepening in his voice.

One that sent a delighted shiver down my spine and warmed me in all the right places. The man might have a dangerous and deadly poison running through his system, but it wasn't doing a goddamn thing to dampen his magnetism.

"That," I said lightly, "depends entirely on the person and their expectations."

"Can you two flirt in private?" Sgott grumbled. "As your surrogate father figure, dear Beth, it's not something I need or want to be listening to."

I laughed and touched his arm lightly. "Sorry."

We continued on in silence, following the winding path past several sets of steps that led back up to the wall before finally reaching an ornate metal staircase that wound up to the bridge that spanned the canal. The waiting ambulance had parked up on the footpath, no doubt to allow cars to pass by on the narrow road. Not that there was all that much vehicle movement, because sane people were no doubt asleep at this hour of the night. Or morning, as it actually was.

Sgott followed the medic into the ambulance and deposited Cynwrig onto the stretcher. After a brief conversation—one I annoyingly couldn't hear—he came out, slammed the doors closed, and then turned to me.

"Well, now, lass, what the devil have you and Lugh been up to tonight?"

"You mean aside from Lugh being poisoned, the Boot being firebombed, and me being attacked by that bastard I knocked down? Nothing much, really."

He snorted. "Are the firebomber and your attacker one and the same?"

"No, although they were both using shadow shields."

"Then how do you know they're not one and the same?"

"Because the firebomber moved a little too fast at one point, and the spell briefly shredded. He had golden eyes and a handlebar moustache. The mugger didn't, and his eyes are blue." I paused. "How is he? Do you know?"

"He was conscious when I left. The medics don't believe there's any skull or brain damage but can't be sure until they get him to hospital and do scans."

"Did you manage to question him at all?"

"No, and a pat-down while he was still unconscious didn't reveal any ID. I've sent a couple of men in the ambulance with him. We'll keep him under guard until we get the all clear to question him."

I nodded. "Do you want me to come to the station and make a statement?"

"I do need a statement, but it can wait until the morning. I've sent a forensics team to the tavern, but you might not be able to open for the lunch crowd tomorrow."

"It'll be longer than that—you know how fussy the heritage council are when it comes to damn repairs."

"You could still open the top bar."

I wrinkled my nose. "Too much hassle. It's not going to hit the bottom line all that much if we close down for a couple of days, because midweek trade in winter is usually abominably slow."

He smiled. "So your mom used to say, and yet whenever I went in there, it was packed to the rafters."

"It's a small place, so it doesn't take many people to do that."

He laughed. "Come on; I'll walk you home."

"I'm fine, Sgott. Really."

"Oh, it's not you I'm worried about. It's any muggers who might make the poor decision to attack you."

I nudged him lightly. "Idiot."

He laughed again. "I notice you didn't deny it."

I could hardly do that when there was more than a grain of truth in it. I'd grown up in a tavern, and Mom had made sure I was well capable of protecting myself. I might not have had any formal fight training, but neither had Mom, and she could bring down the brawniest patron without breaking a sweat.

I'd often wondered if she'd perhaps taken down one too many, and that's what had in the end gotten her killed.

Because she *was* dead. We all knew it, even if none of us were willing to come out and say it just yet.

We made our way back to Eastgate Street. There was an officer in uniform dusting the broken window for prints and another checking for magical remnants.

"Anything?" Sgott asked, as we drew close.

The red-haired, sharp-faced woman shook her head. "Nothing we can use at this point."

Sgott grunted. "Keep looking."

She nodded and got back to her examination. I pressed my fingers against the door, swept the latch up, and then stepped inside to find another two officers photographing and marking the various remnants of the firebomb.

I glanced back at Sgott. "You gave them the code?"

"Aye, lass. You can change it once we're gone."

I nodded and headed for the stairs at the back of the room. Sgott followed me up, the wood creaking under his weight—something it had done for more than sixty years now.

The bulk of the first floor had been given over to a secondary bar and dining area. On the street side of the building, there was another old oak door that led out onto the small terrace walkway that was our section of the Deva Rows.

I continued on past the bar and up the smaller set of stairs to the next floor. I generally kept the door to these locked, not only because this upper area was my living quarters, but also because there'd been a spate of thefts since Mom's death. Thieves had obviously feared her more than me.

Even with the roof height lifted, upstairs was tiny. There was a combined kitchen-living area and two bedrooms—one had been Mom's and was now mine, and the other one Lugh and I had shared as kids and I now used as a spare. The bathroom was the second biggest room in the flat, but it had to be, given that, at one point, four oversized pixies had been using it. Gran had moved out when she'd handed over the tavern's reins to Mom, but before then, she'd slept in the loft, which was only accessible through a hatch and a loft ladder—something that had never worried her, as she'd been remarkably spritely right up until the day she'd passed.

I strode across to the second bedroom and ducked under the doorframe—Gran hadn't altered the doorways when she'd raised the roof—then stepped to one side. There wasn't enough room left for Sgott's bulk, so he remained outside and sat on his heels.

Lugh was asleep on the double bed, his body covered by a blanket, and his sock-covered feet hanging over the end. His face remained pale, but sweat no longer beaded his skin, and his breathing was far easier. Darby dozed in a chair she'd pulled up close to the bed but stirred as we entered.

"How'd it go?" I asked softly.

She scrubbed a hand across her eyes. There were shadows underneath them, and her cheeks looked gaunt— both a result of losing the energy she'd used to cure Lugh.

All magic had its costs, but for healers, it came in the form of physical depletion. Elf history was littered with tales of healers who'd died even as they saved their patients. I hoped Darby never pushed things that far.

"He'll sleep the remnants of the exposure off and should be fine by tomorrow evening, but I thought I'd better remain here until you got back, just in case someone decided another attack was in order." She pushed wearily to her feet. "I take it you didn't catch the firebomber?"

"She might not have caught the bomber, but she did catch a mugger," Sgott replied, amusement in his voice.

"Mugger?" Darby's golden eyebrows rose. "Was it a random event or connected?"

"I'm betting it was connected," I said. "I'll give you all the details tomorrow. Right now, you'd better get home before you collapse."

"I'll drive you," Sgott said. "The car's just around the corner."

"That would be great, thanks."

He nodded and glanced at me. "I'll be back at ten to take your statement."

He turned and went back down the stairs. Darby collected her bag, then walked over and threw one arm around my shoulder, hugging me lightly. "He really will be okay. There won't be any side effects other than a lingering headache for the next day or so."

I smiled and briefly returned the embrace. "Thank you."

Amusement danced in her eyes. "He owes me now, and I have every intention of claiming that debt in sex."

I laughed. "He's master of resisting your approaches. I'm not sure that will ever change."

"Ah, but healing him has given me a whole new insight.

Plus, he had a truth serum in him. I now know how to push *all* his buttons."

"My buttons," came a sleepy comment, "are buried so deep that even you won't find them."

"You," she replied severely, but with laughter dancing through her expression, "are supposed to be asleep."

"How can anyone sleep with you two nattering on? Get out of here and let an old man rest."

Darby snorted but nevertheless headed out. I followed her down the stairs and across the main bar to where Sgott waited near the front door.

"Forensics will be another hour," he said. "I've told them to tape plastic or a tarp over the window for you and then head out the back door when they've finished, so you can lock up here."

"I'll see you in the morning, then."

He nodded and left. Darby wiggled her fingers in a goodbye and followed him out. Once I'd locked up, I grabbed my phone and sent a quick text to my staff, telling them to take the next couple of days off—full pay, of course. Good workers were hard to find these days, and I wasn't about to risk them going elsewhere.

I headed upstairs, checking on Lugh once more before moving across to my own bedroom. I was asleep almost before my head hit the pillow.

A heavy pounding woke me who knew how many hours later. I snapped upright, blinking owlishly for several seconds as my brain scrambled to figure out what on earth was happening. Then it registered—someone was pounding on the front door.

I swore and threw off the blankets. The light filtering in from the skylight above suggested it was morning, and a quick look at my phone confirmed it was nearly eight, which meant I'd had all of four hours sleep, if that. I was going to kill whoever the hell the door-banging idiot was.

After throwing on a sweater long enough to cover my bare butt, I checked Lugh to make sure he was still resting comfortably, and then raced down the two sets of stairs. The banging had stopped by the time I hit the ground floor, and there was no evidence that anyone had tampered with the black plastic that now covered the broken window.

I slapped the dead bolt and the latch aside, and then opened the door.

To see absolutely no one.

I cautiously peered out. There were a few people walking toward The Cross, but none appeared in a hurry, and their appearance and manner of walking suggested they were older rather than young. Not generally the type who'd be banging on retailers' doors just for the hell of it.

There was no pedestrian movement down the other end of Eastgate. Whether that meant the door banger had disappeared down Godstall Lane or into one of the nearby cafes, I couldn't say, and I couldn't exactly go out to investigate when I was wearing nothing more than a longish sweater. I swore and stepped back.

And saw the note pinned to the door.

If you give back what you stole, there will be no further action or consequences, it said. *If you don't, I'll fucking kill you.*

THREE

Anger hit, hard and fast. It wasn't so much the threat as the fact that I recognized the goddamn writing. I had at least twenty notes written in the same old-style cursive text upstairs, though none of them contained any sort of threat. Quite the opposite in fact.

But then, those notes had all been written before I'd dropped Mathi Dhār-Val's lying ass eight months ago.

I didn't rip the note from the door and tear it into tiny little pieces, but only because Sgott would probably want to dust it for prints. It was always possible Mathi *hadn't* written the note, of course, but I seriously doubted it. He and I had been an item for nearly ten years. I knew his writing almost as well as I knew every inch of his gloriously golden body.

I slammed the door hard enough for reverberations to shimmer through the entire building, ran through the dusty tears that rained down yet again, and bounded up the stairs. I might not be able to tear up the note, but I sure as hell could confront the bastard behind it. And it wasn't as if I didn't know where he lived, because he and the wife-to-be no doubt shared the very same house he and I had used for most of the ten years we'd been together.

"Bethany?" came Lugh's sleepy question. "Everything all right?"

"Yes."

"I'm not convinced by that reply. At *all*."

"Someone nailed a note to the door, and it seriously annoyed me, that's all."

"Must have been some note."

"It was." I hesitated. "I have to go out for a little while to grab some stuff. I won't be long."

"If I were a betting man, I'd say 'grabbing stuff' doesn't mean supplies, but rather the balls of the idiot who left the note."

"A statement I cannot deny."

"You need help?"

"No."

"Then be careful."

"Always."

He snorted. And with good reason—being careful wasn't exactly written into our DNA. I might run a tavern rather than hunt relics, but that didn't mean the gene was in any way less dominant in me.

I threw on jeans, boots, and a coat, then, after stuffing my phone, keys, and a credit card into my pockets, headed back downstairs. Once I'd taken a photo of the note, I sent it across to the IIS and Sgott. I didn't tell them who it was from, because I wanted the pleasure of confronting the bastard myself first.

Besides, there was unlikely to be any sort of major confrontation or trouble, because Mathi wasn't normally into that sort of thing. The very few threats I *had* heard him issue over the years were always politely said, and any follow-through generally handled by someone else.

Which *did* make the violent undertone in the note *extremely* unusual.

I locked the door and then headed to the end of Eastgate Street to catch a cab. The main encampment of the light elves—whose true name was Ljósálfar, though few enough used it these days—lay to the east of Deva and comprised a huge swath of land that contained both old and new forests and several vast lakes. Though I'd never been there, I'd seen plenty of photos of the beautiful, magical homes they'd crafted out of living trees.

By contrast, dark elves—the Myrkálfar—were masters of earth and stone, and their buildings reflected that, possessing a presence that was both weighty and wondrous. The dark elf palace was an example of this, though most of the building remained underground, with only the everyday reception rooms and offices visible above. Most did still live in the vast underground compounds, though they weren't the dark and gloomy spaces most people believed them to be, as dark elves had long ago mastered the art of sun tunnels.

Or so Gran had once told me.

Mathi—like many other highborns—maintained a secondary residence within Deva. His was in the Garden Terraces district, which was closer to the main commercial and shopping districts in East Deva.

It was peak hour, so the traffic was vile. Which, in many respects, was a good thing, because it gave time for my anger to cool and let me think more rationally about the situation. And the more I *did*, the more out of character that note seemed—especially when it came to the use of the expletive. Light elves considered swearing to be a coarse and unnecessary use of language, and they weren't into explosive emotion. Or any sort of deep emotion, really. They could be warm and funny once they got to know you, but there was always a remoteness—a reserve—that never entirely disappeared. Many believed they'd become that way because they despised the excesses of human behavior, and while that might in part be true, I thought it had more to do with the sheer length of their lifespans.

Of course, dark elves had the same long-living genes, and by all accounts, there was absolutely nothing remote or reserved about *them*. The little I'd seen of Cynwrig seemed to back that up.

It took us nearly a half hour to reach Garden Terraces. It was a beautiful area close to the canal and surrounded on two sides by community parks—the third reason many of the fair folk had residences there. I paid the cabbie, then climbed out and stared up at the modern brick building. There were four stories in all, but Mathi's apartment was at the top—the penthouse, as he liked to call it. It had lovely views over the city and gardens and was the largest of the twelve in the complex.

I took a deep breath to calm the weird mix of annoy-ance, uncertainty, and nerves, and then walked up to the secure entrance and typed in the code. I didn't expect it to have changed, because Mathi had always been convinced I'd see sense and come back to him.

The door unlocked and clicked open. I shook my head and headed for the private lift. A few seconds later, I was walking through the plush, pale-green foyer to the apart-ment's main door. Once again, the entry code had not changed.

I opened the door, stepped inside, and then said, "Mathi, you here?"

"Bethany?" Sleepiness ran through the silky-smooth tone. "Is that you?"

"In the flesh. Get out of bed, because we need to talk."

His soft but throaty laugh crawled deliciously across my senses and brought back memories of all the nights in which we'd done everything *but* talk.

"Why don't you come in here and get me?"

"I take it that means the wife-to-be isn't here?"

"Why would she be?"

"Because she's your wife-to-be?"

He laughed softly. "Any marriage I undertake is nothing more than a business deal. I've told you that, multiple times."

"Yes, and it makes no damn difference."

"What if I said the wife-to-be is no longer?"

That raised my eyebrows. "Does that mean you're no longer wife shopping?"

"No. It means Mariatta is no longer in consideration. Her family simply asked too much in way of compensation."

Compensation—or a bride price, as it was more commonly known—was a payment the groom's family made to the wife's family and was a peculiarity of the high-borns. "If you're still shopping, you and I are not happening. Are you coming out or not?"

He sighed. "Yes. Go make us a coffee—I cannot function without it at this hour."

"It's just gone eight-thirty, Mathi. That's almost half the morning gone."

"I've always wondered how your tavern makes a profit with math like that." Bedsheets rustled, and I once again found myself fighting the delicious tumble of memories. "Besides, I didn't get to bed until nearly six."

I took off my coat and hung it on the discreetly placed coat stand. "Does that mean you're back to your partying ways?"

He snorted. It somehow managed to be both an amused and contemptuous sound. "I was at a council meeting, not with a woman."

"I wouldn't care if you were. Your womanizing ways are the problem of whoever you're currently targeting, not me."

I headed into the kitchen at the rear of the apartment. Not only was it equipped with all the mod cons, it also had glorious views over the nearby park. Sunshine poured in from the floor-to-ceiling windows, lending warmth to the white-and-gold marble counters and the glossy white cabinetry that now dominated. It had all been glorious old wood when I'd lived here, so Mariatta had obviously redecorated in anticipation of being installed as his official partner. In truth, replacement was probably a good move, given how often Mathi and I had used the various counter surfaces for all manner of things that *didn't* include food preparation or eating ...

I once again shoved the treacherous memories aside and walked across to the espresso machine to make us both a coffee. The slightest stirring of air warned me of his closeness, but before I could react, his arms wrapped around my waist and pulled me back into a body that was warm, wiry, and so very familiar.

"It is such a pleasure to see you again, my dear Bethany."

His breath stirred heat across my skin as butterfly kisses trailed up my neck. It was all I could do to ignore the sweet rush of desire when his teeth grazed my earlobe.

"I'm here to talk, Mathi," I somehow managed to say. "Just talk, nothing more."

And yet I didn't pull away when he slid his hands under my sweater and moved them, with slow, sweet torture toward my breasts. It had been too long since anyone had touched me with such passionate intimacy, and I missed it. More than I actually missed him, if I was being at all honest.

His long, slender hands cupped the weight of my breasts, as if in reverence, then his clever fingers began to tease my nipples, making them harden and ache. I closed my eyes and rested my head against his chest, enjoying the sensations and the desire that rippled through me. Gods, how often had I stood in this same spot attempting to make coffee while he stood behind me intent on seduction? How often had he succeeded?

Every. Single. Damn. Time.

This was dangerous. *Very* dangerous. And yet ...

The breeze of his gentle laugh caressed my neck. "I think we both know talking is not what you have on your mind. Not right now."

Which was just the sort of self-assured, arrogant comment I needed to break the spell of memory and desire. "Mathi, if you don't release my breasts right now and step away, I'm going to bury my heel in your balls."

He laughed again. It remained a sweetly seductive sound. "You don't mean that."

I lifted my foot. He released me and jumped back. "Okay, so you do."

He walked toward the other side of the counter, and it was only then I realized he was utterly and gloriously naked. His golden body was lean and sinewy, his face angelic, and his erection fierce. But then Mathi, like most elves, did have an extremely high sex drive.

I finished making the coffee, then picked up both mugs

and walked over to the long, wide counter, keeping it between us. It was definitely safer that way now that my hormones were primed and ready to go.

It was a truly sad state of affairs that so little could get me so hot.

"Why was the fae council meeting so late?" I asked. "That's unusual, isn't it?"

He accepted his coffee with a nod, his expression remote but the fires of desire unbanked in his eyes. "These are unusual times, apparently."

"Meaning what? It was attended by all fae representatives, not just the elves?"

"Indeed." He took a sip of coffee and sighed. It was a soft sound of pleasure. "If Mariatta had been able to make coffee this good, I might have taken her proposal a little more seriously."

Despite the amused glimmer in his eyes, I suspected he was serious. "And the night council? Were they also there?"

While dark elves did sit on the night council—mainly to bear witness and pass on any pertinent information and decisions to the fae council—it mostly contained representatives from not only the various classifications of shifters and those fae who preferred shadow over light, but also the dwarvin folk and ghuls. The latter two weren't often seen here in Deva, though. Dwarves preferred the more mountainous terrain of the Welsh Mountains to the southwest, and the ghuls tended to haunt older, more remote cemeteries in regional areas.

"Indeed."

I raised my eyebrows. "Something drastic must have happened then."

"Yes, but it's not a specifically recent problem." He eyed

me for a second. "What is it you wished to talk about? Not the late-night meeting of the fae council, I suspect."

"No." I dragged out my phone, brought up the pic of the note, and slid it across to him. "I want you to explain that."

He picked up the phone and studied the image for several seconds. I sipped my coffee and watched him carefully, looking for all the telltale signs that suggested concern or annoyance—the light downturn of one side of his mouth, a tiny but brief narrowing of his eyes. There was nothing.

"To state the obvious, that's a threat." His gaze rose to mine. "To you, or to your brother?"

"You tell me. That's your handwriting, is it not?"

"Why would you think—" He paused, then enlarged the image. "I cannot swear to this without seeing the actual note, but the first section *does* appear to be written by me. The latter part is not, however."

"What makes you say that? Aside from the crudity, that is?"

The slightest wisp of amusement caressed his lips. "Crudity aside, the ascenders are not correctly aligned in the latter half of the note. I would never be so careless, even in haste."

I had no idea what he was talking about and made a mental note to check it out later. "So if someone is imitating at least a portion of your writing, how the hell did they get the actual note?"

"That I can't say."

"But you have sent notes like this?"

Another ghostly smile teased his lips. "To errant members of staff, most certainly."

"Were they sacked?"

"That would depend on what they stole and whether they returned that item."

My eyebrows rose. "You keep thieves on the payroll? Isn't that dangerous?"

He shrugged. "Good help is hard to find these days. Besides, those who are honest enough to return what they stole do deserve a second chance. They are, of course, very aware there are no *third* chances."

Which was something of an understatement given that, in times past, people had disappeared—never to be seen again—from fae businesses for far lesser crimes.

"Do you think one of them could be behind this note?"

"Perhaps, though the staff we use at both the main encampment and within our offices are very highly vetted."

"They can't be too highly vetted if you're sending out notes like this."

"Temptation occasionally gets the better of even the most honest person." A wicked gleam flared to life in the blue of his eyes. "Are you sure the temptation to once again feel my caress is not the true reason you are here?"

"Given my first impulse on seeing this note was to throttle rather than fuck you, I can honestly answer yes."

He tsked. "Such crudity does not become you."

I laughed. "You've spent nigh on ten years trying to knock the tavern wench out of my DNA, Mathi. I suggest it's well past time you gave up."

"I have never believed in giving up."

The determined glint in his eyes only added weight to what was, in its own way, a threat. In coming here today, in reacting to his touch in the manner I had, I'd only fueled his determination to once again claim me as his own.

And there was a tiny part of me that didn't actually mind that prospect. What I needed, I thought wistfully, was a virile and available man to caress away the lingering and very unwise desire for Mathi.

Cynwrig's image rose, and my pulse rate instantly stepped up. While I didn't really need to be going out with another elf who'd never commit to someone like me, a few months of hot and sweaty sex could be just what the doctor ordered.

Of course, the whole problem with that—admittedly delicious—scenario was the fact I'd probably never see the man again.

I took another drink of coffee and then said, as firmly as I could, "I want to remain your friend, Mathi, but I can't be anything else. Not now. Not when you're wife shopping. I will never play the third wheel in any relationship, no matter how much I enjoy your presence and your touch."

He sighed, a sound of acceptance that belied the continuing determination in his eyes. "I take it this note has been given to Sgott and his team for analysis?" When I nodded, he added, "Good. I'll request an update from him."

Meaning his father would. Mathi might hold a seat on the fae council, but his father was Sgott's daytime counterpart in the IIT. I pointed to the phone he still held.

"Have you sent such a note to anyone recently?"

He hesitated. "There is one possibility, though it's not really recent."

"Can I get a name? And an address?"

"You could, but she's unlikely to talk to you."

"Why not?"

That faint smile touched his lips again. "Because she was never pleased with your primary position in my life."

I blinked, even as so many little things that had happened over the last few months of our relationship suddenly made sense. "So aside from courting Mariatta, you had a *third* lover while we were living together?"

"Mariatta and I were never in a sexual relationship. As I have said, it was purely a business arrangement."

"*That* isn't the point. You agreed, at the outset of *our* relationship, to let me know if you were ever considering entering a marriage contract or taking another lover."

"Yes, but I had no desire for you to walk away."

"And yet an elf is only ever as good as his word—how often have you quoted *that* over the years?"

Amusement touched his eyes again. "It is a statement that is *always* tempered by the situation. I do believe that, at the time, I would have agreed to anything to get you into my bed on a more permanent basis."

"That doesn't absolve the promise breaking. At *all*." I took another drink and did my best to control the flare of anger. It wouldn't get me anywhere, because we'd gone over this exact same ground eight months ago when I'd became aware of Mariatta's presence in his life. "Did this third lover steal from you? Is that why she received the note?"

"Goodness, no. The theft simply brought Gilda's ... attributes ... to my attention."

"That's fucked, Mathi."

"I will admit that, in hindsight, you deserved far better treatment from me."

"Big of you," I muttered. "I still need to talk to her."

"As I've already said—"

"It's either me or the IIT," I cut in. "Her choice, but one way or the other, I will get my answers."

He studied me for a moment then pushed back from the counter. "Let me go get dressed, and we'll walk over there."

"Walk?" I said, with just the slightest edge. "Gilda lives *that* close?"

"Yes."

"Always?"

"Yes."

"You're a bastard, Mathi."

"No. I'm simply fae."

Annoyance swirled, more on behalf of the fae whose names he blackened with such a comment. "Not all fae are promiscuous."

"Elves are."

I wanted to fire back "not all elves" but in truth, how could I be sure of that? Especially when the sexual exploits of *dark* elves were the stuff of legends. While I could neither confirm nor deny their prowess, there had to be some truth to the rumors or they wouldn't have persisted down through the centuries.

I swallowed my annoyance and waved a hand at his nakedness. "Go get dressed, then, and hurry up about it. I do have a tavern to get back to."

"Are you sure you don't wish to partake in a little re-familiarization first?"

"Absolutely sure."

The heat in his eyes deepened, and its echo burned through my being, making me hunger for things that were neither wise nor safe.

"Oh, I think you lie, Bethany my darling," he said softly. "Your body betrays you."

I drank more coffee and tried to get my hormones under some form of control. "Sadly for you, my body does not rule my actions."

"It did only a few moments ago."

"You snuck up on me. It won't happen again."

His lips twitched. "I wouldn't bet on that."

Neither would I, actually.

"Go get dressed, Mathi," I said irritably. "I have no desire to waste an entire day in a war of words with you."

"It would indeed be a waste when there are far more pleasurable things we could be doing."

I raised an eyebrow and silently pointed toward the kitchen door. He laughed and strolled out. His erection, I noted, had not eased. But then, he'd always been a randy bastard.

I finished my coffee, put both cups into the dishwasher, and then walked out to the foyer to grab my coat. Mathi appeared a few minutes later, wearing a blue sweater that deepened the color of his eyes, black pants, and a black woolen coat. It was all very crisp and stylish, much like the man himself. He'd never been the jeans and T-shirt wearing type, so maybe that's what I needed to be seeking out next.

Or maybe I just needed to send a wish on the wind for a pixie bachelor of an appropriate height to make an appearance.

Mathi opened the door, waved me through, and then followed. We took the lift down to the main foyer and quickly exited. In the short time I'd been inside, the sunshine had given away to drizzle, and the day had become gray, gloomy, and rather cold. I paused on the foot-path and hastily zipped up my coat. Mathi touched my spine and guided me lightly to the left. Even through the thick layers of the coat, his warm touch had heat stirring through my veins.

I definitely needed a man—*any* man—to get over the desire for this one.

I stepped away from him. He chuckled softly but did keep his hands to himself from that point on.

We turned into the first street on the right. It was a fenced dead end, with the gate leading into a small park. Most of the houses on the street were modern, but there were a couple of gorgeous old Georgians still standing near the park. We stopped at the last of these, and he pressed the bell. It rang loudly inside, but there was no immediate response. After a few seconds, he pressed it again. This time, there was an odd scraping noise—one that had visions of bloody death swirling through my mind.

The instinct to run hit, and it was so damn strong that my body trembled under its force. I didn't want to go inside, didn't want to confront the blood and the death that waited ... and yet the same wisps of second sight that were responsible for those bloody visions were now saying I had no other choice.

Mathi frowned. "It's odd that she's not answering. I know she's home. I rang her before we left."

"Have you got a key?"

"Yes, of course, but—"

"Go in and check on her—but be on guard, as there might be someone else in there. I'll go around the back and check what made that noise."

He briefly looked set to argue and then simply nodded and opened the door. I ran down to the end of the building and into the lane that led into the small parking area servicing the nearby residences.

I slowed as I neared the end, my heart racing, though it was fear rather than exertion. There were three cars parked in the section immediately opposite, but the side fence was too high to see what was going on in the rest of the area.

My appearance was met with a squeal of tires. My head snapped around, and all I could see was the nose of a white van coming straight at me.

I swore and threw myself sideways; the vehicle was too damn close to do anything else. I hit the ground with a pain-filled grunt and skidded along the damp asphalt for several yards, coming to a halt inches away from the sharp edge of the old dumpster bin sitting near the fence.

A rear tire came perilously close to my fingers, and I instinctively tucked my feet back, even though the van had already sped past.

I twisted around and caught a partial glimpse of the van's license plate number as it disappeared down the lane. The asshole didn't stop; the van's tires squealed as he spun it out of the lane and then sped away.

I took a deep, shuddering breath that did nothing to ease the hammering in my heart or the sick churning in my gut. Why had the van driver tried to kill me? He couldn't have known why I was running into that lane, because he couldn't have seen us from the back of the house. I guessed it was possible that he—or someone with him—might have recognized Mathi as we'd approached, but wouldn't they have lain low in the van rather than drawing attention to themselves like this?

I rolled onto my back, heard a soft scratch, and quickly twisted around. Beady eyes stared back at me.

Rats.

There were goddamn *rats* under the bin. I somehow managed to restrain my squeak of horror and slowly edged away. The rats twitched their whiskers, somehow managing to look amused as they strolled away.

I waited until I could no longer see the horrid little monsters and then looked up at the house. Unfortunately, I was too close to the rear fence to see anything useful, though the back gate was open and swinging lightly in the faint breeze. Had Gilda left it open, or had the van driver come through it before his attempt to run me over?

There was only one way to find out. I sat up, and almost instantly a dozen different aches vied for painful prominence. My hands were the worst; I'd skinned them pretty badly when I'd slid along the asphalt, and they were full of muck and bleeding profusely. It was nothing a healer couldn't fix easily enough, but right now, they hurt like a bitch.

My coat was scraped and torn in several spots, but it had at least protected my breasts and stomach from major scrapes. Same with my jeans, though there was a small tear on my right knee that was surrounded by a darker patch that might well be blood. I didn't investigate. It wasn't like I could do a whole lot about it now anyway.

I slowly climbed to my feet, then headed over to the gate and followed the moss-covered concrete path to the rear door. After tugging a sleeve over my bleeding hand— mainly to stop blood getting everywhere more than anything else—I turned the door handle. It was locked, as were the two sash windows on either side.

I stepped back and looked up. The window on the right side of the building was open, but it was one hell of a jump down ... though it wasn't, I guessed, a distance that would worry the average shifter. Or even those fae who were flight capable, though if the latter *had* been responsible for the death that waited inside this house, they'd have simply flown off.

Our window opener hadn't. While the garden bed was covered in those small white stones rather than pine mulch, there did appear to be a couple of indentations. And the winter clematis that hugged the warmth of the wall definitely looked as if someone had half-landed on it.

I walked over to the tap to wash the grime out of my hands and then quickly retraced my steps. As I stepped through the still open front door I said, "Mathi?"

"Up here."

His voice was flat. Monotone. Chills ran up my spine. In the ten years I'd known him, I'd only ever heard that tone once. It had been on the night he'd informed me that his mother had died and that he wouldn't be home, as there was a week-long grieving process to be undertaken. He hadn't been that close to his mother from what I'd seen, but her death had nevertheless shaken him. It was, perhaps, the reason he'd started thinking about his own mortality and led to his sudden decision to seek a wife.

I went up the stairs slowly, knowing full well what I was about to see, thanks to those damn visions, and reluctant to face the brutal reality of it.

"I suggest you stay out there," Mathi said as I stepped onto the landing. "It is ... unpleasant."

"I need to see it, Mathi."

"No, you don't. I've called in the IIT. It would be better if you—"

"Perhaps it would," I cut in gently. "But I'm nevertheless coming in."

Because the wisps of second sight that had shown me this death were now declaring there was something else in there I had to see.

I swallowed heavily, stepped through the bedroom door, and then stopped cold as horror dawned. *This* was far worse than anything the visions had shown.

Gilda had been torn apart.

Totally and utterly torn apart.

CHAPTER
FOUR

There was blood, gore, and body parts everywhere. Legs near the front window, torso on the bed, arms between this door and the rear window. I had no idea where her head was and no intention of looking for it. And yet my gaze went to the far end of the bed and the bloody strands of gold visible there ... Bile surged up my throat. I swallowed heavily and instinctively stepped back, then caught the movement and stopped.

I needed to face this. Needed to find whatever the hell instinct was insisting I find ... though how it expected me to do *that* when all I could see and all I could smell was blood and death, I had no idea.

"Is your ghoulish need to see a rival's end satisfied now?" Mathi said, in a voice so cold it may have well swept off the arctic.

My gaze snapped to his. "After nearly ten years together, you truly think I came in here because of some macabre need to see *this*?" I angrily waved a hand around the room. "That's fucking disappointing, Mathi."

"Then why insist on seeing it?"

"Because my second sight is insisting there's something here to uncover. Something *other* than death."

He studied me silently for several seconds and then said, voice a touch warmer, "I thought second sight was your mother's province rather than yours."

"Well, you thought wrong."

He took a deep breath and released it slowly. It was the only outward sign of how shaken he was by this murder. "I apologize for my outburst, then."

I nodded. In truth, I might well have acted in the same manner if it had been someone close to me so effortlessly torn apart.

I swallowed against the second surge of bile and did my best to study the room. But it was hard to see beyond the gore ... Harder still when I had no idea what I was looking for.

I wished I'd taken more notice of Mom when she'd talked about second sight. Gran had trained her to control and funnel the ability, but there'd never been any indication I'd inherited the skill, so the knowledge had never been passed on. Although, interestingly, Mom *had* started talking about it more in recent years; perhaps she'd begun to suspect I'd be a late bloomer.

"How could something like this"—I waved a hand around again—"happen without anyone reporting it? Surely it wouldn't have happened in silence."

"Both magic and drugs are able to silence someone."

"I'm not sensing any leftover magical resonance here, though."

"A good enough practitioner wouldn't have left one." His voice was back to being remote and very controlled. "If you wish to search the room, I suggest you do so before the IIT get here and lock the scene down."

I crossed my arms and rubbed them lightly. It didn't disperse the chill creeping through me. My gaze fell on the bedside table to the left of the bed. The drawers had all been pulled out and their contents dumped in a bloody pile on the floor, while the bits and pieces sitting on the top had either been knocked over or opened and tipped out. Obviously, Gilda's murderer had been looking for something on the small side. Why else would he—or she—be searching the items on her bedside tables?

"Mathi, did Gilda have a safe or someplace she stored valuables?"

"I don't believe she stored her jewelry anywhere special, or indeed, that she had expensive enough jewelry to require it." He paused. "You don't think this is just a robbery gone very wrong, do you?"

"No, but her murderer was definitely searching for something, given he was ferreting through her underwear drawer."

"Perhaps he has an underwear fetish."

I gave him a long look, and a smile tugged at the corner of his lips, though it failed to melt the ice in his eyes. "Why tear her apart, then? The dead cannot reveal their secrets."

I shrugged. "Perhaps her attacker lost his temper."

"There're certainly a number of shifter subgroups with well-known anger control issues, and all of them would be capable of something like this."

It was said with just the slightest hint of disdain. But then, light elves and shifters had a long history of confrontation, even if things were far more civilized these days.

"Was Gilda human?" I asked.

"No. Light elf." He paused. "From a serving house."

Though most humans believed all elves were equal,

there were actually three distinct class levels: highborn, of which Mathi was one; the foresters, who were the elf equivalent of traders and included healers, wood carvers, and arborists; and the servant class. The latter was generally made up of those elven families who, historically, had no ability to manage flora and nothing in the way of personal magic such as healing.

That didn't mean that either of those skills couldn't occasionally appear in the lower lines, however.

"Do you know if she was able to manipulate wood?"

Surprise flitted through his expression. "I actually have no idea. Why?"

"Because the perfect place to hide something small is in the one place few would ever think to look in a home owned by a woman belonging to a serving house."

"Hiding stuff under the floorboards is not exactly new. Even humans do that."

"Not under. *In.*"

He raised his eyebrows. "If she could manipulate wood to the extent of being able to rearrange the very fabric of these boards, she'd surely have been more than a mere servant. That sort of skill is highly prized these days."

"Unless, of course, she deliberately hid the ability from you." I narrowed my gaze and studied the floor. While a large, patterned carpet square covered the floor under and around the bed, the floorboards in the rest of the room were painted white. There was no obvious intrusion point, so I cocked my head and listened to the murmurings of the ancient woods that made up so much of this house. After a few seconds I heard a discordant note from somewhere to the left. I stepped that way, carefully avoiding all the blood, bits of flesh, and gods knew what else. "How long were you and she lovers, Mathi?"

"Close to twelve months."

"And you never noticed her before she stole from you?"

It was absently said, because I was sensing something else now. Something that vaguely reminded me of the power I'd felt so briefly in the Eye. But fiercer ... brighter. Something that spoke of fire and eruptions rather than death and darkness.

"No."

The discordant murmur seemed to be coming from somewhere near the window. "And you didn't bother rechecking her credentials before you took her to your bed?"

"There was no need to." He paused. "You think her becoming my lover was a setup?"

"It has to be a consideration now, surely."

"But why would they go to all the trouble of setting her up as a possible channel for information and then waste such a valuable resource in this manner?"

"That would depend on what they were after from you in the first place."

I squatted on my heels and brushed my fingers across the floor. There was no answering pulse in the wood, though that wouldn't have stopped Gilda from manipulating its fibers if she'd had that skill. But there was absolutely no indication—no leftover spark of energy—that suggested she had.

"It makes no sense for her to be a spy," Mathi said. "She was carefully monitored when not in my company, and she had no access to any kind of official business. She was never even in *our* home."

"Glad to hear you at least considered our bed out of bounds."

65

"I am not completely without feelings or consideration, Bethany."

No, he wasn't. But he also wasn't capable of the sort of relationship I really wanted, and he *did* have the typical, self-centered, "it's all about me" elf thing happening. If I was being at all honest, our relationship had been based more on sex than anything else.

Of course, it had been damn *good* sex.

The other major factor in the length of our relationship had been the decided lack of other prospects on the horizon. You'd think that working in a tavern would provide a full range of options, but in my experience, the opposite was true. Maybe because I saw them all at their inglorious best.

"Think about it, Mathi. It's rather expensive to buy a place in this part of town, so where'd she get the money from if she was servant class?"

"I presumed she was renting."

"It wasn't something that came up in the vetting probe?"

"No."

"Then maybe it should in future."

"Yes, although I suspect it might be a case of locking the door once the horse has already bolted."

I'd bet he had *that* right. I ran my fingers up the wall. As they neared the windowsill, a faint but jarring vibration teased my fingertips. It was the song of wood fibers torn apart and not repaired.

I shook my head at her thoughtlessness and ran my hand along the sill until I found the nucleus of the song. Then, with my fingers pressed to either side of the tear, I called to the magic that enabled me to control wood and gently but carefully pried the fibers apart.

Something small and red popped out. I caught it with my free hand, then healed the breach—this time knitting the fibers back together so that they no longer resonated a jarring, unhappy note—and held my trophy up to the light. It was a ruby. The fiery energy I'd sensed earlier stung my fingertips and, deep in the ruby's heart, fire burned with explosive energy.

Mathi sucked in a deep breath and then swore softly. I turned to look at him. "I take it you know what this is?"

"Yes." He moved across the room and squatted beside me but didn't attempt to touch the ruby. "It comes from the Éadrom Hoard."

"The *what*?"

A smile ghosted his lips but failed to touch his eyes. "It's basically a hoard of godly relics—one of three within the United Kingdom. The elves have been their guardians for more than a millennium."

Since we pixies had been kicked out of the gods' service, then. "Why are you so sure this stone is a part of the hoard?"

"Because of the energy it's emitting and the fire that burns deep in its heart." His fingers hovered millimeters from its surface, as if he wanted to touch it but didn't dare. "It is one of three stones forged into the shield of Hephaestus, who was the Greek god of smiths, fire, and volcanoes."

"I take it the shield gave the holder control over those elements?"

He nodded. "Which was why the rubies were pried out and stored in separate locations."

"Then how did Gilda get this one?"

"I have no idea how it came to be in her possession, but the vault containing the Éadrom Hoard was broken into six months ago."

The images I'd seen briefly in the Eye came to mind, and I couldn't help but wonder if it was also part of the hoard. It had certainly shown me fire, and this jewel was one of three that could control that element. But surely if it *had* been, Nialle and Lugh's research would have raised red flags within the museum's hierarchy, if not on the fae council itself. Theft might be part of an antiquarian's job, but it was only sanctified when it came to private collections, not state-approved ones such as the vaults.

And yet, it would not only explain Nialle's murder but also the threat on the tavern's door. The elves did *not* take kindly to people making fools of them; if they'd believed Nialle had been part of the plot to steal the hoard, they would have had no qualms about first torturing and then killing him.

It would also explain why the Eldritch hadn't yet interviewed Lugh or allowed him into the apartment to see what might be missing. The Eldritch only answered to was the fae council, and if they also suspected Lugh ...

I took a deep breath and released it slowly. That was stupid. Lugh was too well known—too well respected—for anyone to think him capable of this sort of theft.

"Do you have a record of what was stolen?"

"We have some idea, but many of the smaller items were never recorded." His gaze rose to mine. "Why?"

"Do you know if something called Agrona's Claws were part of the hoard?"

"No, but I'm also not acquainted with the name of every item within the hoard, just the ones the council have had under discussion," he said. "Why do you ask?"

"Because Nialle was murdered recently, and Lugh was poisoned last night. They'd been researching the Claws."

"I take it Lugh is recovering?"

I nodded. "But someone obviously thinks Lugh has the Claws—or, at least, a means of finding them. Why else would they leave that note?"

"And did either Lugh or Nialle successfully procure the Claws?"

I wrinkled my nose. "Nialle *had* just come back from France when he was killed, but more than that, I can't really say."

Mathi frowned. "Your brother wasn't able to tell you anything?"

"He's still in recovery." The temptation to mention the Eye rose, but it was Lugh's possession rather than mine, even if it had been addressed to me. I had no right to say anything until I talked to him first.

The sound of approaching sirens rose above the everyday noise of nearby traffic. Mathi rose. "You should leave this place."

"I can't. I'm a witness."

"Not of the murder—only of its discovery."

"And the murderer might well have been in the van that tried to run me over in the rear parking area." I showed him my hands. "If shifters have been sent, they'll smell the blood."

His gaze slid from my hands to my body, and concern bloomed. He'd obviously been too intent on everything else to realize I'd been hurt. "How bad are your knees?"

"They're scraped, but there's no major damage."

"Then I'll explain what happened and tell them I sent you home. They won't be happy, but I really don't care at this point."

"Maybe you don't, but I—"

"*I* will brook no objections on this matter." He bent, tucked a hand under my arm, and helped me up. "The fewer people who know about the ruby's discovery, the better, for both your safety and that of the continuing investigation."

I followed him across the room, once again carefully watching where I placed my feet. "Are you saying you don't trust the IIT? The very organization your father runs?"

"I have trust in the organization overall, but information *this* important will always escape. That's why all members of the fae council have sworn a blood oath of secrecy."

"One that can't be too binding if you're here talking to me about it."

He led the way down the stairs, his weight barely registering on the old boards. Elves really *did* walk light. We larger pixies, not so much. "Because once you discovered a piece of the hoard, you were automatically included in its terms."

"Handy."

"But necessary, otherwise we couldn't cross-examine any who might be linked to or have knowledge of the hoard." He glanced back at me. "I haven't been able to talk to my own father about it, despite the fact he runs the IIT."

That raised my eyebrows. "Why aren't they part of the investigations? Surely they have the scope and the manpower—"

"As I said, the fewer who know of the theft, the better our chances of recovery."

"It also gives the thieves a greater chance to escape. I would have thought more resources—"

"Oh, trust me, we're not lacking in resources."

The wail of the sirens was now so close, I suspected the vehicles had turned into the street. "And yet they've turned up nothing in six months?"

"I didn't say that. Come on, this way—quickly."

He ran down the hall—something I'd rarely ever seen, and that spoke of his seriousness to get me the hell out of here—then on through the rear kitchen before stopping in the laundry and unlocking the back door.

"Hide that ruby," he said. "Tell no one about it until we can get a specialist to look at it."

"A specialist? Are you forgetting my brother is an antiquarian?"

"No, but I was referring to one of the bibliothecaries responsible for the hoard."

Lugh had mentioned the bibliothèque in the past, always with a distant look of longing. For a researcher and treasure hunter, the legendary library was something close to the holy grail, a place that not only held the history of the elves, but also detailed accounts of all the known treasures, be they godly or not, that had passed through elf hands.

"Surely they could only give you a description or maybe a hand-drawn image. It's not like cameras were around back then."

"No, but the records are so detailed that often pictures are not needed."

"If you're going there anyway, would you be able to check what information there is on Agrona's Claws?"

He hesitated. "I'll see what I can do. In the meantime, you cannot talk to your brother about this find."

"Why, when the ruby might well be connected to Nialle's murder and Lugh's poisoning?"

"That is entirely possible but—"

"I'm not going to lie to my brother."

Annoyance flashed through his expression. "I'm not asking you to. All I desire is that you keep this find to yourself until I get permission from the council to bring you in on the search."

"And Lugh."

He hesitated and then nodded. "Fine. Now go."

He pushed me out the door then locked it behind me. I tucked the ruby into the front pocket of my jeans and then headed out the back gate. I paused briefly, gaze sweeping the parking area, looking for another exit aside from the lane. On the opposite side of the parking area, between two houses, I spotted a pedestrian walkway.

I hurried across, half expecting that at any moment an IIT officer would come busting out of the house after me.

No one did, but the tension nevertheless remained. A bus pulled into a stop just as I came out onto the main street, so I caught that back to Old Deva and then walked down to the tavern. It was only when I entered the main bar and saw Sgott sitting at one of the tables drinking from a take-out cup that I remembered we'd had a ten o'clock appointment.

I grimaced and closed the door. "Sorry. I totally forgot."

"So I gathered." He took a drink. "I also gather your confrontation with Mathi led to the discovery of a rather brutal murder."

Meaning he'd either been listening to the police radio or talking to Ruadhán—Mathi's father. While most night officers headed home to grab some sleep after their shifts, brown bear shifters didn't really need all that much, and they certainly didn't hibernate—but then, their animal counterparts didn't actually go into deep hibernation either. Here in the UK, brown bear shifters tended to take time off in winter—usually February—and went into a regenerative torpor, though they could and did wake up as necessary.

"Yes. And before you ask, and against my protests, he sent me home." I raised my hands. "He didn't want me bleeding all over the crime scene."

"Mathi could no more make you do something against your will than your mother could." Amusement lurked around the corners of his brown eyes. "How'd your hands get skinned?"

I walked over to the bar and grabbed the first aid kit tucked under the counter. "I went around to the back of the house to investigate an odd sound, and some bastard came roaring out of the parking area and tried to run me over."

"Deliberate?"

I nodded. "He didn't stop."

"Did you get the plate?"

I smiled. "A partial one. I was more intent on getting out of the way. Hence the skinned hands."

He grunted and got out his phone. "Ruadhán has asked me to take your statement, so let's start with the plate number and then we'll do the boring bits."

I gave him both statements—one for this morning, the other for last night—while I patched up my hands as best I could. Darby would no doubt be around later this afternoon to check on Lugh, so I'd get her to fix them up properly then.

"You want a sandwich or something?" I stripped off my coat and hung it over the chair opposite his. "I haven't had breakfast yet, and I'm starving."

"When have I ever refused the offer of food, lass?"

I laughed and then headed into the kitchen. Sgott followed, but he leaned against the doorframe rather than coming in. The kitchen was simply too small for someone of his bulk.

"I take it Mathi did write the note?"

I nodded and told him everything Mathi had said about the note and Gilda while I pulled on some gloves and then grabbed the makings of roast beef sandwiches out of the fridge. "The fact the note was pinned on the tavern's door does suggest Lugh's poisoning, Nialle's murder, and now Gilda's might all be linked."

"Not necessarily."

I glanced at him. "You don't believe in coincidences, remember."

He half smiled. "I also don't believe in jumping to conclusions. I doubt the note will provide much in the way of clarity either way, given the only prints we'll probably get will be Mathi's and Gilda's."

"Most likely." I buttered the bread, slapped on some caramelized onions, and then cut the beef into thick slices. "Lugh wants to get into Nialle's apartment to see if anything was stolen."

"I have no sway with the Eldritch, and they're the ones running that investigation."

"You'd think they'd want to know what has and hasn't been taken, though."

"Undoubtedly, but that department has always worked on its own terms and timelines."

"I don't suppose you can at least mention there's some urgency in that matter, given we now have another murder that may well be connected."

"I can try. No guarantee, though."

"Thank you."

A smile tugged at his lips. "I rather suspect that the people behind that note do not understand the force they have unleashed on their trail."

"They poisoned my brother and firebombed my tavern. I have no choice but to track them down now."

"Oh, there are always choices—like leaving the investigation to the proper authorities—but you are very much Meabh's daughter."

My lips twisted. "I just wish I had her knowledge and control when it comes to second sight."

"She always believed you *did* have the ability," he said softly. "She also believed that it—and you—were simply waiting for something."

Something like that black stone, perhaps? Because I couldn't help but think that my errant second sight had only kicked free of its protective shell once I'd held the Eye.

I placed a couple of the sandwiches on a plate and handed them over. "Has anyone talked to the higher-ups at the National Fae Museum about Nialle's murder or the break-in at Lugh's?"

He pushed away from the doorframe and moved back into the bar area. Wood creaked as he reclaimed his seat. "My people did question Rogan, but he naturally denied all knowledge of what either man was up to."

Rogan being the man who had unofficial oversight over all recovery operations. I plated up my sandwich, dumped my gloves into the bin, and left the kitchen. "And off the record?"

A smile tugged at Sgott's lips. "He's pissed off with the delay, because apparently Agrona is a goddess about whom not much is known and yet whose power is written about in obvious awe in the ancient tomes."

Suggesting it wasn't part of the hoard. Or, at least, not a part of the recently stolen items. "Has he any knowledge about the Claws themselves?"

"No." He took a bite of the sandwich and nodded in approval. "But my investigators wouldn't have asked, either, as they weren't mentioned in the report Lugh made."

"Because technically I wasn't researching the Claws." Lugh appeared on the bottom stairwell. "You got one of those sandwiches for me?"

I pushed my plate across the table and rose. "Start on that while I go make a stack more."

He picked up half of the sandwich and proceeded to demolish it.

Sgott laughed. "You're obviously feeling *much* better this morning."

"I am." His gaze rose to mine. "You can tell Darby it's not necessary for her to come over."

"You know she won't take a blind bit of notice to anything I say in that regard." I hesitated, but couldn't resist adding, "Anyone would think you're afraid of her or something."

"Any man with good sense would be afraid of her when she sets her cap on something."

Sgott's eyebrows rose. "She's finally decided to snare her man?"

"Apparently," Lugh said, somewhat glumly.

Sgott leaned over and patted Lugh's arm. "Ah, laddie, it won't be all that bad. And besides, it's way past time you had a good woman in your life."

"I'm very happy in my bachelorhood, thank you very much."

I grinned and headed for the kitchen. "Then just do what you've been doing for years—ignore her."

"I rather suspect that, after last night, that won't be possible."

"What happened last night?" Sgott asked. "Aside from you being poisoned?"

"The poison was also a truth serum. I believe she whee-dled secrets out of me."

"Believe? You can't remember?" I asked.

"It's all something of a blur. I can't really remember anything between following her upstairs and you two plotting afterward."

I laughed. "Then I shall gather the popcorn and watch in delight the battle of wills over the next couple of weeks."

"You're a bitch, sister dearest."

I laughed again, pulled on another set of gloves, and made some more sandwiches. "What were you researching if not the location of the Claws?"

"Containment methods."

"Isn't that sort of thing the province of the museum once the items have been recovered?" Sgott said.

"From the little we uncovered about the Claws, they must be separately contained or the very essence of the earth could be changed. Given we have no idea where the collection is at the moment, I thought I'd get a head start on the best means of transporting them."

"The best means would be separately, obviously," Sgott commented, amused. "I'll also point out that most godly relics have a doom-and-gloom warning attached to them."

"Well, yes." Even though I was in the kitchen, I could all but see Lugh's smile. "But in this case, I suspect it's for good reason."

"So, what, exactly, are the Claws?" I asked. "And if they're so damn threatening, wouldn't they be locked up in one of the elves' precious vaults?"

"I would have thought so, but Nialle seemed to think otherwise. I *can* say that the Claws are actually a crown, a sword, and a ring, the combination of which can give the holder utter mastery over darkness."

"As in, extend it to the point of banishing daylight?" I said, somewhat incredulously.

"So the tomes have said."

"If something like that *had* ever happened," Sgott said, "then surely there'd be a record of it."

"The Greeks and many other ancient civilizations certainly mention the disappearance of the sun," Lugh replied.

I shoved all the sandwiches on a large platter, then once again stripped off the gloves and headed out. "Yeah, but they were simply eclipses, weren't they?"

"That's what we've always believed," Lugh said. "But what if we're wrong?"

I placed the platter in the middle of the table, then walked over to the bar to grab three bottles of mineral water. "Does each item hold a specific power? Or don't we know that?"

Lugh accepted the mineral water with a nod. "In order, it's shadows, darkness, and ruin."

I placed the remaining glasses and bottles next to the sandwiches. "Ruin? That's a bit ambivalent, isn't it?"

"Yes, and there was never any description of what it might entail."

"Not hard to guess, though," Sgott commented. "If shadows and darkness dominate the world, then ruin should surely refer to food production, which cannot exist without sunshine."

"Possibly, but as I said, details are sketchy." Lugh glanced at me. "I take it you've tucked the Eye away safely?"

"If you consider in the pocket of my leather shorts safe, then yes."

"Damn it, Beth—"

"Don't use that tone on my, brother mine. Not when you were a couple of hours away from death at the time."

He blew out a frustrated sounding breath. "Fair enough. Sorry."

"It's not like anyone untoward can get in here anyway," Sgott noted. "Not with the weave of magical protections around this place. Never did understand your mother's insistence on that."

Neither did I, though I suspected it had something to do with her second sight and the missions it sent her on. I grabbed a couple of sandwiches before Lugh could inhale them all. "Talking about the Eye, did it react to you in any way when you held it?"

Lugh's gaze narrowed. "No—why?"

"So you never felt any power in it?"

"Again, no." His expression was grim. "I take it you did?"

I nodded. "It also gave me vague images, some of which were of today's murder."

His gaze narrowed, and I suspected he detected the slight mistruth. "What murder?"

I gave him a quick update on recent events and then said, "The thing that worried me about the stone's response is the fact it was *sent* to me. That implies someone out there currently knows a whole lot more about both me and your quest to find the Claws than either of *us*."

"You still got that envelope?" Sgott asked. "I can get a forensic search done on it."

Lugh tugged it out of his pocket and handed it over. "It's been stuck in my pocket for a while—I'm not sure you'll pick up anything useful from it now."

Sgott shrugged. "The lack of stamps suggests it might have been hand delivered—"

"Which is exactly what I said," I commented, giving Lugh the "told you" glare. He ignored me and grabbed another sandwich.

"Which means," Sgott continued, "that there should be a video record of it. When was it delivered?"

"Two days after Nialle was murdered," Lugh said. "But wouldn't the Eldritch have pulled the video already?"

"They undoubtedly have, but I'll nevertheless get my team to double-check. You never know, we might get lucky."

"If we get lucky, someone in the Eldritch isn't doing their job properly," Lugh commented.

Sgott pulled an evidence bag from his pocket and tucked the envelope into it. "A truth, as far as it goes."

I raised my eyebrows. "Meaning what?"

"Meaning not even the Eldritch are immune to conflicts of interests or corruption."

Mathi had said something similar about the IIT, too. "Have you managed to get a statement from Lord Lùtair yet?"

"Yes," Sgott said. "He claimed not to know how or why he was poisoned."

"Claimed? You don't believe him?"

"I do not—especially when he was given the same poison used on Lugh here. It's unlikely to be a coincidence."

"The Lùtair family are major supporters of the museum," Lugh commented. "Perhaps someone was making a sideways attempt at information gathering."

"Even as a supporter, he's unlikely to know anything useful about your current investigation," Sgott said.

"True, but the people behind the poisoning might not be aware of that—especially if they're also responsible for nailing the note to Beth's door rather than mine."

"You haven't yet been home," I pointed out. "There's no saying one *isn't* nailed there."

"Which brings me to another point," Sgott said. "Given Nialle's murder and the attempt on your life, I think it best you go into protective—"

"No."

"Just until we sort out why—"

"No," Lugh repeated. "I'll take precautions, but if I went into hiding every time someone decided they wanted my research or reclamations, I'd never step foot out on the streets."

Sgott leaned back in the chair, annoyance evident in his expression. "You two are just as bad as your mother."

"As I said only recently, that is definitely a compliment." I finished my sandwich and brushed the crumbs from my fingers. "Is Lord Lùtair still in hospital?"

"Yes, but the fae council have called a special meeting for this afternoon, and he's expected to attend. He'll no doubt check himself out if he hasn't been cleared by then."

"Why couldn't his father attend?"

"The duke's health hasn't been great for the last year, despite the best efforts of both the healers and regular medicine," Sgott said. "He's been leaning more heavily on his eldest children."

Which was a damn good reason *not* to get involved with the man ... except on a short term, sex-only basis. Presuming, of course, I did actually see him again. It was always possible that his "need to shag you now" demeanor was nothing more than natural magnetism and hadn't been specifically aimed at me.

"I don't suppose you know what the special meeting was about, do you?" I had no doubt it involved the discovery of the ruby, but I'd promised not to say anything just yet, and Sgott would think it strange if I didn't ask, given he was well aware how nosy I was.

But if Mathi didn't come through with a clearance within the next twenty-four hours, I'd certainly be telling both my brother *and* Sgott the truth.

"No, I do not." Sgott snared another half sandwich from the platter and then rose. "But there've been a few special —and closed—meetings called over the last six months, so something is obviously going down."

"Odd that no rumors have leaked as yet," Lugh commented. "Especially given what you said about the Eldritch."

Sgott grimaced. "There are ways and means of stopping rumors spreading, laddie, and the elves are not beyond trying them all if it gets them what they want."

A statement that was true in more ways than he imagined, given what Mathi had said about the blood oath. They were pretty nasty things.

"Let me know where you're staying, Lugh," Sgott said, "and I'll get some discreet patrols happening."

"I'll probably just bunk down in the office at the museum—no one and nothing will get through their security."

"Obviously," Sgott said, with a grin, "you've never watched any of those movies about the nasty things that happen when people stay overnight in museums."

Lugh snorted. "Go home and sleep, old man. Your brain is becoming addled."

Sgott laughed and walked out. I opened a bottle of mineral water and took a long drink. "We heading back to your place now?"

"Didn't you hear Sgott's warning not to go there?" he asked mildly.

"Yes, and we both know you have every intention of ignoring it. So, when are we leaving?"

He laughed. "Ten minutes? That'll give you time enough to go upstairs and hide the Eye properly."

"And will you still be here when I get back?"

"Yes."

"Swear on the soul of our sainted mother?"

He rolled his eyes. "Yes, I swear."

"Won't be long then."

I rose and headed upstairs. My shorts were still sitting on the floor where I'd left them and to be honest, the Eye was probably as safe there as anywhere else. There'd be few who would think to look for something valuable in the pocket of a beer-stained pair of shorts. Even so, I tugged it free and once again felt that weird caress of energy. This time, there were no images, but an electric and unpleasant force speared inside me, striking at places that had long been shuttered. Whether it was fully cracking open the second sight vault or doing something else, I couldn't say.

And had no idea how to find out.

We had few enough relatives left—Aunt Riayn and her family had moved to Galway after Gran's death, and we had little contact with them these days. They hadn't even contacted us after Mom had gone missing, which had hurt. Lugh's father had died in a car accident when Lugh was five, and I had no idea where my father was—in fact, all I knew about him was his first name: Ambisagrus. Which was a rather archaic name even amongst those of us who were long-lived. Whenever I'd asked Mom about him, all she'd said was that I was the fortunate result of a brief flirtation, and she had no idea what had happened to him after that.

I'd always suspected she knew far more than she was

admitting, but maybe that was simply wishful thinking on my part.

I pulled the sleeve of my sweater over my other hand and dropped the stone into it. The spears immediately stopped, but I couldn't help remembering the warning that had come with this stone and wished it had been a whole lot more specific.

I took a deep breath that didn't do a whole lot to ease the anxiety then moved across the room to the point where the truss met the external wall. Someone in the tavern's distant past had made various repairs to the old oak frame by using metal straps, which had held the rotting pieces together long enough for my great-grandmother to buy the place and start proper repairs. While the oak beams had been restored to their original condition, she'd created "natural" cavities in the wood behind the remade straps, thereby providing perfect hidey-holes for small items.

The strap in my room was a good three inches deep and three feet long. I caught the domed ends of the bolts at either end of the strap and tugged it away to reveal the foot-long cavity. There was no discordant note coming from the wood fibers here; instead, they hummed with a soft energy that spoke of their mighty past.

I pushed the Eye to the back of the space, then shoved the ruby on the opposite side and waited a couple of heartbeats to ensure there was no reaction between the two.

Once the strap was back in place, I stripped off and pulled on fresh clothing, including a bra. I wasn't likely to see Mathi anytime soon, but the man did have a habit of sneaking up on me, and I wasn't about to risk another breast-caressing episode.

No matter how much I might have enjoyed it.

Lugh was just finishing the last of the sandwiches when I reappeared downstairs. "All good?"

I nodded and grabbed my coat off the chair. "We walking to your place?"

"In this weather? Are you certifiable?"

I snorted. "A lad your size isn't going to be hurt by a little bit of rain."

"No, but the feet might be."

I glanced down. He was once again wearing the cracked and worn brown leather walking boots that were probably older than Methuselah himself. "I really think it's about time you retired those things."

"Why?" He raised one foot and tapped the sole. "Still perfectly good tread in that."

I snorted and motioned him toward the door. After ensuring it was locked, I tugged my hood over my head and followed him down the street to the taxi rank. I didn't have a car, and Lugh rarely used his; parking wasn't practical in the old city, and the public transport system was pretty good these days. If I ever *did* need a car, it was easier to either borrow Lugh's or hire one.

Peak hour had long gone, so it only took ten minutes to get across to Lugh's apartment, which was situated a block away from the Fae Museum. While Lugh paid for the taxi, I climbed out. In the gloom of the torrential downpour, the single-story dark brown brick building was particularly uninspiring, especially when compared to the lovely old terraces further down the street. But this building had one thing they did not—space. It was a decommissioned power substation, and Lugh had jumped at the opportunity to renovate the old building into something befitting a man his height.

I walked down to the black wooden door that was the

midpoint of the long building. It still had all the rusty old electrical warning signs on it, but the door itself was as solid as the day it had been installed. There was no note nailed onto it, but that didn't mean it hadn't been slipped under the door or even through the mail slot.

I punched the code into the screen on the left and then pushed the door open.

As I did, something moved.

Something that appeared wider than it was high.

Before I could move or react in any way, it hit me like a ton of bricks and sent me flying.

CHAPTER
FIVE

I windmilled my arms in a desperate effort to maintain balance but nevertheless felt myself going ... then Lugh caught and steadied me.

"You okay?" he asked brusquely.

"Yes. Go get that bastard."

"Aim to." He stepped around me and hightailed it after my attacker, who may have been short but could fucking move. He was already close to the other end of the street. If he got around that corner, it'd be very easy for him to disappear, as there were multiple streets he could run down. He could even go over the old city wall—dwarves were sturdy bastards, and a drop like that wouldn't trouble him.

I straightened my jacket and then stepped warily inside the building's large, airy foyer. There were two doors leading off it—the one on the left went into the main living area and the two bedrooms, the one on the right into his office and the storage area.

The door to the latter was partially open.

After locking the front door to ensure no one could sneak up on me, I looked around for a note. There was nothing other than advertising flyers for local restaurants in the mail slot.

I walked toward the partially open door but paused again as something scraped across the silence. It vaguely sounded like something being dragged across the concrete, and all sorts of internal alarms went off. I flexed my fingers and wished I'd taken time to strap on my knives. While it wasn't exactly legal to wear them outside the tavern, that had never stopped me before—especially when a long coat could hide their presence.

I forced my feet on. As I drew close to the door, a tendril of smoke drifted past my nose.

Fire. There was a goddamn *fire* in Lugh's office.

I swore and darted in, only realizing after the fact that it could have been a trap.

Thankfully, it wasn't.

But the office was a mess. There were papers, books, and folders strewn everywhere. Lugh's precious collection of relics—the bits and pieces the museum had no interest in—were all on the floor, some shattered, some not. I had no idea whether the mess was the result of the earlier break-in or not, and right now, it didn't really matter. Not when the dwarf had set the pile of papers in the middle of the room alight.

I grabbed the fire extinguisher from the wall, turned it upside down and, being careful to hold it at an angle that didn't spread the paper or the fire, put the damn thing out.

I didn't immediately set the extinguisher down, though not because I was worried about escapee sparks catching alight in the mess. It would make a fine weapon if someone decided to jump me.

I cautiously moved across to the door into the next room and toed it open all the way. No miniaturized steamroller on legs came out at me, and there was no repeat of the odd sound I'd heard.

But my pulse rate remained high, and I flexed my fingers on the extinguisher's grip in a useless attempt to ease the tension.

I slipped inside the storeroom and pressed back against the wall. Four long gray shelving units dominated this area, running the full length of the room and holding an eclectic mix of items. Aside from the expected relics, there were all manner of tools—including gardening, even though the substation didn't have a garden—and a ton of canvases and art supplies. Lugh was an abstract artist in what little spare time he had. Some of his work currently hung in a local modern art gallery, and he could probably have made a decent enough living from it if he ever decided to give up his job at the museum. Which he wouldn't, of course.

I edged further along the wall to check the shelving unit to the far left. No one hid there, and there was no immediate indication that anything had been moved. I repeated the process and checked the shelving to the other side of the door. Again, nothing.

Although there *was* a bit of dust dancing about in the air down the far end of the room, but that could have been due to the rear window being open. Thankfully, the gap was too small for even a miniaturized pixie to get through, let alone a dwarf.

I frowned and swept my gaze across the shadowed area again. What had the dwarf been looking for? Nothing here appeared to have been touched, but if they hadn't found what they were looking for the first time they'd broken in, why wouldn't they search this area instead of going back through the already ransacked office? It made no sense.

But then, we didn't yet understand what exactly they

were looking for. Just because Lugh theorized it was all linked to the Claws didn't mean it was.

I walked back through the office to the foyer but stopped near the door just as the front door opened and Lugh stepped through. He did not look happy.

"The bastard got away."

"Thought he might."

"I had no idea dwarves could move so fucking fast. Shocked the hell out of me." He tugged off his coat and hung it on the hook near the door then stepped into the office. His gaze fell on the burned pile of paper and his expression darkened. "These bastards definitely seem intent on destroying my research. Just as well I moved all the vital stuff online."

"Online isn't all that much safer these days."

"No, but it's encrypted, and only Nialle and I know the code."

"What if they forced it out of Nialle before they killed him?"

"It won't help them, because I changed a couple of necessary keys after his murder."

Which wouldn't stop a dedicated hacker all that long if they had the bulk of the code. I glanced around the room for a second, then frowned. "Why a dwarf?"

Lugh raised an eyebrow. "Why not a dwarf?"

A smile tugged at my lips. "They're not thieves as a general rule. They're usually only employed in situations that involve earth and mining. Hiring one to go through paperwork seems a waste of time *and* money, given they aren't cheap."

"You know, you're right. It *is* odd."

His gaze swept the room, then he moved past me and

went into the storeroom. I put the extinguisher down and trailed after him.

"What are you looking for?"

"Evidence of digging."

"Isn't the concrete in this section several feet thick?"

"Yes, but that wouldn't stop a dwarf."

I guessed not, given digging wasn't only their main skill set but, in many respects, their drug of choice. They really *did* get off on it.

"Why would anyone want to be digging up your concrete, though?"

"Because there are lots of old tunnels around these parts. One runs under this old station, but the access point lies in the property behind."

I blinked. "I take it we're not talking about sewerage or storm water tunnels."

"No." He glanced back at me. "Did you not pay attention at *all* during your history lessons?"

"If they'd mentioned secret tunnels, I might have."

He snorted and continued moving up and down the rows of shelving. I'd already done a sight check, but dwarves were masters of concealing their handiwork, and Lugh knew this area far better than I did.

"There are a number of tunnels that crisscross both sections of Deva, old and new," he said. "There's at least one that links the castle's prison cells to the military court building, as well as a series of military tunnels that were built to provide safe access to the various installations during the Second World War."

"And the National Fae Museum is situated close to the military museum, the castle, and the Crown Courts," I said. "Does the tunnel underneath the power station head up that way?"

"Yes."

He moved down the final lane, his steps slowing as he neared the end. I couldn't see anything out of place, but that odd haze of dust continued to swirl, so something had obviously gone on.

"Maybe they thought you had access to that tunnel," I said. "And that they could use it to bypass the museum's security and search Nialle's effects there?"

"Or maybe they thought I hid valuable items down there."

I raised my eyebrows. "And did you?"

He glanced at me. "The tunnels are dark and dank. Not a place a man my size would ever willingly enter, even to hide precious items. Besides, unless said items were properly protected, the dampness would destroy them pretty damn quickly."

"Doesn't discount the possibility they're searching for a sneaky way into the museum."

"Definitely not."

He squatted down and carefully brushed his fingers across the concrete. After a moment, he grunted and slipped his fingers into what looked to be a thick crack. With very little effort, he lifted a three-foot-wide square chunk of concrete up and propped it up against the back wall.

Revealing a hole that dove down into the ground.

"You want to grab me the flashlight from that shelf over there?" He vaguely waved his hand to the left.

I scanned the shelf that ran along the sidewall and, after a moment, spotted it. After fetching it, I flicked it on and then handed it to Lugh.

"Thanks."

He shone it into the hole. I couldn't immediately see the

bottom but eventually caught the flicker of movement. Rats. There were *rats* down there.

I shuddered. "Well, even if we did belong to the branch of pixies able to miniaturize themselves and fly short distances, there'd be absolutely no hope you'd get me down there to investigate."

He snorted. "Rats don't eat pixies, small or not."

"And you know this how?"

"Because I've studied the history of our various lines." He glanced at me, frost-green eyes gleaming with amusement. "And because I was once reliably informed that miniaturized pixies taste like old boot leather."

I blinked. "Informed by who?"

"A drunk shifter who wandered into the pixie section of the museum."

"I hope you threw his ass out of said museum in a not-so-gentle manner in honor of the pixie he taste-tested."

"I did indeed." He motioned to the hole. "From what I can see, it's more a crawl space than a tunnel. Our dwarf friend might get through, but neither of us would."

I frowned. "So why break into the tunnel from here? There have to be multiple other places they could have used —why alert us like this?"

"For all we know, they *have* broken into other areas." Lugh grabbed the edge of the concrete block and dropped it back into place. "Maybe they—whoever the hell 'they' are —are using the old tunnels as a means to move across the city without being seen. It would certainly explain why none of the security cams caught anyone entering either Nialle's building or mine."

Nialle had lived in a Victorian end-of-terrace close to the racecourse but within walking distance of the museum. It was an area that was still classified as being within the old city, even though the walls along that section of the racecourse had been partially destroyed a long time ago. The wealthy types who'd lived in the apartments back then couldn't have anything restricting their view of the racecourse, after all. I had no idea why the heritage council had allowed it, given how shitty they'd gotten with Gran over the roof raising. Unless, of course, the council members responsible for making the decision at that time also happened to live there.

"So if that dwarf used this tunnel to get in, why wouldn't he have used it to escape?"

Lugh brushed the dust from his fingers and rose. "They usually work in pairs for safety reasons, so I daresay he ran to draw our attention away from his partner and this tunnel."

I recalled the odd scraping I'd heard when I'd entered. Had that been the other half of the dwarf team going back down the hole and closing it up? More than likely.

"So why would they have come back here? Surely that was a big risk to take when the investigation is still ongoing."

"Maybe they thought their end goal was worth it." He motioned to the first in the row of four-drawer filing cabinets lining the back wall. "Help me move that over here."

I followed him over, and between the two of us, we managed to maneuver the heavy thing onto the concrete block.

"That'll stop them from using this entry point, but not from creating another," I said.

"No, but I'll ask Morris to come here ASAP."

Morris was the local locksmith who ran a profitable sideline in protection spells. He worked out of a shop only a block away and was responsible for the spells that ran around the tavern.

"I'm surprised you didn't ask him to do that after the first break-in."

"Didn't think they'd come back," he said. "And it's not like there's anything truly valuable in this area. I mean, while I love all my bits and pieces, they're basically museum rejects."

"Some of which would be worth a fortune on the black market."

"Well, yes, but they didn't go near any of them, either the first time or, I suspect, this."

He led the way back through the office and over to the living portion of the old substation. Nothing appeared out of place here—Lugh might be a messy worker, but he was pin neat when it came to his living quarters. Any mess or search would have been immediately obvious.

"Check the spare bedroom," he said, as he walked toward the main bedroom. "Just in case something has been left or taken."

I did. There wasn't.

We met back in the kitchen. He made a quick call to arrange for Morris to come over and then said, "I'll head over to the museum once he's done. We'll have to get a team in to check for entry points along the tunnel's path."

I nodded. "I'll head back to the tavern, but keep me updated."

He glanced toward the window. There wasn't much to see because the rain was still torrential. "You want me to drive you? Or call you a cab?"

I smiled. "Unlike you, I'm not afraid of a bit of water."

"That," he said, with a hand wave to the window, "is

hardly a bit. You're going to arrive home a sodden, chilly mess."

Undoubtedly, but it would take longer to get there in a cab than it would to walk. Besides, I wasn't really in the mood to handle cabbie small talk right now.

"There are such things as hot showers, brother mine. You should try them occasionally. They do a great job of warming chilled bones."

He snorted again and pushed me lightly toward the foyer. "Be gone then, woman."

I grinned, pulled up the coat's hood, and left. By the time I reached the tavern, both my boots and my coat were sodden enough that they were no longer repelling water. My feet were like ice, and both my sweater and the shirt underneath were damp. I still didn't regret not getting a cab, however. There was something almost ... soothing ... about the peace that descended onto Old Deva on storm-clad days like this.

The tavern was on the chilly side, so I lit the fire in the main bar as well as the one in my living area—saying a gentle prayer of thanks to the wood even though its song and life had long ago left—then headed into the bathroom and had a nice, long, hot shower.

Once fully dressed, I let Darby know she'd find Lugh at the museum this afternoon and asked if she could drop by briefly to fix my hands if she had time. After spending an hour or so carefully repairing the burned sections of floorboards by reconnecting and healing the singed fibers, I spent the rest of the day dealing with the heritage council and their stupid rules in an effort to get the window fixed. Which, as predicted, would not happen until Thursday, at the earliest, despite the fact they had specialized glaziers on contract who could step in at a few hours' notice in order to avoid businesses located in the rows being out of action for very long.

They'd very definitely *not* got over Gran's ignoring their wishes.

Darby appeared just before five.

"You want a coffee?" I called out as she came through the rear door.

"Is the weather positively shitty?" she replied dryly as she ran lightly up the steps.

I snorted and shoved another pod into the coffee maker. "How'd it go with Lugh?"

"Your brother is resisting the inevitable."

I grinned and, once the second coffee was made, carried them both over to the small living area. "He has been for at least the last ten years. He's nothing if not determined."

"Yes, but I now know he really *is* attracted to me. Like, seriously attracted."

"You didn't need a truth serum to know that—a blind woman could have seen that."

She laughed and motioned toward my hands. I held them out, and she began unwinding the bandages. "Well, yes, but a girl does like to be sure before she plans a full-on assault."

"I almost feel sorry for my brother. Almost."

She laughed again. "He's not going to know what hit him."

"Excellent." I paused. "I don't suppose you know anything about Cynwrig Lùtair, do you?"

She nodded. "He was at the hospital last night. Not in my ward, sadly, but his presence caused quite a stir." She studied me speculatively for a second. "Why?"

"I hauled him out of the canal last night."

"And it was lust at first sight?"

"Very definitely. But after the whole Mathi thing, I'm not sure it would be wise to get into any kind of relationship—even just a sexual one—with a highborn."

Which was something of a lie, because I had every intention of getting that man into bed—but I also wanted to know exactly what I might be getting into. Darby worked at the only specialist fae hospital in the region, so she was perfectly placed to hear all the chatter.

"And yet, according to the gossip mill, you were seen with Mathi today."

"For business, not pleasure," I said dryly.

"Bet that didn't stop him trying to merge the two."

I laughed. "No, it did not."

Her gaze became a little distant as she began to heal my hands. Energy washed across my skin and made my fingers twitch and tingle. "Well, I can tell you one important difference between highborn Ljósálfar and Myrkálfar—the latter are far more in tune with their emotions."

"And you know this from experience?"

"A brief but glorious one." She released my hands and sat back with a grin. "Not a Lùtair, sadly, but they're all magnificent specimens, and I highly approve of a relationship with one. Especially when you have so many cobwebs to get rid of and continue to resist Mathi's wiles."

"Sadly, I think today only strengthened his resolve to get me back into his bed."

It was gloomily said, and she raised her eyebrows. "Oh yeah? Do tell?"

I smiled and picked up my coffee. "Nothing serious happened—the cobwebs remain. Is Cynwrig as wild as rumors have us believe?"

She pursed her lips. "He certainly *did* have a reputation for running with the wrong crowd when he was younger, but he and his sister have taken over the day-to-day running of the encampment for their father, and I can't say I've heard too many recent rumors of wildness."

"Which might just be a result of no one wanting to badmouth their next king."

"*If* he is to be king. That's no certainty, given he's a twin, and the Myrkálfar do have a far more progressive attitude when it comes to female rule than my mob." She sipped her drink. "Interestingly, although multiple nurses were making plays for the man last night, he did not reciprocate."

"That you know of," I said wryly. "He might have collected all their numbers and even now be working his way through them."

"Possible, although if that had been the case, there would have been gossip. Trust me."

Which made me feel a little better, though in truth, even if he were the biggest player around, it wouldn't stop me from at least spending some time with the man. As Darby had noted, there were cobwebs to get rid of.

The conversation moved on to the movie we were going to catch at the cinema over the weekend and, at six, Darby headed out for her evening shift at the hospital.

I was settling in for an evening watching my favorite show on Netflix when the back door buzzer rang. I pushed up from my chair and walked over to the intercom. "Who is it?"

"Mathi. Let me in."

"Last time I let you in, you seduced me."

He laughed. "Good times, hey?"

Well, yes, but that was beside the point. "What do you want?"

He sighed, a put-upon sound if ever I'd heard one. "Your presence has been requested by the council."

Requested, my ass. He was here to make sure I went. "Tonight, I take it?"

"No, tomorrow," he said sarcastically. "Why else do you think I'm here?"

"For the same reason you're usually here?"

"Not this time. Let me in, Beth."

"No."

"You don't trust me?"

"To keep your hands to yourself? Certainly not. I'll be down in ten."

"Bring the ruby," he said. "And may I point out it's freezing out here? It's very uncivilized of you to make me wait in such weather."

"I'm a bar wench. We tend to be uncivilized."

I released the button, cutting off any reply he might have made, and quickly moved into the bedroom. After grabbing the ruby from its hidey-hole, I pulled on a pair of boots, picked up my long coat and purse, and headed downstairs. But I didn't immediately head for the back door, walking over to the bar instead. By all rights, I shouldn't need my knives, given the fae council's premises was probably one of the most secure places within Deva, but something within was suggesting I take them, and I wasn't about to gainsay it. Not after the last couple of days.

I strapped them on, then did up my coat. It was long enough to cover my knees and bulky enough that no one would notice I was wearing the knives unless they knew what they were looking for.

Mathi was leaning against the external wall, his arms crossed and expression as cold as the night air. "You have the ruby?"

"Yes." I resisted the urge to kiss away his annoyance—it was born of habit more than any true desire to mollify him —and motioned him to lead the way. "I take it you have a car waiting?"

"Of course. It is too unpleasant a night to be walking."

He flicked open a large umbrella and held it up to cover us both. While I had no desire to be that close to him, I also didn't want to get soaked again. Besides, the boots were new.

He hurried us down the lane to where his driver waited in a small but gorgeous silver Mercedes. Once I was ushered in, he folded the umbrella and sat beside me. The driver moved off the minute we both had our seat belts on. There was no conversation on the ten-minute drive, but that wasn't surprising given what Mathi had said about being unable to talk about the hoard in the presence of anyone who wasn't either blood sworn or already aware of the theft. I doubted his driver would fit either category.

The fae council's headquarters was located next to the Deva City Council offices and, just like that building, was an uninspiring red brick and concrete construction. The driver pulled up beside the entrance, and a doorman held the door open for us. Mathi led the way up the bland but functional stairs to the second floor and down a long gray corridor. The guard who stood to one side of a sturdy-looking double door nodded and keyed us in. As I followed Mathi through, magic swept my body, and my knives reacted, quickly nullifying it. But not quite fast enough. A light immediately began to flash.

Mathi stopped abruptly and turned, his expression a mix of surprise and disbelief. "You're armed?"

I reluctantly undid my coat to reveal my knives. "Yes."

"Why?"

"My brother was poisoned, his place has now been ransacked twice, and someone threw a firebomb through the tavern's window and then stuck a threatening note on my door. Why the fuck shouldn't I be armed?"

"But ... the council is no threat."

"Then I'll have no need to use the knives, will I?" I motioned toward the next door. "Are we moving on? Or am I going home? Those are the only two options here, Mathi."

His gaze narrowed, but after a moment, he made a motion with his hand—dismissing the warning magic, I suspected—and continued on. The next set of doors opened as we approached, revealing a long, utilitarian room. Though it was the size of a grand hall, there were no decorations, nothing in the way of wall hangings or crests, and the large oval table was plastic rather than wood or metal. That surprised me, at least until I remembered that the council was made up of people who could control many natural elements. Plastic furniture gave no one an edge when it came to possible weapons. And while that normally would have given the shifters a serious advantage, the magic rolling around the edges of the room actually prevented shapeshifting.

Council meetings were *not* as harmonious as they would have the general public believe.

The table was packed, which meant not only were there representatives from the six light elf *and* the seven dark elf lines, but also six shifters, a dwarf, and even someone from one of the smaller pixie lines—the Malloyei, if the blue tint to her hair was anything to go by. That there was no one representing the other four pixie lines wasn't exactly surprising, given that even today most of us tended to keep our noses out of anything representing officialdom. Also unsurprisingly, there was no one here from the ghuls. They liked to feed on the flesh of the dead, and that tended to make most people nervous, even shifters, who'd never be in any danger of being overwhelmed by the pale, insubstantial beings.

Most of those sitting at the table were strangers, but one was not.

Cynwrig.

He was wearing a black jacket with a white shirt that was partially undone and revealing tantalizing wisps of dark chest hair, and a smile that was devilish. My pulse immediately skipped into a much higher gear. There might be six other dark elves in this room who were equally impressive in size and looks, but my hormones only had eyes for one.

"Lovely to see you again, Bethany," he said in that soft, smoky, and oh-so-sexy tone of his.

I felt rather than saw Mathi's sharp glance. "You know Lord Lùtair?"

"I hauled his ass out of the river last night." My gaze remained on Cynwrig's. "Best catch I've had from that waterway in a very long time."

Cynwrig's amusement deepened, even as desire flared in his eyes. It was a wave of pure heat that washed across my senses and made me ache in all the right places. Which the shifters in the room would no doubt smell, and which would have been embarrassing had I cared about such things.

"Being kissed back to life was certainly a memorable experience," he said. "And you do know what they say about a life saved."

I smiled. "You owe me nothing, Lord Lùtair."

"Oh, I most certainly *do.*"

An older, gray-haired elf sitting in the middle section of the oval table banged a gavel lightly.

"Can we please stop this nonsense and proceed?" She gave Cynwrig a stern look—which seemed to amuse him more than anything else—then returned her attention to me. "Young lady, do you have an enhanced weapon in your possession?"

"You already know I do, and there's not a chance in hell I'm giving them up. Sorry, but too much shit has happened over the last couple of days, and I'm not inclined to trust strangers right now."

"Even if you're hot for one of them," someone murmured.

Not Cynwrig, someone else, though I couldn't immediately pick out who.

"Desire doesn't mean I won't stab him with said weapons if he does anything untoward."

"And I do have confirmation of that fact from Sgott Bruhn," Cynwrig commented, his tone lazily amused.

The older woman cast another exasperated look Cynwrig's way. This time, he gave her a nod.

"Please be seated, Ms. Aodhán," she said crisply. "We do have a bit to get through."

I followed Mathi across to the vacant seat at the "head" of the oval table; he pulled out a plastic but comfortable-looking chair and sat me down, then moved around to the left to sit next to the older woman who was obviously running the show this evening. I had no idea who she was, although I did know that the various representatives took turns in being meeting convener.

"Do you have the ruby in your possession?" she asked.

And just as obviously, I was not going to be formally introduced to anyone here. Had I been dealing with anyone *other* than a light elf, I might have considered it nothing more than manners slipping in the urgency of the situation. But this was deliberate. Highborns could be assholes like that.

I reached into my pocket, pulled out the ruby, and tossed it lightly onto the table. It burned briefly to life in the artificially bright room, and a soft but collective murmur ran around the room.

It suggested few here had ever actually seen it.

"Now, young lady," she added, her voice even cooler than it had been before, "please explain to council how you came to possess this item."

I raised an eyebrow. "Mathi hasn't told you?"

It was said simply to be annoying, and her gaze narrowed a fraction. "He has, but we wish to hear it in your own words."

I dutifully gave them the bare bones of the story. A light elf opposite the convener shifted—deliberately, I suspected, to catch my attention—and said, "And you've not felt this energy before now?"

"No."

Which wasn't a lie, as the Eye had a very different type of energy.

"And you found this ruby via second sight?"

"No. It was more the song of abused wood fibers that led me to the ruby's location."

"And yet you told Lord Dhār-Val otherwise," a shifter said.

I frowned. "No, I told him instinct—or second sight, if you want to call it that—was telling me there was something in the room to find. It wasn't responsible for leading me to the ruby's location."

The convener raised an eyebrow, clearly not believing

this. "So you claim to have inherited none of your mother's skills?"

"That is currently an unanswerable question." I leaned forward and crossed my arms on the table. "Let's cut the bullshit—why was I called here? What do you want of me?"

"We have a few more questions to ask before we get to that." The comment came from another dark elf, one with just the faintest flick of silver in his dark hair but lacking the overall refinement of the man sitting at the far end of the table.

My hormones were very definitely fixated.

"What sort of questions?" My voice sounded perfectly normal and undistracted. Go me. "I can't tell you anything more than I already have."

The convener interlaced her fingers and said, "Does your brother hold the second sight skill?"

I frowned, not sure where this was going but definitely not liking it. "You know he does. Why?"

"Your brother is the most successful reclaimer the museum has ever employed, and your mother—" The convener paused thoughtfully. "Your mother had a stellar reputation for finding what no others could."

There was something in the way she said that that had me thinking the elves were not only familiar with Mom's reputation but had used her services on multiple occasions.

Something Mom had said nothing about. But then, there now appeared to be a whole lot of things Mom had said nothing about.

"And was she working for you on the day she went missing?" I said, my voice surprisingly even.

"No," the convener said. "She was not working for us."

Which didn't mean she wasn't working for someone

else in this room, but a quick glance suggested I wasn't going to get a different answer from anyone else.

My gaze landed on Cynwrig's again. There was just the faintest hint of warning there, though I wasn't entirely sure about what.

"And were you aware that a singing bowl from the missing hoard mysteriously turned up in the museum's crypts a few weeks ago?"

The speaker was an elf with a sharp nose and deep green eyes, which said he was from the Gila-Ken line. They were the only ones who had eyes that color.

"Yes. Lugh told me about it."

And he'd been interviewed about it extensively, by both the museum's security division *and* the fae council's.

"Did he say how it got there?"

"No, but I know the investigation is still ongoing." My gaze swept them as unease continued to grow. "Why are you asking me these questions? Lugh's my brother, but it's not like we live in each other's pockets."

"No, but siblings do talk," the Gila-Ken elf said.

"I'm still not seeing the relevance."

"He was not willing to undergo formal questioning," the convener said. "We are merely trying to establish whether he told you anything different to what he told the museum or us."

I frowned, the thick sense of unease so strong now it sat like a weight in my gut. "Formal meaning magical, I take it?"

The convener nodded. "It is considered normal in situations such as this."

"Yes, it is, and that's why the museum called in truth seekers to interview *all* staff. Why would he or anyone else put themselves through the physically draining effects of being mind-read like *that* again when the results would be no different?"

"It *is* possible for truth seekers to be foxed. Our methods are more ... reliable."

I stared at her for a second and then slowly asked, "And is one of those methods Dahbree? Were you the bastards who poisoned my brother?"

The convener raised pale eyebrows, her expression mildly offended. "We would not stoop so low as to use that drug. Not when there are far safer ones."

It wasn't a declaration that really comforted me, because we all knew they could and would stoop that low if it got them what they wanted.

"I still don't understand what this line of questioning has to do with the hoard. Unless, of course, Agrona's Claws were part of it." I glanced at Mathi. "Did you check?"

"Yes," he said. "They weren't listed, though it is possible that they were taken in a previous raid."

"There's been more than one?" I clucked my tongue. "We were fired for less than that."

"You," a sharp-faced, red-haired shifter said, "or rather, your long-dead ancestors, were fired because you stole from the old gods."

"And have been doing that exact same thing ever since," another shifter muttered.

Anger flared, and it took a gigantic effort to keep my voice even as I said, "And many of the pompous assholes sitting here at the table have made good use of those skills over the years. To repeat, what is the goddamn point of these questions?"

"There is no point," a smoky voice said. "And certainly no sense."

My gaze found Cynwrig's again and saw anger. Not at

me, but rather what was happening here. Why I was so sure of that I couldn't say, but relief nevertheless flicked through me. At least I had one ally, though I wasn't entirely sure it would do any good.

"The point—" the fox shifter paused, as if searching for the right words, though something in her sharp expression suggested it was merely done for effect. "—is that a few weeks *after* your brother's team began researching the Claws, the vaults were raided and the contents subsequently vanished. Then, a few months later, a bowl mysteriously appears in the museum's crypts, and now this ruby is miraculously found. By yourself, the woman with no second sight or finding skill."

I stared at her for several long seconds while I digested exactly what she was implying. Then my gaze flicked to Mathi. "You brought me here for *this?*"

He had the grace to look uncomfortable, but it was the convener who said, "It is a reasonable question that has to be asked before we can proceed any further."

"Reasonable? *Reasonable?*" I slapped my hands on the table and thrust to my feet. "That ruby was found in the home of Mathi Dhār-Val's lover—a lover he took to his bed only a few months *before* the hoard was stolen. How about you throw some of these accusations *his* way?"

"They have," he said evenly. "But you need to see this situation from their point of view—"

"No, I don't. In fact, they can take their point of view and shove it where the sun doesn't shine."

I turned and strode angrily toward the door. There was a scrape of sound, and I said, without looking around, "Anyone who attempts to follow or stop me will get a knife in their goddamn guts. I mean it."

"Bethany," Mathi said. "Please, the questions are more

informational confirmation than accusations, and your reaction is uncalled for."

"Uncalled for?" I stopped and swung around. "You're implying my brother is responsible for the theft of the hoard and that my discovery of the ruby means I'm in on it. Fuck you all."

And with that, I slammed through the doors and strode out of the building.

CHAPTER
SIX

The weather hadn't improved any, and I was perfectly fine with that. The chill wind and torrential rain were probably the next best thing to alcohol to help ease the incandescent fury that burned through me.

I buttoned up my coat, nodded a thank-you to the guard who unlocked and opened the external door, then shoved my hands into my pockets and stepped out into the wet, cold night.

How *dare* they.

Lugh had worked all his life—and even *risked* his life—to retrieve and keep safe precious antiquities, be they of the gods or not. And while theft very definitely was part of his job, it was only used in situations that involved items illegally procured by private collectors. Not other museums. *Never* other museums. And he'd certainly never touch the vaults of the gods. For fuck's sake, we pixies had spent eons protecting godly items. It was in our blood, something we could not deny even if we no longer held that duty; it was what still drove Lugh and, I suspected, my mother, to do what they did.

To imply that Lugh could be party to such a theft and then pile on top of that by suggesting my finding the ruby was something *other* than a coincidence was insulting. Slanderous, even.

But what angered me more than even *that* was Mathi's reaction. He may have looked uncomfortable with the whole situation, but he'd nevertheless toed the party line, even though he'd been a part of my life for nigh on ten years and knew Lugh better than most.

Bastard. They were all bastards ... even Cynwrig. Though he did at least speak up toward the end. And, in truth, the voice of one man would not have made any difference to the council's decision to interrogate me in such a manner.

Though I guessed I should be thankful they didn't slap me down with magic and tear the answers from my brain ... but maybe my knives had a lot to do with that. The convener had *not* been happy about their presence, and I was sure Mathi would have mentioned their ability to divert magic. She'd called them enhanced, after all, and the probe I'd walked through was nothing more than a basic weapons alarm and wouldn't have provided that sort of information.

I walked into the lane that would take me from Hamilton Place to Northgate Street. The old buildings on either side loomed above me and cut the force of the wind. In that sudden stillness, awareness surged. The frisson of heat that came with it told me exactly who it was.

"Did you not get the memo?" I said, without looking around. "Fuck off. I'm not in the mood to talk to any of you right now."

"Understandable, given what was said. But for better or for worse, the Ljósálfar are not known for their tact."

His voice was dark silk and as soothing as hell. Unfortunately for him, I did *not* want to be soothed right now.

"It wasn't a light elf that implied my brother was a thief."

"No, but there was a general consensus the question had to be asked."

"Define general."

"There were five who disagreed."

"You were one of the five?"

"Of course, and it had nothing to do with you saving my life. My family is a major donor to the museum. I'm very familiar with both their work and that of your brother."

"Then why didn't you speak up when the question was asked?"

"I was not the convener, and I am bound to honor her rule. Those of us who disagreed with the direction of the interrogation were ordered to remain silent." Amusement ran through his tone. "I did, however, have something to say after. You just didn't hang around long enough to hear it."

I snorted. "Did I mention I'm not inclined to trust any of you right now? So, to repeat, fuck off."

His laugh was a warm, rich sound that fizzed brightly through the cold, wet night. "Oh, our relationship is definitely going to be a satisfyingly fiery one."

His words had wanton images of our naked bodies and entwined limbs flashing through my brain. I softly cleared my throat and tried to concentrate. "You're getting a little ahead of yourself, aren't you?"

I could almost feel his shrug. I could certainly feel his closeness. Though he made no sound on the wet cobblestones, the heat of him caressed my senses, and his musky, earthy scent teased my nostrils. It was a scent as delicious as the man— *Nope.* Not going down that path. Not yet.

"That," he said softly, "is the way of Myrkálfar when we feel an attraction this fierce."

I harrumphed, though it was gratifying to know that the attraction went two ways and wasn't just a result of his natural magnetism.

I swung onto Northgate Street and strode toward The Cross. Light gleamed off the red stone, but no one sat on its steps, and there didn't appear to be anyone moving through the square. No surprise, given the overall shittiness of the weather.

"Can we go somewhere out of this rain and talk?" His voice hummed with calming power, and just for an instant, I felt my anger slipping.

Bastard.

"We *are* talking. And quit using that persuasive shit on me or I *will* stick you."

His amusement washed over me again, a sensation as fierce as the hunger that burned between us. "So, the savage beast is not calmed by words. Can she be calmed by a good whisky?"

She most certainly *could.* "Why do you want to talk?"

"Because you need to understand what the council intended, and I need to spend some time with you."

Need. It was a nice word when applied that way. I blew out a breath and felt a lot of my anger leaving with it. "Fine. Where?"

He lightly touched my spine; it felt like I was struck by lightning. Whatever this thing was between us, it was damnably strong.

"This way."

He guided me to the left, and we ascended a small,

somewhat rickety set of stairs to the upper level of the Rows. None of the stores here were open at this hour, but he didn't hesitate, leading me down to the left and through a late-night, hole-in-the-wall coffee place. At the back of this was an ornate but ancient wood and metal door that had a key-coded lock to one side. Cynwrig punched in some numbers and the door creaked open, revealing an old-fashioned, gorgeously ornate speakeasy.

"I've lived here my entire life," I said, unable to disguise my surprise, "and I had no idea this even existed."

"Few do." He guided me down steps lit by faint light strips. "It caters to a very specific clientele."

My gaze did another sweep of the shadowed but lavishly decorated room. It was long and narrow, with an ancient-looking oak bar lining one side of the room and behind that a wall of alcohol, some of the bottles so old they belonged in a museum. On the other side of the room was a series of small wooden booths, with heavily carved privacy screens that ran to the ceiling. The slight shimmer in front of each booth suggested there was also privacy magic being employed.

"The insanely wealthy, I'm guessing?" I said. "And perhaps even those up to no good?"

"Those two definitions would definitely cover ninety-five percent of the bar's patronage." He walked close enough that his breath brushed my ear as he spoke, and tremors of delight skipped through me. "The other five percent are souls who—like me—simply wish to enjoy the full range of alcohol available here."

Yeah, believing that. He was a dark elf with a reputation for playing hard and fast, even if said reputation was earned more in his past than his present.

He guided me down to a booth at the far end. The

wooden table was darkly stained, but the song of its past remained strong, even if it was filled with an odd sort of melancholy—a result of having centuries of alcohol stain its timber, I suspected. It spoke of an ancient forest that had once held a life and consciousness of its own, from a tree cut down in its prime by humans who could not hear her song, and who had no understanding of what, exactly, they were destroying. There were less than a handful of such forests left across all of England these days, but they were fiercely protected by the pixies and wood elves— who were considered forester class—living in or near them.

I ran my fingers gently across the table's edge, lightly acknowledging the life of the old tree. Its song sharpened in response.

"Do you wish to hang up your coat?" Cynwrig asked softly.

I jumped and then tugged the wet woolen coat off and handed it to him. He knew about the knives and wasn't worried about them, so I didn't either. Maybe weapons were a necessity in a bar that regularly handled high-level shady deals.

I slid onto the plushly padded red-leather seat and glanced at the rear wall. The old-fashioned wallpaper looked to have been red at one point in its past but was now so darkly stained with age and smoke that the patterns were barely discernible. What surprised me was the crest that dominated the center of the wall; it was a hammer and anvil, which, from memory, belonged to the Lùtair family.

"Your family obviously conducts a lot of business here if you have a personal booth."

Cynwrig draped his cloak over mine and claimed the seat opposite me. A move I was happy about. Mostly.

"There's no place safer in Deva to conduct a certain kind of business," he said. "Would you like a drink?"

"You promised whisky—I do hope you're not a man to go back on his word."

He smiled, raised a hand, and made a come-here motion. A waitress moved out of the shadows and said, "And what would you like tonight, Lord Lùtair?"

"We'll have the Macallan '79, thanks."

I raised my eyebrows. While the '79 wasn't the most expensive single malt Macallan made, a bottle of the stuff was going for three grand or more these days. It certainly wasn't a drop I'd be serving in my tavern. But then, my customers were obviously in a very different socioeconomic sphere to those who frequented this place. "A choice to impress or to apologize?"

He raised an eyebrow, amusement lurking around the corners of his smoky silver eyes. "You don't seem the type to be impressed by an expensive drop."

An apology, then. "So, what is it that they've sent you here to say?"

"What they sent me to say is a waste of words, but that doesn't negate the need for you to understand what is truly happening."

"Did their words involve a threat?"

"A veiled one, yes." He paused. "Did you really have a ten-year relationship with Mathi Dhār-Val?"

I raised an eyebrow, amusement stirring. "And what has that got to do with the matter at hand?"

"Absolutely nothing. I simply wish to understand how you could survive that long in his company. His conversation range is ... unimpressive, to say the least."

I laughed. "He's not *that* bad."

Which was true, even if part of the reason I'd never

moved full-time into his apartment was the fact it would have led to a little too much of his "out of bed" self-interested conversation time.

"I find the man a bore, but he obviously had some worthwhile talents to hold a woman of your caliber for so long."

I laughed again. "Now *that* is the comment of a man who wants to get me into his bed."

"Desperately," he said, his solemn tone belied by the amusement in his eyes. "I take it you split when he decided to go wife shopping?"

"Yes—although I would have left earlier had I known he'd another lover on the side." I eyed him for a second. "You're not contracted or married, are you?"

A smile tugged at his luscious lips, but the amusement in his shadowed gaze fled. "There's two major differences between us and the Ljósálfar—we marry for love, and when we do so, there are no others."

"So that would be a no, then?"

"I would not be flirting with you if I had committed my heart to another."

"Good to know."

I glanced up as the waitress reappeared with our drinks and placed them on the table. I smiled in thanks, then picked up the thick-based round glass and "nosed" the mahogany liquid. Oh lord ... the smell. It was almost as divine as the man sitting opposite.

"Wait until you taste it," Cynwrig said, his smile touching his eyes again.

I did so. There were heavy notes of rum-soaked raisins, nutty spices, and orange first up, and then it got spicier, with hints of cloves and pepper. It was long coating and rich on the tongue, with an aftertaste that spoke of black-berries and old oak.

"I believe the appropriate comment here is ... wow. Apology well and truly accepted."

His laugh was warm and rich, and delight skimmed across my skin. "At least I now know how to get back into your favor after an argument."

"Depends on how serious an argument we're talking about." I raised the glass to the light and admired its rich color. "And you're still getting ahead of yourself."

"Oh, I don't believe I am."

His gaze moved from the whisky to my lips. That hunger stirred again, a pull so fierce that I found myself leaning forward, a bee drawn to nectar she could not resist.

"You," I said softly, "need to stop with the magnetism."

"This," he countered, voice just as soft, "is not of my doing."

Meaning he could control it no more than me? Interesting. I forced myself back. "Do the council truly believe that Lugh is behind the theft of the hoard?"

He hesitated. "There are some who claim the coincidences are too great to be ignored."

"And are these people the reason the Eldritch have not yet interviewed Lugh? Or allowed him into Nialle's apartment to see what might be missing?"

"Yes. They wish a full background check of your brother's finances and movements over the last year done first."

I snorted. "Lugh's an antiquarian. If anyone knows how to cover their tracks, it would be him."

"They're aware of that."

"Then what is their theory on Nialle's murder? I suppose they believe Lugh did that too?"

"No, they do not. That is but one of many confounding factors in this whole matter."

I took another sip of whisky and briefly closed my eyes. Lord, I really was going to have to track down a bottle of this. "And what about Gilda? Are her background and finances going to be more thoroughly checked now?"

"Yes, although it's likely to be too late, given whoever is behind her murder has had the time to cover their tracks."

"Meaning there were no unexpected DNA traces or other evidence found in her bedroom?"

"What evidence they found is still undergoing forensic examination."

"And Mathi?"

"Was cross-examined by a seeker this afternoon. He was not a willing participant in the theft of the hoard."

I raised an eyebrow. "Meaning they think he was an unwilling one?"

"There were traces of Borrachero in the blood sample taken."

"And that is?"

"A truth serum, of sorts. When given, it puts you into a sort of twilight zone halfway between consciousness and unconsciousness and makes you more chatty and disinhibited. But when you wake, you have no memory of what you were talking about."

"Meaning Gilda or whoever she worked with was milking him for information?"

"It would appear so, although it remains unclear how it would have helped the thieves in regard to the hoard. Mathi might be highborn, but he was never advised of the vault's location."

"Were you?" I asked curiously. "You *are* your father's heir."

"One of them," he said. "But the Ljósálfar are responsible for the security of the Éadrom Hoard, not us."

"Then who does know?"

"The kings or rulers of each fae or shifter line are aware of the location of all three hoards. Leaders aside, only the assigned guards and the bibliothecaries were aware of the location. In the case of the former, they do not have full access to the entire site, only the perimeter."

When the numbers were toted up, that was still a fair few people. "I take it both the bibliothecaries and the guards underwent regular security checks?"

"Yes, but one of the bibliothecaries went missing after the hoard was stolen, so it's possible he was involved."

"His family has been fully vetted?"

"Of course."

"And the guards are all accounted for?"

"Yes. Not that that means anything—Mathi is a prime example of how it's possible to steal information without the giver being aware."

I nodded. "He might also be the reason no one has yet been able to find the missing bibliothecary or even the hoard itself. He's on the fae council and privy to all decisions regarding the investigation. He could have supplied the people behind the theft with every move and decision the council made."

And he wouldn't be the only one on that council being unknowingly used in such a manner, I'd wager.

"Yes, which is why all councilors must now undergo regular seeker screenings and blood tests."

"I do hope the latter is being done in a controlled environment."

He raised an eyebrow. "You really aren't the trusting type, are you?"

"That depends on the situation and the person." I took another sip of whisky. "I still can't believe that the council, with all the resources it has at its fingertips, hasn't been able to uncover anything about the thieves or the hoard to this point."

I knew enough about Lugh's work tracking stolen relics —as opposed to the truly lost items such as the Claws—to know that there was *always* some kind of trail, be it small tells, magic that could be traced if you had the skill, or even an old-fashioned paper trail.

"I'm of the personal belief that the thieves haven't dared move or sell any part of the hoard thanks to the alert that was immediately put out, and the fact that all known legal and illegal channels are being monitored."

"That still leaves unknown channels, doesn't it?"

"The shifters and even some fae seem to believe there are smuggling channels we Myrkálfar know nothing about. I assure you, they are wrong."

A smile tugged at my lips. "I thought your lot had given up that line of work eons ago?"

"To the degree that many of our businesses are now registered and legitimate, yes." His gaze gained an intensity I felt all the way down to my toes. "Our familiarity with the black market and all the various shipping routes is the reason I'm sure your brother had nothing to do with the theft. I've used many of his contacts myself, and trust me, had there been even the slightest whisper of his involvement, I would have been informed."

"Then why do some on the council believe otherwise?"

"Because the Ljósálfar think in terms of black and white. He has the knowledge and the skill, so therefore must be proved innocent rather than guilty."

"Bastards, as I said." I stretched out my legs and lightly

touched his. The move might have been casual, but the response was anything but. It felt like skin on skin. Felt like a prelude to something bigger and stronger. Something that was both dangerous and undeniable at the same time.

I couldn't ignore it. Didn't *want* to ignore it.

Not tonight.

Not when I might soon be washed away in a wave of danger and death.

I frowned lightly. If second sight was now warning that the shit was about to hit the fan, I wasn't about to ignore her; she might be new, but she certainly had a good prediction record so far. And if she was warning I'd better enjoy a night in the arms of this gorgeous man while I still could? Well, that was a step I was more than happy to take.

Of course, it might not be second sight at all. It might simply be my sex-starved hormones making damn sure I didn't let this opportunity or this man slip by.

My gaze rose to his. Saw the passion and rich awareness there. Knew he was every bit as determined not to let this night end with either of us being alone or lonely.

I took another drink and then said, in a voice that was husky with wanting, "Was I hauled in front of the council simply to prove my innocence? Or was there another reason?"

"There was another. There always is."

"And that was?"

"They wish your help to locate the hoard."

I stared at him for a second and then threw my head back and laughed—a short sharp bark of disbelief. "Why would they think I'd go out of my way now to even *spit* on them, let alone help them locate the hoard?"

"As I said, the Ljósálfar are linear thinkers. Once they

cleared you of any involvement, they could see no reason for you not wanting to work with them."

"Mathi could have told them otherwise."

"He did say it perhaps *wasn't* the best road to take if we wished your help."

"Understatement in the extreme." I finished my drink and crossed my arms on the table. "Was my finding the ruby the catalyst for deciding I might succeed where everyone else they've employed had failed?"

Cynwrig motioned for another round. "That, and Mathi saying you'd inherited your mother's skills." He studied me for a second. "Was your denial a lie or the truth?"

I raised an eyebrow. "You couldn't tell?"

"I thought it might have been a bit of both, but I haven't known you long enough to be sure."

"Well, I do believe *that* is something we'll have to correct."

"Tonight?"

"If you wish."

"It is *not* just about my wishes, dear Bethany."

I smiled. "I rather suspect that if we do nothing to ease this fire, I might well combust."

"That feeling is mutual."

"Excellent." I smiled at the waitress as she brought us both another shot of whisky. "Do you have a theory about either the singing bowl or the ruby's reappearance?"

He pursed his lips briefly. They really were utterly kiss-able. "In times past, we Myrkálfar diverted attention away from our movements by planting one or two minor items in the homes of innocents. By the time they were cleared of any wrongdoing, we were well gone."

"Which makes sense in the case of the singing bowl, but

not the ruby. Not if they were using Gilda to milk Mathi for information."

"Yes, but given what you said about the ruby's location, it's likely Gilda got a little light-fingered and paid the price for it."

"If that's true, she was far closer to the thieves *and* the hoard than her background checks have so far revealed."

He nodded. "I've got my people working on it."

I raised an eyebrow, amusement lurking. "Your people? Would this be family, or shadowy underground criminal types?"

"In some respects, the two are one and the same. As I said, not all of our businesses are legitimate." He paused. "We do not, however, deal in drugs or flesh, despite the old rumors that keep resurfacing."

"No drugs aside from alcohol, I take it?"

"High-end alcohol is to be savored, not binged."

"Says the man whose DNA will not allow him to consume vast quantities."

"And that," he said, picking up his glass, "is probably a good thing, given the quality of the alcohol we transport."

I glanced at the wall of booze. "I take it you supply this place?"

"And many others you might not be aware of. Not all fae are happy to keep the company of humans."

Or shifters, I'd guess. "If the council actually wants my help, then they're going to pass on any and all information they have about the theft to me. And I'll tell you here and now that I will *not* take a blood oath. I need to be free to talk to whoever I deem necessary."

"They are unlikely to agree to that."

"Then, to repeat a favorite phrase, fuck them."

Another of those sexy smiles teased his lips. "I take it you nevertheless intend to uncover what is going on?"

"In regard to Nialle's murder, Lugh's poisoning, and the fucking note left on the tavern's door? Yes. If, in the process, I stumble on anything regarding the hoard, I'll pass it on." I studied him for a moment. "Why were you poisoned? What were you doing on the wall walk?"

"I was following a suspect."

"Related to the hoard?"

He hesitated. "Unclear."

There was something in his expression that suggested the matter was more personal, but he went on before I could question him.

"But that same night, someone left a note and a large moonstone in my apartment. It might be connected to the hoard—"

"Might?" I cut in. "You haven't had it confirmed by the council?"

"No."

"Why not?"

"Because of those who still believe the Myrkálfar are behind this robbery. A stone turning up unexpectedly in my apartment would be confirmation in their eyes."

I snorted. "That makes about as much sense as Lugh being behind the theft. I mean, you're smugglers, amongst many other things. I hardly think you'd be dumb enough to keep even the smallest item anywhere close to you or your family."

"Yes, but after the hullabaloo raised over the appearance of the singing bowl, I'm reluctant to reveal the gem's appearance and possibly confirm anyone's unwarranted suspicions."

"And besides," I added, "you want to see what crawls out of the woodwork if you don't mention it."

The sexy smile got stronger. "It is amazing just how well you understand my thinking when we are little more than strangers."

We wouldn't be strangers for long; not if I had any say in it. I drank more whisky and felt its delicious burn all the way down. But it was nothing to the burn being caused by this man. "So where is this moonstone now?"

"At my apartment."

A smile tugged at my lips. "How very convenient."

He expression gave little away. "Do you wish to relocate?"

"I think it would be foolish not to."

"With that, I concur."

He finished his drink, then moved to my side of the table and offered me a hand. His fingers were warm against mine, his touch firm but enticing; I had visions of them sliding down my stomach, pressing past my panties, touching and teasing ...

I downed the rest of the whisky in one go, but it did little to ease either the low-down ache or the unsteady thumping of my heart. My gaze rose to the shadowed brilliance of his. The desire so evident there had tremors of anticipation shooting across my skin.

I wanted this man as I'd wanted no other. Not even Mathi.

I licked suddenly dry lips, and his gaze followed the movement. Then he smiled, lowered his face to mine, and whispered, "May I?"

I didn't answer, just tangled a hand in his thick, dark hair and pulled him closer. Our kiss was long and sensual, a teasing prelude to what was to come, and yet so much more. It was heat and passion and promise, and by the time he pulled away, I wouldn't have objected to being taken right here at the table.

He stepped back, his breathing unsteady as he plucked my coat from the hook and helped me into it. His fingers briefly brushed the back of my neck, and once again, it felt like I was being struck by lightning.

He signed for the drinks, and we left the bar. The full weight of the storm hit as we stepped out into the Row, and it went some way to easing the inner heat. I shivered and quickly did up my coat. "How far away is your apartment?"

"It's in Watergate Street."

Which was near the racecourse, close to the remaining section of wall in that area. "We'll need to order a cab then."

I normally wouldn't have minded walking, but arriving in a frozen, pruney state at his apartment wasn't optimal for immediate seduction.

"Already taken care of."

I glanced at him, eyebrows raised. "And just when did you do that?"

He guided me toward the steps. "There's a private car for guests to use on nights such as this."

"Handy."

"Very." The heat of his gaze washed over me, and the wave of desire that followed had my knees threatening to buckle. "Especially when urgent business is at hand."

"Oh, I hope I'm a whole lot more than merely business, Cynwrig."

"I very much suspect you will be."

Something in the way he said that had me glancing at him sharply. "Was seducing me part of the council's orders?"

He raised an eyebrow, smoky gaze giving little away. "And if it was?"

"I'd fuck you, but I wouldn't trust you."

He laughed. "As it happens, I was ordered to charm the truth out of you, not the pants *off* you. Though I will admit that I've also been assigned as your council liaison."

"I'm surprised Mathi didn't volunteer for that job. He's certainly been desperate enough to get back into my good books."

"And bed?" Cynwrig asked, one eyebrow rising.

"Always."

"Well, I guess I have to give him points for having good taste, even if good sense is somewhat absent."

"Something I learned *way* too late. And you didn't answer the question."

"I didn't?"

I gave him a long look, but he merely smiled. Which suggested to my mind that there'd been some kind of argument over the matter. If that *was* the case, I was glad Cynwrig had won. I was still a little annoyed with Mathi for not warning me about the council's intentions or speaking up for either me or Lugh. And while I was aware he might not have had the option to do either, it didn't ease the annoyance. My feelings weren't always logical when it came to Mathi.

I tried again. "Can they actually order a Myrkálfar prince to do something like that?"

"We are all of equal standing on the council. We have to be for it to work."

"And the liaison duty is one you took oh-so reluctantly?"

"So reluctantly," he said casually, "I threatened to kill any who attempted to take it from me."

I glanced at him with a laugh that abruptly died. "You're serious?"

He quirked that eyebrow at me again. "And why does this surprise you, given the force that burns between us? I am utterly helpless before it, dear Bethany."

"Helpless is a word I would *never* use in conjunction with you." My voice was dry. "And I say that barely even knowing you."

"And *that*," he said, his soft voice so deep, so sultry, and vibrating with so much passion that, for several seconds, I could barely even breathe, "is a situation I fully intend to rectify tonight."

A dark blue Audi pulled up to the curb as we stepped onto the street. Cynwrig opened the door and ushered me in, then ran around to the other side.

"The apartment, please, Joseph."

"Yes, sir," the gray-haired driver replied.

The car took off smoothly, and the privacy screen slid into place. Not that it was required, as neither of us said anything. For my part, the weight of desire and need had simply become too great to form a coherent sentence—a situation that wasn't at *all* helped when he slid his hand over mine and our fingers twined.

His apartment was situated in a grand, three-story, double-fronted Georgian building. The entrance hall was large, airy, and opulent, with entrances to the two ground floor apartments to the left and right, and an ornate, obviously original, red-carpeted staircase in the middle. He led me toward it then up to the second floor.

"My sister owns the apartment on the right," he said, an odd vibration in his voice that suggested anger and briefly made me wonder if the twins had fallen out. "But we have the entire floor to ourselves. She's taken over the full duties of the crown at the encampment while I've been working with the council on the theft."

He keyed the apartment door open and ushered me through. The living area beyond was one large living space, with a fireplace dominating the far wall and ceiling-high bookcases either side. The sash windows at the front of the room offered views over the treetops and the buildings on the other side of the street, while the kitchen to the left was large and surprisingly modern. There was a laundry and bathroom to one side of this, and a big old sofa and four comfortable-looking chairs in the central area, facing the fireplace and the TV above it.

What I didn't see was a bed, nor a staircase leading up to another floor. Neither of the bookcases looked to be the type that pulled down into a bed.

He accepted my coat, then hung both his and mine in the discreet coat cupboard situated at the end of the ceiling-high cupboards that ran the full length of the room on the door side. "Do you wish to see the moonstone first?"

"Only if I have to."

"There is no 'have to' tonight, Bethany. There's only want and need to."

Oh, he was smooth, there was no doubt about that.

"Then I want and need to explore every inch of your glorious body."

He laughed and tugged me across the room. When we reached the left bookcase, he stopped and pulled down what looked to be a ratty old dictionary. There was a soft click, and the bookcase silently swung open.

"A concealed door?" I said, amused.

"I'd like to say it is a by-product of my family's shady past, but in truth it was here when we bought the building twenty years ago."

"Bet it comes in handy for your more nefarious activities."

I followed him into the shadows and up a set of stairs that creaked under our weight. Behind us, the concealed door closed, briefly wrapping us in darkness before tiny lights recessed into the brick wall flickered to life.

"Any activities and deals that walk the line are handled at the encampment," he said, amused. "I only deal with the legal stuff here."

"I guess that means the secret door is not so secret?"

He glanced at me, amusement twinkling in his shadowed eyes. "Are you suggesting I have a very high number of lovers?"

"Well, the Myrkálfar *are* well known for their sexual appetites."

He laughed, a sound as smooth and as rich as honey, and just as enticing. "I will admit *that* particular rumor holds truth, but there's a very comfortable and quite large pull-down bed built into the cabinetry near the door that is used for such activities."

I raised my eyebrows. "So why am I being honored with a tour of the inner sanctum?"

"Because," he said, with a glance so filled with heat it curled my toes, "I believe you and I will be far more than one night."

I didn't dare read anything into that statement, even if the weight of what lay between us was obviously something more than *just* desire. If my time with Mathi had taught me anything, it was not to expect too much, no matter how long the relationship. Besides, Cynwrig was heir to the crown, even if that crown technically no longer existed. Like all highborn elves, he would eventually marry within his own race. It was only the lower classes that sometimes married out of it.

"I would hope so," I said lightly. "I've got a lot of cobwebs to get rid of."

He laughed. "Then the men in this town are fools. But I shall do my best to get rid of them."

With a wicked grin, he increased his pace, and we all but raced up the last few steps to the loft area. It was a surprisingly large space; the pitched roof was higher than it had looked from the outside, and the dormer windows allowed just enough streetlight to wash away the darkness. A large bathroom lay directly opposite the stairs, while the main room was divided into two distinct areas; there was an office with three desks—one a massive but beautiful antique oak with a leather top, and two smaller ones that acted as side returns—in the front half, and a bed the size of a boat in the other. Low storage cabinets divided the two spaces, while a line of wardrobes dominated the far end wall. The rear wall—directly opposite the boat—had a series of folding doors that led out into a small balcony. Even from where I was, I could see the magnificent views out over the city's rooftops.

He led me into the bedroom and stopped near two well-padded and very comfortable-looking leather chairs that sat between the boat and the doors. "Would you like a drink?"

"No." I gently wrapped a hand around his neck and pulled him toward me. "But I *would* like a kiss."

His smile was achingly beautiful, and his eyes bright with the same fierce heat and desire that pulsed through me. His lips met mine, and time seemed to slow. Nothing existed beyond this man, this kiss, and the energy that swirled between us, gradually building to an explosive peak as we tasted and explored with mouth and touch.

Then his lips left mine and moved to my neck, branding me with butterfly kisses. When his teeth grazed my earlobe, I shuddered, a soft gasp escaping my lips.

He chuckled softly, his breath so warm on my skin. "I would kiss far more, but this bulky sweater is not conducive to such activities."

"Then perhaps," I said, flicking several of his shirt buttons open and slipping my hand past the silky material to explore the wonderfully muscular flesh underneath, "we should remove our clothing."

"At the same time? Or shall we assist each other?"

I pursed my lips, pretending to think on the matter when there was only ever one possible answer. "I believe the latter would be best. These boots are new and a bitch to get off."

His laugh was a low and sexy sound. "Then perhaps we should start with them?"

He pressed a couple of fingers against my diaphragm and gently pushed me back into the chair.

I dropped into the deep cushion and draped my legs over the arm. "Perhaps we should."

He caught my right foot and tugged off the boot and sock, tossing them onto the other chair before repeating the process with my left. Then he knelt in front of me, raised one foot to his lips, and began to kiss and suck each of my toes. I'd never really gotten the foot fetish thing, but maybe that was because I'd never had a master of seduction apply his full attention to my digits before.

It was glorious. Devastatingly so.

I have no idea how long his attention lasted, because I was too lost in the sheer pleasure of it. When he finally pulled away and rose, I almost groaned in disappointment.

He offered me a hand and pulled me gently to my feet. Without comment, he slowly began to undress me, teasing and tasting each newly exposed piece of flesh with lips and teeth and fingers before moving on. By the time he slipped my panties over my hips, I was close to meltdown.

Then he kissed me right *there,* and I jumped and groaned all at the same time.

His chuckle had a decidedly evil edge. "Didn't taste any cobwebs, dear Bethany. Perhaps I should delve a little deeper?"

"No." If he did, I'd come, and I wanted to bring him to the same desperately aching state as me before any sort of release happened. I took a deep, shuddering breath in a vague effort to control the need pulsing through my veins and stepped out of my panties. "I believe it is time now for you to get naked. Prepare to be tortured as thoroughly as you tortured me, my lord."

He stepped back and lightly bowed. "I am yours to do with what you wish."

"A vow you might yet regret."

"Oh, I seriously doubt that."

"A challenge. I like it."

I started with the remaining shirt buttons, flicking them undone one by one while I held his gaze and watched the slow burn become wilder, fiercer. I didn't immediately push the material from his shoulders, instead exploring the muscular planes of his chest with hands and mouth, trailing kisses across his dark flesh and capturing first one nipple, then the other, with my teeth, gently biting before soothing the sensation with my tongue. He shuddered, and the burn between us increased. I ignored it and continued to taste and tease him as thoroughly as he had me. Finally, I pushed the shirt from his shoulders and down his arms to the floor, then trailed kisses across one shoulder to his back. I paused, pressed my breasts against the heat of his spine, and slid my hands around to his washboard abs and then down, undoing his belt and the button at the top of his jeans before slipping my hand past the elastic on his silk shorts and lightly caressing the heated and oh-so ready hardness still constrained by cloth.

A shudder ran through him, and he all but groaned, "*That* is unfair."

"*Nothing* is unfair, my lord. You are mine, remember?"

He made a low sound that could have been either a growl or a desperate half laugh but said nothing more. I continued to caress and tease his erection, until the shudders in his body grew fierce and desperate. Then I pulled away and continued my kisses to his other shoulder and on to the front of his body before working my way down his washboard abs, this time with lips rather than hands, following the happy trail of hair downward.

He made another of those incomprehensible sounds when I slowly slid the zip on his jeans all the way down, but otherwise didn't move. I hooked my fingers through the waist of both his jeans and silk shorts, then pushed them down to his thighs. His cock sprang free, thick, long, and oh-so-ready for action.

I lightly swirled my tongue around its tip, and he shuddered, groaning. I chuckled softly and continued, using mouth and tongue to bring him to the brink before pulling back. I took off his shoes and socks and then tugged his pants the rest of the way down his legs.

He kicked them off, caught my hand, pulled me up, and kissed me fiercely but all too briefly. Then he led me across to the bed, lightly pushing me down before straddling me. But for the longest time, he did nothing more than kiss me, slowly and so very passionately. Waiting, I suspected, for the heat in both our bodies to ebb so that the seductions could begin again.

It was a suspicion that proved correct. Once again he began the slow, exquisite journey down my body, using mouth and tongue and teeth with devastating effect.

When his tongue flicked over my clit, I bit back a groan but couldn't stop myself arching into him, wanting more, *needing* more. He chuckled softly, his breath so cool compared to my heated, aching flesh, and then complied. Sensations flowed like liquid fire through my veins, building to a fierceness that would not be denied.

"Oh ... gods." My voice was little more than a fractured whisper. "Please ..."

His tongue caressed my clit one more time, and my climax hit, stealing breath and thought as shudder after delicious shudder ran through me.

But it wasn't enough. I wanted—*needed*—him inside.

"Please," I repeated, through the still fierce echoes of pleasure. "I need ..."

The words trailed off as the vague sounds of foil rustling registered, and then he slid slowly into me. The feel of him—so thick and hard and long—had the barely ebbed waves of pressure building anew. His heat penetrated every fiber, enveloping me in a force that was basic, pure, and so very powerful.

I groaned in utter pleasure and wrapped my legs around his hips, moving with him, even as I drove him deeper inside. The pressure continued to build as his powerful body stroked deeper and harder, until need and desire became so fierce it was nigh on explosive.

My orgasm hit again, and I gasped, unable to breathe as sensation swept over me. He came a heartbeat later, his body thrusting deep into mine even as a groan was torn from his lips.

For several minutes afterward, neither of us moved. Then he stirred, slipped to one side, and took care of the condom before gathering me in his arms.

He kissed the tip of my nose and then said, his eyes liquid silver in the shadowed light, "*That* was an absolutely amazing entrée. Shall we move on to the main course?"

I laughed and threw a leg over his hips, drawing him closer. The man was already half erect. "I've heard rumors about the sexual stamina of the Myrkálfar. I fully intend to see if the reality lives up to them."

He chuckled softly, wrapped a gentle hand around the back of my neck, and drew me into another long and explosive kiss.

I learned, over the long and glorious course of the night, that the rumors had definitely *understated* the stamina of the Myrkálfar.

Cynwrig wasn't in bed when I finally woke. I scrubbed a hand across my eyes in a vague effort to erase the lingering tiredness and peered somewhat blearily around the room. Light shone wanly through the sliding doors opposite, and the sky was gray and threatening. It had at least stopped raining, but the heaviness of those clouds suggested it wasn't going to remain that way for long.

I pushed up into a sitting position, shivering a little as the cool air caressed my bare skin, and spotted the note sitting on the nearby table. *Nipped out to get fresh bread for*

*our breakfast. Feel free to make yourself a coffee or grab a
shower. Won't be long.*

I smiled, tossed the blankets aside, and padded across
to the bathroom. There were whispers of soreness coming
from various parts of my body, but I wasn't about to
complain. The man hadn't only blasted away the cobwebs,
but well and truly worked out numerous muscle groups.
And he certainly had an imagination that went way beyond
the bed ...

I found a big fluffy towel, soap, and toiletry items
waiting for me in the bathroom, and couldn't help but
smile. The lady traffic was definitely high if he had toiletry
bags ready and waiting for every new "guest."

I grabbed the soap and washcloth, then stepped into
the enormous double shower and flicked on the hot water.
By the time I'd finished, the delicious smell of bacon filled
the air, and my stomach rumbled.

I hurriedly got dressed, then padded barefoot down the
stairs to the main room. Cynwrig stood in front of the stove,
flipping eggs in one pan while bacon sizzled in the other,
but glanced around as I entered. He was wearing dark jeans
that fit enticingly over his butt, and a gray sweater that
somehow emphasized the lovely width of his shoulders.

His gaze skimmed my length and came up heated. "You
look good enough to eat."

"I believe you already have, and multiple times." I
planted a kiss on his bristly cheek, then reached past him in
an attempt to snare a bit of bacon.

He lightly slapped my hand away. "No stealing, wench.
Go sit at the island, and breakfast will be served in a matter
of moments."

I harrumphed but nevertheless did as ordered, leaning
my arms on the counter as I watched him cook. There was

something very sexy about a man who knew his way around a stovetop.

Once he'd served everything up, he joined me at the table and slid the breadboard holding the freshly cut slices of sourdough and the butter dish toward me. "Ladies first."

I picked up the crust, slathered it with butter, and took a bite. It was still warm, and damn delicious.

"So, is there actually a note and a stone? Or was that all one big story to get me here?"

One dark eyebrow winged upward. "I'm offended that you think I'd stoop so low."

I nudged his knee with mine. Though the contact was brief, desire surged. Last night had not eased the fire, not in any way. "No, you're not."

He laughed. "It's upstairs, on my desk."

"What did the note actually say?" I started in on the mountain of bacon and eggs. To say I was hungry was something of an understatement.

"Only those who can see can find. Only those who trust will win. Seek the seer."

I blinked. That was almost as cryptic as the note that had come with the Eye, and it made me wonder if they'd come from the same source. "And do you know a seer?"

He glanced at me, shadowed gaze serious. "Your mother was the only person who could have claimed the title of seer in Deva, but I never personally met her, and I don't think my family ever used her services."

I wrinkled my nose. "She was more a diviner than an actual seer. She didn't see the future, per se, just possibilities."

"That still falls within the broader definition of seer."

True. I scooped up some bacon and munched on it

thoughtfully. "Tell me, did the note happen to be written on a scrap of vellum?"

His gaze sharpened. "Yes—how did you guess that?"

I hesitated. While it was Lugh's secret rather than mine, I had a bad feeling this whole thing was already far bigger than he or I could handle—especially when he remained on the suspect list. We needed to put our trust in someone who not only knew about the hoard but who also knew what steps the council was taking to uncover it. At this point, that meant either Mathi or Cynwrig. I was more inclined to trust the latter than the former. Which could be a huge mistake, but …

"Lugh received a note regarding something called the Eye a few days after Nialle's death."

"And the Eye is?"

"No idea." I picked up the remaining bit of crust and ran it through the egg remains. "But Lugh thinks it's why Nialle was killed and his place trashed."

"Huh." Cynwrig's expression was thoughtful. "I can't remember seeing anything called the Eye being mentioned, but I'll double-check."

"That would be helpful, although Lugh also believes it's connected to the Claws and, as far as I'm aware, he doesn't know about the hoard."

A flicker of surprise ran through his expression. "You didn't mention it?"

"No, because Mathi asked me to wait for council clearance." I smiled wryly. "Now that I haven't got it, I will of course be telling him absolutely everything."

He snorted, but a sharp buzzing cut off any reply he might have made. He rose, moved across to the door, and pressed the intercom. "Who is it?"

"Detective Kazan, Eldritch division. We have a warrant to search your premises, Lord Lùtair."

My gaze shot to Cynwrig's; his expression burned with fury, but none of it showed in his voice as he coolly replied, "And why might you have that?"

There was a brief pause. "We received an anonymous tip that an item belonging to the hoard might be found at your premises."

I slid off the stool and quickly but quietly gathered the plates and cutlery, then moved across to the dishwasher. I couldn't be found here, nor could there be any evidence that I *had* been here. It would only deepen the council's suspicions. Though, if they *did* suspect Cynwrig, why on earth would they have appointed him my liaison? Something was very off in all this.

"I find the timing somewhat interesting," Cynwrig drawled, "and will be requiring a full report on this so-called tip from your commanders."

"Naturally," the voice behind the door said. "In the meantime, you need to let us in, Lord Lùtair."

"Of course. Give me a few seconds to get dressed first."

"Yes, of course."

He released the intercom and padded softly across the room, quickly placing the sourdough in the nearby breadbox and then sweeping the crumbs into his hands and tossing them into the rubbish bin. Then he caught my arm and guided me across to the still-open concealed doorway.

"There's no guarantee they won't know about this door or the loft," I whispered.

"I suspect they will, given this has the stink of a setup." His expression remained fierce. I wouldn't want to be the person behind the search warrant. "Collect the note and the gem, and then leave via the balcony doors. Cross over the next two balconies, take the fire escape down to the rear lane, and then make your way home. I'll call when I'm able."

I kissed his cheek, then ran silently up the stairs. The concealed door closed behind me, and the shadows moved in. I shivered, hoping it wasn't an omen, and quickly but quietly moved over to the gorgeous old antique desk. The envelope sat on top of a stack of folders and was a replica of the one Lugh had received, down to the typed address. I tipped it up to check the moonstone was inside; the minute it rolled onto my hand, my skin crawled. Then energy stirred, whispering secrets.

There was magic both in and around the stone.

And the *latter* was a tracking spell.

If I took this stone with me, whoever had sent the Eldritch after Cynwrig would soon be hunting me.

CHAPTER
SEVEN

P anic surged, but I flexed my fingers and breathed deep in an effort to control it. If there was one lesson I'd learned over the years, it was that decisions made in the midst of panic never helped *any* situation. In fact, they were more likely to land me deeper in trouble than get me out of it.

From downstairs came the sound of conversation—hard-edged questions mingling with Cynwrig's softer but tightly controlled replies—and multiple footsteps echoed on the old floorboards. Most moved to various sections of the room but at least two strode straight toward the concealed door.

I had to get out, and fast.

I shoved the envelope and note into my pocket but kept a grip on the stone as I padded quietly over to the seating area. As I pulled my knives from underneath my coat, the blades reacted, their hilts glowing a deep, rich purple. *That* meant the tracker on the stone came from a darker source of magic.

I slid one knife free and touched the moonstone to the

blade. There was a bright flash, followed by a faint wisp of smoke that smelled slightly acidic, and my skin stopped crawling even though energy still stirred in the deeper heart of the moonstone. Obviously, the soul of this stone was not born of darkness. I nevertheless shoved it into the bottom of the sheath, just to ensure there was no chance of it being tracked magically, and then strapped the two knives on.

At the base of the stairs, there was a soft scrape as the concealed doorway opened.

I was out of time.

I grabbed my coat, boots, and purse, then ran lightly across to the sliding doors. Their frames were wood rather than metal, which was a decided bonus for someone like me. I slipped out and closed the door, then moved out of the direct line of sight and pressed my fingers into the joint between door and track. The song of the wood was faint, tarnished by time and pollution, but she heard me. I gently wove the fibers of the two together, creating a bond strong enough to prevent the door from opening.

Footsteps vibrated through the floorboards inside the loft. I rose and walked across to the small wall that divided Cynwrig's apartment from his sister's, climbed over that, and then ran on. Behind me, someone pulled at the door; the wood creaked in annoyance but held firm.

I scrambled over the next, much higher wall, and then dropped down behind it to pull on my boots and coat. Once I'd swung my purse over my shoulder, I walked on, finding the fire escape in one corner. It was old and rusty, and the metal creaked and swayed as I swung over onto it. By the time I'd reached the ground, I felt like kissing the cobblestones in sheer relief.

I looked around to see if there was anyone taking any

interest in me, then went right. There was no other option; going left would take me close to the corner of Watergate and City Walls Road, where Cynwrig's apartment building was, and there'd undoubtedly be guards positioned out front watching both roads. The Eldritch did *not* take chances.

Of course, there was no guarantee there wouldn't be watchers on the road ahead, but it was at least a little less likely.

Thankfully, there were quite a few people walking through the Mews, including—if the number of cameras was anything to go by—a large group of tourists. I tucked in behind them and followed them left into the street. After casually looking around to ensure no one was taking any undue notice of me, I crossed the road and walked into the walled-off parking area. Once hidden from the immediate sight of anyone watching from the street, I sprinted through the cars and up the ramp to the road on the other side. The storm that had been threatening ever since I'd woken chose that moment to unleash, and with such ferocity that I could barely see where I was going. The weather gods, it seemed, had decided to test my love for storms.

I called a cab. While it wasn't really that far to the tavern from here, I had no desire to walk in a storm *this* violent.

By the time the cab finally arrived, my boots, jeans, and hair were all soaked, and moisture seeped through the thick woolen coat. The cabbie tossed me a towel to put on the seat before I got in, but kindly dropped me as close as possible to the lane that ran to the back of the tavern. Once I'd paid him, I sprinted down and dripped inside.

The wet boots were damnably hard to remove, even

with the help of a bootjack. I placed them on a shelf to dry, then hung up the coat and headed down the narrow corridor between the kitchen and storage areas. The air was icy, but that wasn't surprising, given the age of the tavern and the fact it had never been designed to retain heat, especially when all the fires would have burned down overnight. If I didn't re-light them quickly, the place would be an icebox this evening.

I rubbed my hands in an effort to get some warmth into my fingertips, but as I stepped into the main room, the sudden sharpening in the song of the old floorboards had me stopping abruptly.

I had a visitor.

She was seated at one of the tables in the center of the room, glaring at me from over the top of a take-away coffee cup she held in one hand while drumming the fingers of the other on the table. It was a sharp sound of displeasure that vibrated through the fibers of the building. She was on the short side—though far too slender to be a dwarf—with sharp brown features, a thick nest of wiry steel-gray hair, and an aura that echoed the ferocity of the storm that raged outside.

I had no idea who she was, but I definitely knew *what* she was.

A *hag*.

I swallowed heavily and resisted the urge to reach for my knives. While most myths said hags were a grotesque and disfigured type of fairy—or even a shapeshifting witch of immense power—they were, in fact, ancient goddesses who'd been locked into human flesh as a form of punishment. There were only half a dozen who remained earthbound today, and four of those could be considered minor goddesses with little power. The other two, however, were

Brid and Beira—the goddesses of summer and winter respectively.

Given the intensity of the storm that had followed me home and the tumultuous glow of her aura, this *had* to be Beira.

"Well, you took your fucking time, didn't you?" Her voice was guttural and unpleasant—nothing like the dulcet tones I'd always imagined a goddess would have, though I guess it *did* fit the whole hag persona. "Do you think I've got nothing better to do than to wait on the pleasure of your company?"

Despite the fear her presence naturally stirred, amusement rose. Of all the things I'd expected a hag to say, chastising me for lateness definitely *wasn't* one of them. Of course, it was possible she talked to everyone this way. It wasn't like I'd ever had the fortune—good or bad—to be in the presence of a goddess before.

I cleared my throat and then said, as respectfully as I could, "If I'd had any warning you'd be here, I'd have ensured—"

"I sent you a notice *days* ago," she cut in crossly. "I can't be expected to do anything more than that."

"There *was* a note nailed to my door, but it just threatened to fucking kill me if I didn't return what I stole—"

"If I'd intended to kill you, young woman, I could have done so without risking an appearance."

Always nice to know. "Then the only other note I've seen is the one that came with the Eye, and *it* was delivered to the tavern's post office box rather than to me."

She wrinkled her nose, a movement that somehow managed to make the wart at the end of it appear even bigger. "*That* was an unnecessary piece of subterfuge used by a younger counterpart, and one that could have gone badly given events still playing out. She has been repri-manded." She hesitated, curiosity touching her expression. "Though I do have to ask, *did* you steal something? It's something of a family tradition, after all."

"No, I did *not*." I walked over to the hearth and began stacking the kindling. It, like the bigger bits of wood used in the fire, held no life or song, but I nevertheless said a silent prayer of thanks for its sacrifice.

She harrumphed. "Then perhaps I'm the reason for *that* particular note."

I lit a match then glanced at her. "Why would someone threaten me over an item you stole? It's not like you and I have even been introduced, let alone met before now."

"Ah, yes, remiss of me. I'm Beira, the mad bitch in charge of winter and storms." She cackled, a grating sound that revealed surprisingly straight white teeth. "And while you may not remember me, young Bethany, I certainly know you."

My stomach started doing mad flip-flops again. "I take it that means you knew Mom?"

"Since she was a wee snap of a thing. Her unexpected disappearance caused great sadness amongst us all."

All? She'd known all *six* hags? "Then why—"

"Have you not seen me before?" She wrinkled her wart-capped nose again. "I never thought it wise, but that was your mother's choice."

The fire caught, so I absently started throwing larger bits of wood onto it. "Did she ever say why?"

"It was uncertain as to whether you'd inherited the gift and, until that changed, she wished the darkness kept well away from you." Beira grimaced. "The Eye would have confirmed the matter, but I think she feared to know. And then, of course, it was all too late."

My breath had caught somewhere in my throat. "Have you any idea what happened to her?"

"No." Sadness and perhaps annoyance shone in her eyes, and it was that, more than anything, which made me believe her. It was an inclination that could have been a mistake, given hags had a rep for being unhelpful more than helpful. "It was a whisper on the wind that led me to the missing Eye, but the woman who held it could shed no light on the circumstances of your mother's disappearance."

I swore and scrubbed a hand across my eyes. All we ever seemed to hit were dead ends. "Then how did the Eye come into her possession?"

"She could not remember."

"Convenient."

"More a memory wipe." She grimaced. "Whoever did it held a power and precision I've not seen in ages."

And if *that* worried her, it scared the hell out of me. "Who whispered to the wind, then?"

"Another thing I do not know, but there are few in this world capable of directing her in such a manner."

"A storm witch could."

"There's only one left, and she did not send the information. It's a mystery."

And she hated mysteries, if her expression was anything to go by. "Why would anyone want to steal the Eye in the first place?"

"Because it is the truest means of finding the lost treasures of the gods."

"Then why have I never seen it before?"

She scowled. "I've already answered that question—do I need to be cleaning out your ears?"

The storm in her aura flared as she spoke, and outside,

thunder rumbled ominously. The building shook under its intensity.

Note to self; do *not* annoy the hag too much. "If Mom used the Eye the day she went missing, do you know what she saw or where she went?"

"No. We only realized something was wrong when the light in our Eye died."

A statement that basically confirmed our fears that she was dead. "There're *two* eyes?"

"Why does that surprise you? Eithne—the original hag and a great prophet—was gifted with two, just the same as everyone else. What shows in one echoes through the other."

I stared at her for a second, torn between horror and disbelief. "They're *actual* eyes?"

"Eye flesh is delicate and never does last, so we turned them to stone." Her tone was matter-of-fact, but the twinkle in her dark eyes left me uncertain as to whether she was joking or not. "Eithne also became stone, incidentally, though I'm not entirely sure why. Her soul was never going to hang around, given her time in this world was over, but she always did like a monument, and it does still hold remnants of her power, even if it is not one we hags can access."

I raised my hands to the flames and tried to warm them. "So Mom used the Eye to find missing treasures?"

"For the most part," Beira said.

"And when she found them, then what? Did she return them to the elves for safekeeping?"

She snorted. "Those bastards couldn't organize a raffle in a pub."

I couldn't help the laugh that escaped. "Then why were

they appointed guardians of sacred sites *and* the hoards after we were booted?"

"Because they were the only sensible choice. The rest of the fae and even the shifters were too short-lived to make it worthwhile. As for the humans, well, when it comes to theft, they'd already developed it to a very fine art." She shook her head. "I *never* agreed to the removal of pixies, by the way. One minor theft should not have tarnished the whole race."

That had my eyebrows rising again. "You were there?"

"How do you think I got stuck in this skin suit? I was defending your asses, and my contemporaries were unimpressed."

Which maybe explained her continuing contact with my family ... "Then who *did* steal the treasure? Us or the Tàileach?"

She shrugged. "That was never confirmed."

"That's rather odd, isn't it?"

"Gods are not infallible," she replied, voice dry. "And, rather sadly, security cameras weren't invented back in those days."

The image of all the gods clustered around a security screen rose, and I barely restrained another laugh. "I take it you're aware the Éadrom Hoard was stolen the day Mom went missing?"

"I am, but there was nothing we could do. We're restricted when it comes to our ability to fully interact with this world, especially when the Eye is dark."

"So why did you come here? I'm no seer—"

"Perhaps not by training, but the blood of the old gods runs in your line."

Meaning the rumors were true. "It'd be a very tenuous

link these days, though. I mean, they haven't had anything to do with us for eons."

"True, and your mother's claim *was* distant, even if the blood ran true in her. You, however, are a direct descendant on your father's side."

"This would be the father I know nothing about?"

"You don't need to."

I gave her a wry look. "To be a direct descendant, said father or even my grandfather would have to be an old god, and *that* is simply impossible."

"Nothing is ever truly impossible, and gods have a long history of begetting children on human or fae."

"Yes, but that was when the gods were a heavy presence here on the earth. I can't imagine one of them suddenly deciding to pop down from Valhalla or wherever else they've all retreated to, just to spend a few pleasant nights with my mom."

"There you go, questioning me again. It's decidedly annoying, young woman."

A smile twitched my lips. "Sorry, I don't mean to. It's just ... it's a lot to download all at once."

She harrumphed. "Which is why I wished your mother had been more open about her work and her skills." She stretched out short legs, revealing old-fashioned lace-up leather half boots that looked like they'd come directly out of the Regency period's fashion handbook. "But in this case, he wasn't a returning god. He was a curmudgeon."

I blinked. "My father was a bad-tempered, vile old man?"

"Of course *not*. Give your mother the credit of more taste than that. A curmudgeon is the male equivalent of a hag and, aside from whatever powers they had as a god, they could shape shift. Men *always* get the better end of the deal, even when it comes to these goddamn flesh suits." She sniffed. "There are only three of them left, by my reckoning."

Another smile twitched my lips. "I had no idea they even existed."

"That's because history is written by men, and they love piling crap on the stronger sex rather than their own."

This time, my smile broke free. I really was beginning to like this woman. "What was my father the god of?"

"If your mother never said, I cannot."

Meaning she didn't know? "She did say his name was Ambisagrus."

"Really?" Her expression became surprised. "He would have been my last guess, but it would perhaps explain the whispers on the wind."

I waited, but when she didn't add anything else, said, "Why?"

"Because he's a minor god who ran with storms and lightning. As far as I'm aware, he hasn't been active for hundreds of years. In fact, none of them have. Might be wrong, of course."

Her expression suggested she didn't believe that was the case. "Why aren't they active?"

"Because men are always leaving women to clean up their messes. Now, what did you see when you touched the Eye?"

I hesitated. "Nothing specific. I mean, I saw a bloody death and I did end up finding that, along with a ruby from the shield of Hephaestus, but that discovery was due more to the song of the wood than the Eye."

"Do you still have the ruby in your possession?"

I shook my head. "Returned it to the fae council yesterday."

Her responding hiss was a sharp sound of displeasure. "That's unfortunate."

"I take it you trust the council as much as you trust the elves?"

"We don't trust *anybody* as a matter of principle. Makes things far easier in the long run." She raised her cup and drained the last of her drink. "In this particular case, however, I'm of the opinion the council has been infiltrated by our foes."

"Hags have foes?" Who knew?

She shrugged. "Be it in our divinity or this wretched form, when have we not? But the foe I refer to in this matter are the Ninkilim."

"Who are?"

"A secret society who worship the teachings of Ninkil— a minor rat god who believes the sacred items of the gods should not be hoarded by a few but rather shared around the many."

"The 'many' including his followers, I take it?"

She nodded. "The thing is, the Ninkilim have become worryingly active in the recent year."

"Are they behind the theft of the hoard?"

"We have no proof, of course, but it has all the hall-marks of their style, even if many of the items within the Éadrom Hoard are little more than psychic enhancers."

"There are some pretty damn scary psychic gifts out there in the world."

"Well, yes," she growled. "But compared to the more mainstream powers of the gods, they are but ants in the wind."

Amusement stirred through me. While this old woman could no doubt smite me with a mere flick of her fingers, my fear of her was definitely receding. Besides, if Mom *had* worked with the hags for decades, they obviously weren't as bad as their reputations made them out.

Of course, hags were also very good at lulling their targets into a false sense of security.

"What makes you think the fae council has been infiltrated?"

"Unsettling whispers on the wind, mainly." She shrugged. "Ninkil might be a rat god, and duplicitous in the extreme, but he was fair of face and manner, and silver of tongue. Many of his followers possess the same attributes. It would not be hard for them to infiltrate any organization they desire."

Up until yesterday, I would have said the council had enough checks and balances in place to prevent such a thing, but the whole business with Mathi had certainly planted doubts.

I threw a log on the fire. "Are you simply here to introduce yourself, or is there more to this visit?"

"There is always more, young woman."

Which was an echo of what Cynwrig had said and made me wonder if the dark elves had regular contact with the hags. "Does that 'more' involve a note left at Cynwrig Lùtair's and a moonstone?"

"It does not." She frowned. "What did the note say?"

I tugged the envelope out of my pocket and gave it to her. "Who would have sent him the stone, if not you?"

"I don't know." She pulled the note free and quickly scanned it. Her frown deepened. "The writing certainly doesn't belong to a fellow hag. You've checked it for darkness and tracking?"

"First thing. The power that remains in the stone is clean."

She didn't look any happier. "There are many forces

who walk this world that we have no influence over; it's more than possible one of them has decided to get involved in the battle that looms."

"One of the long-absent curmudgeons, perhaps?"

She folded the note and handed it back to me. "Or even a mage."

"I thought they'd all been wiped out?"

"That's the rumor, but mages are experts when it comes to subterfuge. It is never wise to discount them."

I sighed and rubbed my forehead. Despite all the information being given, it weirdly felt like I was going around in circles and getting nowhere fast. "So, what do you actually want from me?"

"To take up the mantle left by your mother. To seek what has been lost, and to confront the darkness in whatever guise it takes."

I stared at her. "But ... I don't even know how to use the Eye. I've certainly never been trained to use whatever sliver of second sight I might have."

"I know, and it is decidedly unfortunate, but there is little we can do about all that now." She shrugged. "You will just have to learn on the job."

"But—" I waved a hand in something close to exasperation. "That could take *years*."

"We haven't got years. Darkness rises, young woman, and so must you."

"And if I say no?"

Mirth lurked around the corners of her eyes. "What comes will not be stopped by any unwillingness on your part to assume the mantle that is yours by birth."

"But I have the tavern to run—"

"So did your mother. She managed." She pushed to her feet. "I'm aware this is all very sudden, so I'll depart and give you time to think on the matter. But do not take too long, young Bethany, or darkness will find you before you are ready."

Was that a warning or a threat? It rather sounded like the latter, and given hags did *not* like to be thwarted, perhaps it was.

I licked suddenly dry lips and said, "How do I contact you if I need to?"

"Reach out through the Eye. We will hear its echoes through ours."

And with that, she strode to the front door, moving through both it *and* the protective magic as if neither existed. And perhaps, for her, they didn't. She was a goddess after all.

I took a deep breath, then headed upstairs to light fires in the other hearths. Once I'd tucked the moonstone into my storage space with the Eye, I had a long, hot shower that did absolutely nothing to wash away the chill settling deep within. Darkness was coming, she'd warned, and my newly wakened second sight seemed intent on emphasizing that.

The rest of the day passed slowly. The heritage council rang late in the afternoon to say the restorers would not be here for another few days, but I could open the upper level tomorrow if I wished. I resisted the urge to swear at them, knowing full well it would only cause further delays, and made arrangements for Ingrid—who'd been the tavern's manager for as long as I could remember—the kitchen staff, and those who worked in the upper bar to come in while extending leave for everyone else. Thankfully, no one was too worried by this development.

I was in the kitchen getting dinner ready when my phone rang. I didn't recognize the number, so I rather warily pressed answer and said, "Bethany Aodhán speaking —how may I help you?"

"Oh, I can think of a dozen different ways to answer that particular question," came the deep, velvety reply. "But we'll start with you opening the front door and letting me in."

"And why would I do that?" I pulled the fry pan from the flame, then stripped off my gloves and headed into the main room. "My mother always warned me against letting strangers into my home."

"After last night, I hardly think we can be deemed strangers."

I laughed. "And how did you get my phone number? Or is that a stupid question, given the council have been investigating me and Lugh?"

"I can hardly be your council liaison if I'm unable to contact you now, can I?"

"I guess not." I bounced up the steps and swung the door open. He was wearing a long burgundy coat that emphasized the width of his shoulders and black jeans that hugged his hips and powerful thighs in a rather delightful way. His short dark hair glittered with diamond-like droplets of misty rain, but it was his smoky gaze that caught and held my attention. His eyes burned with such heat that my breath caught deep in my throat and sweat instantly skittered across my skin.

I needed to lose myself in that heat. *Now.*

I tugged him inside, slammed the door closed, then wrapped my arms around his neck and kissed him fiercely. He made a low sound deep in his throat, then wrapped an arm around my waist, dragging me closer, pressing me so hard against his big, powerful body that I could feel the rapid pounding of his heart and the growing thickness of his erection.

As a counterpoint to the strangeness of the day, it was absolutely perfect.

I had no idea how long we stood there, tasting and teasing each other with lips and tongue; it seemed like forever but was probably little more than a few minutes.

Eventually, he pulled back and lightly brushed unruly strands of red hair away from my cheek. "Now that," he said, voice delightfully husky, "is a welcome a man could get used to."

"It's been a very trying day," I said. "I needed the release."

Devilment danced through his smoky eyes. "A kiss hardly provides that, however delightful it might be."

"I know, and I would normally drag you upstairs to have my wicked way with you, but I'm in the midst of making dinner, and I hate wasting good steak."

"Should I come back later?"

"Hell no. I've food enough for two ... if you'd like to eat something, that is?"

"I *always* like to eat."

It was said in a manner that said he wasn't talking about food, and the desire to just shove the steak back into the fridge and do what my hormones were begging me to rose. I ignored them with great effort, tucked my phone away, and motioned him to follow me. The floorboards hummed pleasantly under his weight even though he moved with no sound.

I walked around to the stove and placed the fry pan back onto the flame. "What happened with the Eldritch this morning?"

"They were rather disappointed to have found absolutely nothing. They *did*, however, ask multiple questions about the person who'd shared my bed, and I rather suspect they knew it was you."

I placed two pieces of steak into the pan and then added more chips to the basket before dropping it into the hot oil. "It's possible they were already watching me, given the mess with Nialle and Lugh."

"Possibly, and I did make it clear to everyone on the council what I'd do to anyone who bothered tailing *me*."

Despite the lightness of his tone, there was something in his expression that suggested getting on the wrong side of this man would *not* be a good idea. I flipped the steaks and then shook the basket. "Did the warrant specify what they were searching for?"

"It simply said an artifact believed to belong to the hoard. I've called a meeting of the council tonight and *will* get to the bottom of this."

And someone, I thought grimly, *would* pay. "If you were being set up, why the note? That makes no sense."

"Oh, I don't think they were looking for the moonstone. I think they were looking for this." He reached into his pocket and pulled out a small, somewhat ratty-looking brown statue.

"I take it that's no ordinary statue?"

"It's commonly known as rat-man and was carved from mammoth ivory."

"Why on earth would a statue of a rat be in the hoard?" Given what Beira had said, it was easy enough to guess who the statue represented, but it never hurt to be sure.

He placed the ratty thing on the metal benchtop. Though there was no obvious ebb and flow of power, just looking at it made my skin crawl. "It's a statue of Ninkil, the god of rodents, and is said to imbue his followers with the ability to shift shape into a rat."

I shuddered. "Then I won't be touching the fucking thing."

The smile that teased his lips was seriously sexy. "A rat in a kitchen is never a good idea."

"A rat fucking *anywhere* other than dead and buried is never a good idea." I plated up the two steaks, then let them rest while I drained the basket of chips. "When did you discover it?"

"A second or two before I allowed the Eldritch inside. It had been placed on the display shelf near the door, amongst some other—legal—statues I possess. If I hadn't been alert to problems, I might not have seen it."

"Where did you hide it?"

"I didn't. I simply slipped it into my pocket."

Surprise ran through me. "That was a bit of a risk, wasn't it? If they'd had a sniffer, you'd have been in trouble."

A sniffer was a canine shifter capable of sniffing out magic. They were mostly used in crimes where the cause of death was inconclusive.

"Oh, they did, but the main living area is magically null."

But not the loft area, obviously, as my knives had still been active. It did make sense given his office was located up there. I tossed the chips in a bowl, salted them up, and then added them to the plates. "Meaning you haven't employed protection spells? That seems odd given your family's rep for illegal activities."

"Protection spells and even wards are easily enough gotten around if you have the know-how—and many do. Nulling is a different matter entirely."

"Nulling won't stop regular old thieves, and espionage is a thriving business these days—as you're no doubt aware." I placed cutlery on his plate and pushed it across. "Let's head out to the main room."

He picked up his plate and followed me out. "This is a perfect meal for a man heading into battle."

I snorted. "As if the magics around the council room will allow anything more than heated discussions."

"The magic is reactionary rather than prohibitive, so it *is* possible to kill if you're fast enough. The problem is, far too many people forecast their intentions before they actually do anything."

I sat down and gave him a long look. "Speaking from experience, are we?"

"As much as I *do* want to kill many there, I haven't as yet." He sat next to me and placed the meal and the statue on the table. "It happened in my father's time, though he wasn't involved. A word to the wise—never annoy a bear shifter. They're not as slow as many believe."

I'd seen Sgott in full flight more than once and could absolutely second that statement. I scooped up some chips and munched on them for a second. "Did the warrant give any clue as to who might have set the Eldritch onto you?"

"No, but it was issued not long after the meeting you attended, with a requested raid time of 9:00 AM."

"To give them time to place the statue?"

He nodded. "Which they did, at seven this morning. I suspect that's what actually woke me, and the security cams confirmed entry into the building by a person or persons unknown."

"They were concealed?"

"Light shield."

I frowned. "How did that hold up once they were in your apartment, though?"

"It didn't, but they were fully masked and wearing a bulky coat that hid their form."

Of course they were. "Has something like this happened before? If not, why now?"

"I think the answer to that is pretty obvious—someone there was unhappy about my becoming your liaison and wanted me out of the way."

I gave him another long look. "Mathi would *not* do something like that. Besides, he was read, and he has no knowledge of the hoard."

"Doesn't discount him from not wanting me anywhere near you."

"Mathi does *not* do jealousy."

"He is a light elf, and they don't easily walk from things they consider theirs."

I rolled my eyes. "He doesn't want me *that* badly."

"If you honestly believe that, then you do not truly know the man."

"No non-elf ever truly can. You're a secretive lot."

He chuckled softly, but there was an odd light in his eyes that had my insides quivering—and I wasn't entirely sure its source was desire. "Well, this is one elf who is utterly determined to ensure you and I know each other as thoroughly as any man and woman ever could."

"Oh," I said lightly, "I think we ticked that box last night."

"*That,*" he said, his voice a whisper of heat that crawled deep inside and lit inner fires, "was merely a start."

And despite the lingering trepidation that could have been born of fear or foresight or simple wariness of trusting this man too much before I really knew him, I couldn't wait for the exploration to begin.

I concentrated on eating for a few minutes, but eventually said, "What time has tonight's meeting been called for?"

"Eight." He glanced at the clock at the wall. "No time for dessert, unfortunately."

Amusement slithered through me. "There is *always* time for dessert."

He shook his head, that devilish light back in his eyes. "It's very unseemly for sex to be in any way hasty when a relationship is in the fledgling stage."

"Oh, so this thing is now a relationship?"

"Only if you so wish. I most certainly do."

My pulse rate leapt at the mere thought. I considered him with mock seriousness for several seconds. "I'm afraid I'll have to fully test the goods on offer before making any firm decision."

He laughed and nudged me lightly with his shoulder. "I'm more than happy to comply with any test you so wish."

"Excellent." I speared more chips. "So why did you actually come here this evening?"

"I was wondering if you'd had the chance to examine the moonstone."

"Not really." I hesitated. "I did notice a tracking spell on it, though. I had to disable it before I left your apartment. I'm surprised you didn't notice it when it was sent to you."

"I would have if it had been active, but I suspect it only went 'live' just before my apartment was raided."

I frowned. "Why?"

"I spent the afternoon doing some research, and there's a possibility it came from the Crown of Shadows."

Not only would *that* be too much of a damn coincidence, but it would also back Beira's worrying comment that there were unknown forces at work. And if that spell was activated minutes before the raid, it confirmed my suspicions that they knew I was there, and meant it was aimed at tracking my movements rather than Cynwrig's. "What makes you think that?"

"Nothing more than its description, which mentioned a six-pointed silver crown with an inset moonstone split by a thin vein of ragged black at the front of it."

Which was an exact description of our stone. "Moonstones are generally used to harvest the energy of the moon and promote healing and balance, which isn't really compatible with the crown's reported ability to control shadows."

"You're forgetting the crown was created by a goddess of war and death who wished to extend the shroud of darkness over the entire world. Why would she not use the power of the moon in such an endeavor?"

I shrugged. Put like that, it did make sense. "How do you research or even find an item that was lost centuries ago and no longer recorded in the archives?"

"By searching in the Myrkálfar archives, of course."

I frowned. "Why there? Wouldn't the central bibliothèque give greater access to information?"

"The bibliothèque is the Ljósálfar archive. It does not hold the histories of my people."

"And this is important because ...?"

"Because we are responsible for the security of the Tenebrous Hoard, not the Ljósálfar."

Which was something I hadn't known. "And the Claws were a part of that?"

"Once, though they disappeared long ago. The more

interesting discovery was the fact that someone else accessed the same information five and a half months ago."

My pulse began to beat a whole lot faster. "Just a few weeks after the Éadrom Hoard was stolen? That surely can't be a coincidence."

"*That* is an unanswerable question, because Jalvi, the woman who conducted the search, completely disappeared after accessing the information."

Dead ends seemed to be all we were hitting right now. "How did she even access the information? I thought it was restricted?"

"Current details, yes. But information on items listed as missing is freely available. It's in our best interest to have a wide range of people aware of their details, just in case said items ever come onto the black market."

"Have they ever?" I asked curiously.

"Occasionally. Said sellers were dealt with appropriately."

"Meaning they didn't survive the sale?"

"It depends entirely on how the item came to be in their possession."

Suggesting that many *did* die. But then, dark elves did have a reputation for that sort of thing, even if they didn't hold the patent on murderous behavior. In all truth, light elves were the more efficient at killing, because their emotions were less likely to be involved.

I finished my steak, then leaned back in the chair to study him for a second. "Have you any idea what the connection is between the Claws and the stolen hoard?"

"At this point, I don't believe there is one."

"But you have a theory?"

His smile was decidedly sexy. "There you go again, reading me as few others do."

"Reading body language when you run a tavern is a necessary trait if you want to avoid trouble."

My voice was dry, and his smile widened. "Can't pixies magic people into obedience?"

"Not all people."

"Elves?"

"No. Otherwise, I might have gotten the truth out of Mathi sooner."

"Huh. I had no idea."

"You've obviously led a very sheltered life if you were unaware of such a minor fact."

He laughed. "If there's one thing my upbringing could never be described as, it's sheltered. It's just that pixies are a rare breed here in Deva."

That was a sad truth, and indeed the reason why I'd gone out with so many fae and shifters before I'd gotten a little too comfortable in my relationship with Mathi.

"What's your theory?"

"That we're actually dealing with two parties—one responsible for the theft of the hoard, and the other looking for the Claws."

"And have you any evidence for this belief?"

He hesitated. "Nothing concrete. But between the hoard's theft and Jalvi accessing our archives, there was an incursion from Annwfyn."

Surprise hit so hard it felt like I'd been punched in the gut. "There was no mention of it on the news."

"It was deemed best if the general population didn't know. It would only have caused undue stress."

"Not entirely undue. Not if it was the first of a new range of attacks from them."

"If it was, there would have been subsequent attacks. There hasn't been."

"So, it was simply a matter of bad timing and bad luck?"

He nodded. "The five hit were all women—three highborn Ljósálfar and two of my cousins. They were celebrating a milestone birthday."

Which for elves was either one hundred—the coming of age—or five hundred, which was when they were considered to have reached the midpoint of their lives. I reached out and gripped his arm; his muscles were like steel under my fingers. "I'm so sorry, Cynwrig."

He grimaced. "They should have been safe. They were in a private residence with full lights and protecting magic. Alva was also a gate monitor and well experienced in dealing with the Annwfyn. But they were caught unawares, and it was ... brutal."

"I take it there was a dark gate nearby?"

He nodded. "One that had been inactive for centuries and downgraded on the watch list." His lips twisted. "It is fair to say, we opened that bastard up and let rip with a few rockets."

I blinked, though why I was surprised the dark elves could get their hands on bazookas, I couldn't say. They did trade in the black market.

"Were all five killed?"

He took a deep breath and released it slowly. It didn't ease the tumultuous wave of energy surrounding him. "No. One of them—Jalvi's sister, Telyn—is missing."

"Oh, fuck—she was taken?"

That would be a fate worse than death if true, because the women and men taken back to Annwfyn were used in much the same way—and for much the same reason—as we used cattle and sheep.

"We think so." He scraped a hand across his bristly chin.

"There's no evidence to suggest she was eaten at the scene."

Suggesting the others had been. Horror shuddered through me. The Annwfyn preferred their meals alive and wriggling ... I swallowed heavily against the rise of bile. "Do you think Jalvi's search on the Claws is connected to what happened to her sister?"

"I think it very likely."

"But why? The Claws can't save her sister—they're nothing more than a means of controlling darkness."

"I know." He took another deep breath and released it slowly. There was a whole lot of fury in that soft sound, and it echoed through the light that shone in his eyes. That light was furious. *Murderous.*

It was yet another reminder that no matter how well I might know his body, I didn't actually know *him*.

I studied him for a few seconds and then said, "There's something else, isn't there?"

"Yes." His voice remained even, despite the violence that still shone in his eyes. "There was a second attack, only this time it wasn't Annwfyn. It happened on the same night your brother was drugged."

"Who'd they attack?"

But even as I asked the question, I knew. The answer was right there in his eyes.

"My sister." His voice was low but vibrated with fury. "The bastards went after Treasa."

CHAPTER
EIGHT

"**W**ho was it, if not Annwfyn?" I asked.

"Thugs for hire."

"Then they're obviously not very bright. I mean, I don't know much about dark elves, but I sure as hell know you're all big believers in revenge and retribution."

I kept my reply low and calm. He stared at me for a heartbeat and then made a soft sound that wasn't quite a laugh. "Perhaps they hold to the current view that we have all been civilized."

A smiled teased my lips. "Oh, I think we proved *that* to be a lie last night."

This time, his laugh was rich and full, and that fierce wave of fury began to ebb. Relief slithered through me. Anger could make even the most placid of people unpredictable—something I knew from growing up in this place. "I take it your sister is okay?"

"Her leg was broken and her ribs bruised, but yes, she's fine."

I studied him for a minute, sensing a touch of guilt

under the anger and suddenly realizing why. "The attack on her was just a distraction, wasn't it?"

"I now believe so. When I think back, I remember seeing seven people, but only six attacked Treasa."

"Six against one? That's overkill, isn't it?"

"In truth, had they known anything at *all* about my sister, they would have sent more. She'd taken three down by the time I'd run out of the bar to help and would have taken out the rest if not for the bastard who hit her from behind and stomped on her leg."

"Note to self—never piss off your sister." I paused. "Have the six been questioned?"

"Yes, but they could shed no light on who employed them. That particular portion of their memories has been wiped." Frustration flitted through his expression. "And while a warrant has been placed for the seventh person, there's been no sign of him."

"Then they were all men?"

He hesitated. "The six who attached Treasa were, but to be honest, my attention was on the men attacking my sister rather than the person hanging back in the shadows. My bad, as it turned out."

"And it was the seventh person you were chasing?"

He nodded. "I have no recollection of how I ended up in the canal, though. I was obviously hit from behind, but I never saw or heard my attacker."

"If your attacker was the same person I was chasing, then that's no surprise given the shielding he was using."

"They are unlikely to be the same. The timing is all wrong."

"True." I pushed up and walked over to the bar. "Drink?"

"A mineral water would be good. I need to keep a clear head for the meeting."

I pulled two bottles from the refrigerator, then walked back and handed him one. "So, the attack on your sister was merely a distraction to ensure they could drug and question you about the Claws location?"

He took a drink. "I would presume so."

"Assuming Jalvi is working with the people seeking the Claws, why would they think you'd have more access to information than her?"

"Because there *are* certain files only an heir can access. Perhaps they thought that applied to the Claws, given how little Jalvi would have found in the general archive."

"And is the attack on your sister and Jalvi's actions one reason why you were so determined to be my council liaison?"

He gave me a rather sexy smile that had my insides quivering. "I would think it pretty obvious *why* I wanted to be your liaison."

"Sexual attraction is beside the point, and you well know it."

"Sexual attraction *this* fierce is never beside the point," he countered. "But yes, it was pretty obvious that you and your brother are caught up in the same mess as me and my family. The note with the moonstone only confirmed my decision to keep close."

"I'm no seer, Cynwrig, and I have no idea how to control what little second sight I might have inherited. I may not be of any use at all when it comes to finding the crown or understanding what is going on."

"Perhaps, but you are the daughter of a seer, and someone out there obviously believes you're ready to fill her shoes."

"Yeah, a bunch of old hags," I muttered.

He raised an eyebrow. "The hags have been here?"

"Beira has, but she denied sending you the note or the moonstone."

"And she had no suggestion as to who had?"

"No." I hesitated. "She did say she feared the council had been infiltrated by the Ninkilim."

"Something I'd already guessed given the statue." He picked the ugly thing up then rose. "I'd better go. Thanks for the dinner."

I nodded and followed him across to the door. "What are you going to do with the statue?"

"I've an archivist meeting me. He'll deal with it."

I wished that meant destroyed, but that was unlikely given its age and probable value. Besides, destroying relics of gods never went down well with said gods. "Are you dropping by later?"

His gaze met mine, and the desire so evident there curled my toes. "If I'm invited."

"You are."

"Then I will." He paused. "I have no idea how long the council meeting will run. It could be very late before I get here."

"That's okay. I can only open the first floor tomorrow, and Ingrid—my manager—is well able to look after things in my absence."

He nodded, then dragged me close for another of those mind-blowing kisses. "Shall I ring when I arrive?"

"Just knock. I'll hear the echo through the wood, and it won't startle me as much."

"Will do."

He kissed me again, then opened the door and strode out while I crossed all things that the council meeting didn't go on and on. Which it probably would now that I'd put that thought out there.

I grabbed the plates and cutlery and returned to the kitchen to clean up before heading upstairs. After throwing a few more logs onto the living area fire, I walked into my bedroom to grab the stones. But the minute my fingers touched the Eye, it burned to bright life, and a broken reel of images began to play through my mind. *Silver glinting in the cool light of a moonbeam, piercing blue lost in a sea of darkness and hate, a standing stone wreathed in old man's beard, the tufted balls of white ringing the stone's top making it seem as if it was wearing a crown, cold steel flashing down through darkness with deadly intent—*

My fingers twitched in an instinctive response to protect myself, and the images stopped so abruptly it tore a gasp from my lips. I staggered backward, hit the bed, and sat down hard, my heart pounding so fiercely, it felt like it was about to tear out of my chest. For several minutes, I did nothing more than suck in air; in all truth, I wasn't sure I could do anything more. My limbs trembled, and hot pokers of pain were shooting through my brain, making my eyes water and lose focus.

How the fuck did Mom use this thing so regularly if this was the result? Or was it more a matter of me being untrained and therefore unprepared?

No power pulsed through the Eye now, but the purple lightning still flickered deep in its heart, and it had an ominous feel.

I swore and shoved it into my jeans' front pocket. Almost instantly, the world seemed brighter.

Was that what the warning in the note had meant? That using the Eye without a specific purpose could draw the seer's mind to darker places or even darker deeds?

And yet, aside from the knife, nothing I'd seen spoke specifically of foul deeds or even death, even if the stone's ominous pulse suggested darkness was nevertheless coming at me, and fast.

I took another of those useless deep breaths, then pushed to my feet and walked back to the storage space. This time, I tugged my sleeve over my hand before I picked up the moonstone. Given what had just happened with the Eye, I wasn't about to take any chances. Not until I was ready, at any rate.

I returned to the living room, dropped the moonstone onto the coffee table, and then moved over to the kitchenette to make myself a pot of tea. After grabbing a block of Cadbury's Toffee Whole Nut out of the fridge, I moved back and contemplated the moonstone from the safety of my comfy old armchair while I ate several rows of chocolate.

Once suitably fortified by both tea and chocolate, I reached out and tentatively touched the stone. The energy within it pulsed, as if in acknowledgement, but nothing else immediately happened.

The inner tension didn't in any way ease.

I warily picked the moonstone up and rolled it through my fingers. Still nothing. The inner pulse of power I'd sensed earlier was absent. Maybe I needed to use the Eye to actually get anything concrete from the moonstone, but I did *not* want to tempt fate or darkness any more than I already had tonight.

Not unless it was absolutely necessary.

I frowned and tried to remember what Mom used to say about scrying. It wasn't her main gift, but she had on occasion run "psychic" nights here in the tavern where, for a fee, she'd either find missing items or tell a person's future using a personal item. If I'd inherited any of her skills at all, then scrying was the most likely. Both my grandmother and my great-grandmother had been able to scry, so it was obviously a skill that was handed down through the females of our line, even if I suspected it was more a variation of our ability to connect to—and control—people than any true psychic talent.

I tucked my legs up and crossed them, making myself as comfortable as possible in the big old chair. Then, with the moonstone held securely, but not tightly, in my right hand, I began the slow breathing yoga routine I'd seen Mom do before she began the psychic nights.

An odd sense of calm descended, and after a while, it felt like I was floating. I focused on the moonstone, pressing its cool surface into my palm with a little more force. Gradually, awareness of my immediate surrounds faded even as other senses sharpened and expanded, moving beyond the tavern and into the powerful thrum of the night. The rich scent of rain filled my nostrils, wind played lightly through my hair, and the sharp electricity of the oncoming storm had sparks dancing across my skin. Though a thick blanket of clouds hid the moon's cold light, I could feel her; *touch* her. Not physically, but mentally. Somewhere deep within, fear stirred, but I pushed it aside and called that cold incandescence to me. She responded with such eagerness, a gasp was torn from my lips and my fingers twitched, as if battling to hold the force being called into the moonstone.

It burned to fierce, bright life.

And in the heart of that light, through a crack of black, a hall house appeared. A *broken* hall house. It sat high on a hill, in a clearing surrounded by trees that raised stark limbs to the sky, as if pleading for help. The vision shifted and thrust into deeper darkness. The air was damp, musty, and water dripped, an unpleasant sound that spoke of age and decay. A pale glimmer of a lonely moonbeam briefly shone on slime-covered stone stairs. Another shift, this time into a cave. Water whispered past toes that didn't exist in this place, and the air was ripe with death. Movement whispered through the shadows; large round eyes gleamed with malevolence as yellowed claws scraped against stone.

Annwfyn.

Then, in the glow of another moonbeam that had illogically found its way into this place, was a point of silver.

The point of a crown. The *moonstone's* crown.

Buried so deeply in the earth that nothing other than that one point was visible—and only then, I suspected, thanks to the never-ending rivulets of water that ran down the wall and washed to the center stream.

I frowned and tried shifting the point of view in an effort to get some idea where the broken house was located. The moonstone pulsed in response, then the images fractured and the light in the stone died. I swore and rubbed a hand across my eyes. The red-hot pokers were hitting my brain with renewed vigor, and tiredness trembled through me. I ate more chocolate, then wearily pushed to my feet and staggered more than walked into my bedroom. It honestly felt like a truck had hit me—absolutely everything hurt.

Mom was definitely made of sterner stuff than me.

Once I'd stashed the moonstone away, I went into the bathroom to do my teeth and grab some painkillers. My strength was slipping away so quickly, I barely made it back to my bedroom. I stripped down to my T-shirt and knickers, then climbed into bed and fell into a deep, deep sleep.

It was the song that woke me who knows how many hours later.

Wood song, humming through the floorboards, speaking of soft movement. I frowned and stirred, but my mind was still caught in the cobwebs of sleep and didn't really register what it meant.

Then the bedroom door creaked open, and I knew.

A stranger had not only entered the tavern but also my room.

My eyes flew open, and I saw the shadow.

Then silver, flashing down.

The exact image I'd seen in the Eye.

I instinctively threw the blankets up at the knife, hoping like hell they'd tangle around the blade enough to impede its deadly descent but not bothering to hang around to see if it had worked. I rolled out of bed and scraped a hand across the bedside table, grabbing my knives but sending my phone and a glass of water flying. The latter crashed to the floor, a sound that echoed sharply in the tense, dark silence.

The song of the floorboards sharpened again.

Two intruders, not one.

The shadow lunged at me from the other side of the bed. I swore and rolled under it but wasn't quite fast enough; the blade sliced past my calf and buried itself deep into the floorboards. Its song changed to one of hurt, and fury pulsed through me. I slapped a hand against the floor, closed the wood fibers around the knife so he couldn't draw it free, then drew my own and lashed at the hand attempting to pull the captured blade from the floorboard. *My* blade sliced through flesh, muscle, and bone with equal ease, severing several fingers. A deep howl of pain rose, but no blood spurted. The smell of burned flesh told me why— the silver in the knife had sealed the wounds. My assailant was a shifter.

His weight shifted quickly from one side of the bed to the other. I rolled underneath and, as one foot touched the ground, grabbed his ankle and growled, "Don't fucking move. Not an inch. And don't fucking speak until I tell you to."

He froze. He had no other choice, not when I'd used pixie magic.

The floorboards quivered as the second intruder ran out of the bedroom and down the stairs. I scrambled from under the bed and gave chase, my steps fast and sure on the old boards, guided not only by their song but also by the pale light that pulsed from the knives.

That light said not only was there a *third* person in the tavern, but he was casting a spell in the main room.

I increased my pace, all but flying down the stairs. The second intruder was cat fast; even now he raced toward the front window, and I hadn't even reached the lower landing.

I jumped down the final few steps, glimpsed a bright, arrow-like flash to my right, and threw myself forward, hitting the floor with a hard grunt but nevertheless rolling back up into a defensive crouch. The light in my knives flared out, encasing me in an arc of protective blue. The incandescent spear that had been aimed at my body hit the blue shield hard and exploded, covering the floor with tiny sparks of broken magic.

The caster had already scrambled out the window that no longer had the plastic covering, the shadows unrolling down his body as he fled to the left. The shifter leapt through after him and headed right.

I pushed up and raced over to the window. Neither the shifter nor the shadow was visible, but that didn't stop the desperate urge to jump out and chase at least one of the bastards. But the spells protecting the tavern had been torn down, and I still had a prisoner upstairs.

And he *would* give me some damn answers.

I ran back up but headed into the bathroom first. I'd been damn lucky in that the cut on my calf hadn't hit anything major and wasn't particularly deep, but it was bleeding like a bitch, and the last thing I needed was to be leaving big pools of blood all over the place. I grabbed the first aid kit and, after washing the wound, sprayed on some antiseptic, then applied a bandage.

With that done, I went into the kitchen to grab a couple of zip-lock bags and finally returned to my captive. His cat-green eyes held the promise of retribution rather than any sort of fear, which was curious given his situation. Or did he think whoever had sent him here would protect him? If he did, he was an idiot, given whoever was behind all this seemed to have a liking for either erasing minds or erasing lives.

I gave him my sweetest smile—which, to anyone who actually knew me, would have been a warning to back the hell away because trouble was about to hit—and moved around to the other side of the bed. After picking up the broken glass—which, thankfully, had only shattered into three large pieces—and putting it out of the way on the bedside table, I gripped the intruder's knife just under the point where the hilt met the blade and pulled it free. It would leave my prints on the metal but at least meant any prints on the hilt would remain undisturbed. And while those prints would undoubtedly belong to my captive, he wasn't wearing any sort of knife harness, and that meant there was a very slight chance his companion might have handled the blade.

I dropped the knife into one bag and the two severed

fingers in another. If he hadn't tried to kill me, I might have put them on ice, but I wasn't really in a generous sort of mood. He was lucky they were all he'd lost.

After healing the wound in the floorboards, I sat on the edge of the bed and rang Sgott. The wave of fury coming from my prisoner ramped up even more, but I continued to ignore him.

"I'm thinking," Sgott said, with a mix of amusement and concern evident in his voice, "that you calling me at this ungodly hour of the morning is not a good sign."

It was only *then* I noticed it had just gone 4:00 AM. Not only had I totally and utterly crashed, but Cynwrig had not made good on his promise to drop by. And there was definitely a part of me more upset about *that* than being woken by intruders.

"Three people broke into the tavern, and one of them attacked me with a knife," I said. "He's currently in a frozen state in my bedroom, but the other two—a shifter and a witch—escaped out the broken window."

Sgott sucked in a sharp breath. "Are you okay?"

"Other than a minor cut on my calf, I'm fine."

"I'll call in the medics, then, because I've seen your definition of minor—"

"Honestly," I cut in, "it's really just a scratch. I'm not even limping."

He harrumphed, a disbelieving sound if ever I'd heard one. "Fine. I'll be there in ten."

Which meant he was close. "Thanks."

I hung up and made another call, this time to Lugh. If he was asleep, he wouldn't be happy, but he'd be even less so to hear about this incident from Sgott or someone else.

But he wasn't likely to be asleep. Not given his determination to uncover what was going on.

He answered with an absent, "There's a problem?"

"Yeah, you're concentrating on something else rather than your only sister."

His laughter ran down the line. "Sorry, I was trying to translate a scroll. What's happened?"

"Plenty, but first and foremost is the fact someone just broke into the tavern and tried to kill me."

"*What?* Fuck, Beth, are you okay?"

"Yes. I managed to catch one of them, and I've called Sgott. I'll start interrogation when he gets here."

"I'll be right over."

"Good, because that's not the only thing that happened tonight. A stone came into my possession, and I believe it's the—"

My prisoner made an odd sound, drawing my attention. His cat-green eyes were filled with amusement, and my gaze snapped around to the storage compartment.

It was open.

"Hang on, Lugh," I added abruptly. "I need to check something."

I raced over and swept a hand through the space. No stone. *That's* what the second intruder had been doing.

But how the hell had they known about my hiding place or the moonstone? Or was it a simple matter of mistaken identity? Had they been looking for the Eye and just decided to take whatever stone lay in the storage space? That was very possible, especially when the note pinned to the front door was taken into consideration.

"Beth," Lugh was saying, "you need to tell me what's happening."

"They fucking stole a stone—one I believe belongs to an item you're currently looking for." I had no idea if my captive actually knew what they'd stolen, but I wasn't about to give them any more information than necessary.

"*What?* How the hell—"

"Long story," I cut in. "Just get over here."

I hung up on his affirmative then strode over to my captive. Before I could ask him anything, the creak of a floorboard told me Sgott was in the building and on his way up.

He stepped into the room a few seconds later, his gaze sweeping me and coming up relieved. "Nice to see you weren't exaggerating about being okay, but the medics will nevertheless be here in a few minutes to make sure."

I smiled, unsurprised he'd ignored my assurances, and reached for a dressing gown. The fire had obviously died down overnight, and the air was on the icy side. "Good, because my friend here lost a couple of fingers in our scuffle and will need to be looked at."

Sgott's gaze moved to my captive, and recognition flashed through his expression.

"Well, well," he drawled, "fancy seeing you here, Danny-boy."

"You *know* him?" Which was a somewhat superfluous question, given he obviously did.

"His full name is Danny O'Conner, and he's a cat burglar—quite literally, in this case." Despite the amused tone, there was a gleam in Sgott's eyes that should have had a sensible thief quailing. Danny-boy merely looked belligerent. "Hate to tell you this, laddie, but you've chosen the wrong place to raid this time. Bethany here is family, and you know how I feel about family being targeted."

Danny made a low sound deep in his throat but couldn't actually say anything. I didn't release him—his expression suggested he didn't have anything polite to say.

"He didn't come here alone—as I said, there was another shifter and a witch with him."

"The shifter is likely to be Danny's brother, Cillian—they always work as a team. Employing the services of a witch is a new angle, though."

"I don't believe they employed the witch, as I think he's the same one who attempted the firebombing the other night." I glanced at Danny. "And if the other thief *was* your brother, you'd better hope he runs hard and fast. The witch has a habit of either killing those he employs or erasing their memories."

Danny stared at me for several seconds, his expression a mix of disbelief and consternation.

"Did Cillian get away with anything?" Sgott asked.

"Yeah, a stone belonging to one of the items Lugh was looking for."

Speculation rose in Sgott's eyes. "How'd you get hold of that? I thought those items were lost?"

"They were. *Are*." I shrugged. "I think the more pertinent question here is, how did the witch know I had it, given it only came into my possession yesterday morning?"

"Perhaps Danny-boy here can answer that." He took out his phone and hit the record button, then read my captive his rights and said, "Okay, let him speak, Beth, and make sure he does so honestly."

I smiled. There was no way I was actually going to give Danny the option of answering *dishonestly*. I walked over, touched his shoulder lightly, and said, "Danny, I need you to answer every single question you're given with absolute honesty. You may also climb off the bed and stand fully upright but move no further."

He shifted position and then uttered a string of curses,

amongst which were a number of "I know nothings" and "this is against all my legal rights."

Sgott ignored him and simply said, "Why were you sent here this evening, Danny?"

The shifter sucked in a breath, obviously fighting the compulsion to answer. He didn't have a hope in hell.

"We were here to get something called the Eye."

Thank gods I'd forgotten to put it away, then.

"Then why try to kill Bethany?" Sgott asked. "Murder is usually beyond your purview, Danny. It should have remained that way."

"I wasn't intending to kill her," he muttered. "Just scare and distract her while Cillian found the damn storage place. We weren't told she was a fucking pixie."

"Well, it's no damn secret, given the tavern has been in pixie hands for centuries," I said, amused despite the continuing wash of anger. "So you obviously didn't do your homework."

"*That* is one of the many reasons why he and his brother have ended up guests of Her Majesty's specialized prisons so often. Who employed you, laddie?"

His face screwed up in yet another obvious effort to stop the reply, but he nevertheless growled, "The job came through the regular channels."

"Through Kaitlyn?"

Danny nodded. I glanced at Sgott. "Who's Kaitlyn?"

"She runs a shop over on Falkner Street and calls herself an entrepreneur, but she's basically a broker of services, legal and not. If you want something bought, traded, or stolen, Kaitlyn is your woman."

"If her services are less than legal, why is she still operating?"

"Because she's a wily old bird." There was a touch of

grudging admiration in Sgott's voice. "And she has fucking good lawyers."

I laughed. "I guess in her line, she probably needs them."

"And I'd place good money on the fact she had no idea the job involved you. She knows better than that."

Which suggested that she had once taken a job that involved his family. If she was still in business, it obviously hadn't been anything major.

I returned my attention to my prisoner. "Who was the witch who was with you tonight?"

"I wasn't given a name, just a description. We were ordered to meet him here and then grab the stone while he dealt with the protecting magic and anyone who might be staying here."

"Can you give us his description?" Sgott asked.

"I could, but it won't do you any good. He was using a transforming spell and those colored eye contacts. I couldn't even swear to the fact that he *was* a he. Could have been a she for all I know."

I frowned. "How do you know he was using colored contacts?"

"Arrived at the meet point early and saw them being put in."

"So you *did* see his true eye color?"

Danny shrugged. "With the spell, couldn't be sure."

"But?" I asked.

"But, they looked blue."

Which didn't really tell us anything, given light elves—as well as many shifters and humans—had blue eyes.

"Where was Cillian supposed to deliver the stone?" Sgott asked. "Back to Kaitlyn?"

"Yes."

"And the spellcaster?"

He shrugged. "Don't know, don't care."

Sgott stopped recording and then glanced at me. "Release him."

I did so and then added, "Do you need a little pixie magic to help Kaitlyn talk?"

"Won't do any good." Sgott cuffed Danny and then pushed him toward the door. "She's part elf."

"Ah, bugger." I picked up the bagged items and followed the two of them down the stairs.

Sgott opened the front door and thrust Danny toward the two medics who were walking toward us. "He's severed a couple of fingers, so will need to be checked. Frankie, go with them and make sure he cooperates."

Frankie was a wolf shifter, from the look of her. She nodded, caught the bagged fingers I tossed to her, and then followed the three men toward the waiting ambulance. Sgott's gaze returned to me. "You going to be all right here alone?"

"Of course." I rubbed my arms against the chill coming in through the front door. The dressing gown wasn't doing a whole lot to ward it off. "Lugh will be here in a few minutes."

"Good." He motioned to the broken window. "When is the council fixing that?"

"Whenever they decide to get around to it."

"I'll put a rocket up their ass for you, then." His smile flashed. "What's the use of being a head of the IIT if you can't abuse the power every now and again?"

I laughed, rose onto my toes, and kissed his hairy cheek. "Thank you."

He nodded and said, somewhat gruffly, "Family looks after family, lass. No matter what."

Then, with a quick nod, he left. I smiled and locked the door behind him. Which was pretty pointless, really, given the open window. I frowned at it for several seconds, then turned and strode down to the older of our two storerooms, where we kept the various bits and pieces that were no longer in use but too good to throw out. Mom had been something of a hoarder, and it was a habit I'd also fallen into.

As I rummaged through the dusty bits and pieces, the floorboards gave me warning of Lugh's approach.

He appeared in the doorway a few seconds later, crossing his arms as he leaned lightly against the frame. "Why are you rummaging through the store wearing little more than a dressing gown?"

"Because I haven't had time to pull on anything else."

"You could have gone upstairs before you came in here and stirred up all the dust."

"The protection spells are down, and it's too early to call Morris, so I wanted to find something to make a stronger temporary seal across the broken window than plastic."

"The council won't be happy if you in any way damage that window."

"Right fucking now, I couldn't give a fig what the council think. If they'd moved their asses earlier and repaired the thing instead of dicking me around, I wouldn't even be doing this."

He smiled and motioned to the rear right corner of the room. "There's some heavy timber planks sitting over there —they should be both long and sturdy enough to create an effective barrier."

I glanced around but couldn't see the planks thanks to

all the other rubbish in the way. "How do you know they're there?"

"Who do you think broke the table they came from? Now, tell me, what the fuck happened tonight?"

I filled him in while I picked my way toward the corner. The table he'd killed had obviously been more an ancient trestle type than the round ones we currently used, and the boards were both thick and heavy. I handed him three before making my way back with a fourth.

He led the way back to the main room. "Why are you so sure the moonstone came from the crown?"

"Because I did a scrying."

His head snapped around. "*You* did?"

"Apparently, I *did* inherit some of Mom's skills after all."

"Well, fuck. I mean it's good, but it's also odd that the ability appears now, and not before."

"I never touched the Eye before. I think the stone has woken something inside of me."

"Well, that would have pleased Mom." He placed the three bits of wood on the floor under the window and then reached for one end of mine. "She always did want you to follow in her footsteps."

Then why had she never wanted me tested? Had she been waiting for some sign, or was Beira right in thinking that she'd wanted to keep the darkness away for as long as possible?

We held a thick bit of wood against the window and carefully attached it to the supporting frame that ran around the window rather than the window itself. At least that way there'd be less of a chance of doing any damage to it.

"And was the scrying successful?" Lugh asked.

I nodded as we picked up the next board and attached it and then told him what I'd seen.

"Why the hell would it be buried in a cave under an abandoned building?" he said. "That makes no sense."

"I guess it depends how long it's been there and who owned the building before it was abandoned. According to Cynwrig Lùtair, the crown has been missing for decades, and there's been no sign—not even a whisper—of its presence through any of their channels in all that time." We attached the third board. "It's also possible that the hall house I saw has nothing to do with the location of the cave and the crown."

Lugh's eyebrows rose. "You've been talking to Lord Lùtair?"

I grinned. "I've actually been doing a whole lot more than talking to him, brother."

He blinked. "Since when?"

"Since I was hauled in front of the council and cross-examined."

"Christ, it would appear I've missed more than a few updates."

"Yeah, sorry, but things just got away from me." I quickly filled him in on the murder, the ruby, and the interrogation as we finished attaching the last board. "Let's head upstairs so I can put on something warmer while you make a pot of tea."

"What about the Eye?" he said as he followed me up. "Was it also taken, or is it safe?"

I flashed him a grin over my shoulder. "I presume it's safe—I left it in the pocket of my discarded jeans rather than the storage hole."

He half laughed. "Well, I guess there *are* few thieves

who'd search a pocket before a pixie's safe. Did you also scry the Eye?"

"No." I walked into my bedroom and quickly checked the Eye was still there. It was. "But it's not a key, Lugh. At least, it's not one that's directly connected to the Claws."

The water pipes rattled lightly as he turned on the tap. "How can you be sure of that if you didn't scry the thing?"

I stripped off my dressing gown then pulled on a fresh pair of jeans and my thickest, warmest sweater. "Got a visit from a hag yesterday afternoon; she told me all about it."

"Which hag was it?"

I shoved my icy feet into slippers and then headed out. "You've met them?"

"Not really; I've just seen them a couple of times." He poured hot water into the pot, then put the old tea cozy Gran had knitted over it. "Once with Mom when I was young, and another time here, about a year ago. I believe I walked in on an argument because, oh boy, was there some tension in the air."

I walked over to the fire and turned around to warm my butt and legs. "And the mother of all storms outside?"

"Yes."

"Beira then."

"Yes, though I was never introduced and Mom didn't answer any of my questions afterward."

I wondered if that argument had been about me— about Mom's determination not to drag me into her world. If it had been, I couldn't help but wish Mom had listened. Maybe then I might not be feeling so lost and out of my depth.

He walked over with a tray containing two mugs, a small jug of milk, and the teapot, placing it down on the table. "Shall I be Mother?"

I smiled. "You're doing a fine job of it so far."

"Mom trained me well."

"Because why have kids if you can't train them to wait on you?" I intoned, dropping my voice to echo Mom's deeper tone.

He laughed, poured milk into the mugs, and then picked up the teapot. "I think that was Gran's favorite saying, too."

He handed me a mug and then retreated to the sofa. "What did Beira say?"

"That the Eye belonged to Mom, who used it to track lost items of the gods. Apparently, she'd been working with the hags for a very long time."

Lugh stared at me for several seconds, then scrubbed his spare hand across his face. "Well, fuck, my own mother was a relic hunter and I never knew?"

I took a sip of tea and winced at its lack of sweetness. I added some sugar and then said, "That's not exactly true. She never hid the fact that she used her abilities to find missing items, and that those items sometimes included relics."

"Yes, but never relics of the *old* gods. Even when I began working for the museum, she never once mentioned she was in the same line."

"Because the stuff she hunted was dangerous."

"It's *all* dangerous, old gods or new." He eyed me for a second. "Is *that* what she was doing the day she went missing?"

"Beira couldn't say. Apparently, there are two Eyes, and what Mom sees usually reflects in theirs. It didn't that day."

"Of course not."

His voice was filled with the same sort of frustration that had echoed through me earlier. I grimaced and said, "I don't suppose you have any idea where that hall house is, do you?"

"No, but it shouldn't be too hard to find." He dragged his phone out of his pocket. After a few minutes, he said, "There're three in the county."

"That's presuming the one I saw *is* in this county. I didn't see anything suggesting it was." I walked behind the sofa to check out the images over his shoulder. "That last one is the most likely, given all the trees."

"Then we'll start there, and if it's a bust, we'll check the other two. Are you opening the tavern tomorrow?"

"Partially, but Ingrid can handle it."

"Good," he said. "What about the Eye? Did you see anything in it?"

I told him. "The knife thing was obviously a warning, but nothing else makes sense."

"No." His expression was contemplative. "The description of the standing stone does ring a faint bell, though. I might head back to the museum and run a check on the heritage listings."

"Not all of them are listed or protected."

"No, but the most important ones are, and why would you see it if it wasn't important?"

"That is an unanswerable question right now, brother mine."

"Hence the research." He paused. "Are you going to be okay here alone? Or would you rather I stay?"

I smiled. "I doubt anyone will chance a second attack tonight. Besides, if I know Sgott, he's probably ordered his people to keep a watch on the place."

"Now that you mention it, there was a shifter loitering in the rear lane." Lugh gulped down his tea and then rose. "I'll check on my way out. If we have no luck finding the right hall house tomorrow, you might have to try using the Eye to refine the location, otherwise we could be searching the length and breadth of the country."

"I have no idea how to control what I see, so that might not help."

"Still worth trying. We need to find the crown before whoever stole the moonstone does."

"Our thieves were after the Eye, not the crown."

"That doesn't mean they won't know what the moonstone is, or that they're not in a position to use it as you did. Better not to take any chances."

True. I followed him down the stairs and over to the back door. "How'd you do with the security check on the tunnels under the museum?"

"No incursions have been found so far, but they've one more to analyze. It'll happen tomorrow."

"And you're being careful when you're there? We both know how little you pay attention to your surroundings when your nose is stuck in research, and I don't want you disappearing on me anytime soon."

"That's not something I'd be keen on, either." He reached into his pocket and drew out what looked to be a small silver flash drive with a small black button sitting on the top of it. "Proximity alert. Once set, anyone getting within six feet without me noticing will set off an alarm."

I raised my eyebrows. "Six feet gives you time to react, but it's going to cause problems in daytime situations."

"It can be adjusted, but these bastards have so far shown no inclination to attack during the day."

"So far being the operative words there." Especially since it was possible that whoever had attempted to set up Cynwrig was connected.

"Yes, but there's little use second-guessing possible

future movements. Not until we know a little more about their intentions and motives." He opened the door and tugged up his collar. "I'll pick you up at nine."

He hunched his shoulders against the cold and strode down the lane. I half closed the door, then caught a brief flash of movement and hesitated. A dark figure momentarily stepped into the light and spoke to Lugh, who then gave me a thumbs-up. As I'd guessed, Sgott had left watchers.

As I locked the door, my phone started ringing, the tone telling me it was Mathi. I bolted up the stairs and dove over the bed to grab it from the bedside table.

"Mathi?" I said, slightly breathlessly. "What the hell are you doing ringing at this ungodly hour?"

"Mathi is unable to come to the phone right now," came a cool, calm-sounding voice. "I'm afraid he's a little ... incapacitated."

My breath caught in my throat, and for several seconds I couldn't breathe. Couldn't think.

"What have you done to him?" I croaked. "What do you want?"

"You're a smart woman. I think you can guess what we want."

"I ... I don't understand."

Which wasn't a lie, because I had no idea if he meant the Eye or something else entirely. Given everything that had happened over the last few days, it could have been fucking anything.

He sighed. It was a very put-upon sound and reminded me somewhat of a long-suffering teacher being confronted with a normally bright student being inexplicably obtuse.

"We want you, obviously. And the rest of the fucking rubies, of course."

Rubies, not the Eye. Thank the *fuck* I hadn't mentioned it, then. "The only ruby I had, I gave to the council. I can't give you any of the others."

"For young Mathi's sake, I hope that's not true."

"Damn it, I can't give you what I don't *have*, no matter how much you might wish otherwise."

"Well, let's hope you can find the rest of them, then, otherwise your man is dead. You have fifteen minutes to get here, or we'll start cutting off appendages and throwing them out in the street for the rats to eat. Oh, and no knives. And if we hear the slightest whisper of the IIT, he'll be dead and we'll be gone before anyone gets here."

And with that, he hung up.

CHAPTER
NINE

I drew in a deep breath and released it slowly. It didn't in any way help ease the twisting fear, but it at least helped calm the tumbling array of erratic, panicked thoughts. Which was good, because if I didn't think clearly, Mathi might well die.

The first thing I needed to do was contact both Mathi's father and Sgott. I might have been warned not to, but there was no way known I was going to walk into this situation without IIT support. I wasn't a fool. These bastards obviously believed I had the same seer ability as Mom, so it was doubtful they'd let me go if I did happen to find the missing rubies.

In truth, they couldn't afford to.

Then another thought hit—had Cynwrig also been snatched? While it was more likely he'd simply gone home after the council meeting, I couldn't discount the possibility.

I quickly scrolled through the recent calls list until I found his number and, after adding it to my contacts list, rang him. It immediately switched to voice mail, which didn't ease the worry any. I left a quick message telling him what had happened and asking if he was okay, then scrolled through my contacts list to find Ruadhán's private number. I'd never really had that much to do with Mathi's father—he was, like most highborn light elves, a distant parent—and the only reason I had his number at all was thanks to a call he'd made uninviting me to an event Mathi had invited me to. He was charming like that. Mathi had apologized, saying he hadn't realized it was elf only, and I did believe that even if I suspected the event had only become so after Ruadhán was made aware of my invite.

Once again, the call switched over to voice mail. I left another message, then shoved the phone into my pocket, pulled on my boots, and strapped on my knives. They'd most likely be taken from me, but I couldn't *not* take them. They were tuned to my touch and resonance, so it was remotely possible their magical protection would work even when I wasn't holding them.

I guess I'd find out soon enough.

I headed out of the room. The thug on the phone hadn't given me an address, but he could only be at one location, given the mention of rubies and rats.

If I was at all wrong, Mathi would pay with limbs if not his life.

I shoved my arms into the sleeves of my waterproof coat as I raced down the stairs and out the back door. The shifter I'd spotted earlier once again stepped out of the shadows and said, "Is there a problem, miss?"

"Mathi Dhār-Val is being held captive, and unless I get there within the next ten minutes, they'll start cutting off bits of him."

The shifter—a whip-thin man with a beak nose and

feathery brown and gold hair—swore and immediately dragged out his phone.

I placed a hand on his, stopping him from making a call. "Using regular contact channels to contact the chief inspector isn't advisable right now, as I've been ordered not to contact the IIT." Not to mention the fact I had no idea if the thugs had inside sources. "I'll contact him on his private number and explain the situation, but in the meantime, can we please get moving?"

The shifter hesitated, then nodded abruptly and said, "Follow me," as he took off down the lane.

We reached his car—a silver Vauxhall—and climbed in. As the engine roared to life, I gave the shifter Mathi's address and then called Sgott.

He answered with a growled, "What did they demand?"

A comment that suggested he was already aware of Mathi's kidnap. I gave him the rundown of what they'd said and then added, "I know they're using him as bait, but I can't not appear, no matter what else you plan."

"I know that, but we'll nevertheless take every precaution. See you at Mathi's in ten minutes—"

"I've only just over ten minutes before they start hacking bits off him."

"We'll make it, but not without making you safe as we can first."

He hung up. I put my phone away, my stomach twisting painfully as we sped through the streets, lights on but no sirens. It didn't take us long to get to Mathi's, but Sgott was already waiting. Two women—a blonde and a redhead—stood to his right, while a small man stood to his left.

I climbed out of the car. The wind was bitter, filled with the promise of more rain, and the brightness of dawn seemed a long way off yet even though it had to be close to six now. I shivered, wishing I'd brought some gloves as I shoved my hands deep into my pockets.

Sgott glanced at his watch and then said, "Right, we've three minutes. We'll need to tape those knives of yours to your spine. If they've tortured Mathi for answers, it's likely they're aware of their protective power and will be looking for them."

The two women stepped forward, one of them holding what looked for the world like a roll of duct tape—and probably was, given how little time they'd had to gather anything more suitable. I took off my coat and tossed it to Sgott, then handed my knives to the blonde woman and tugged up my sweater.

"I'm not going to be able to use them if they're taped to my spine," I said. "And I really don't like going in there without a physical means of defense."

"And I don't like the idea of you going in at all, but here we are," Sgott growled. "We're bugging you, so the second anything untoward happens, we'll hit the place."

"What happens if they search me and find the bug?"

"They may pat you down, and they may well find the knives, but they won't find the bug. It's the latest in nanotechnology and indistinguishable from a mole unless you know what you're looking for. It's unlikely these men do."

"And you won't be alone," the smallish, gray-haired man standing next to Sgott said. "We've already got two people watching the place closely, and I'll be following you down the street."

"How on earth—" I stopped, suddenly registering his thin appearance and longish gray whiskers. "Rat shifter?"

"Indeed," Sgott said. "Rats are prevalent enough around

these parts thanks to the nearby river that few would look twice at them."

I nodded, though the knowledge that help was only a squeak away didn't really ease the trembling inner fear. The two women finished wrapping the tape around my body, and I tugged down my sweater. "I need to go."

Sgott glanced at the blonde who'd attached the bug. She was studying her phone but nodded. "Signal's coming through clear."

"Good." Sgott returned my coat. "Go then, but please, be damned careful. The minute you tell us Mathi is in there, we'll hit the place."

I shoved my hands into my coat pockets again—more to hide their shaking this time—and walked on, trying not to think about what would happen if he *wasn't* there. The streetlights created warm puddles of brightness through which to walk, even if the park at the far end of Gilda's street lay wreathed in shadows. The lights there were obviously out, but it wasn't like any sensible person would be strolling through there at this hour of the morning.

Of course, a sensible person wouldn't exactly be walking into a trap like this, either.

I casually glanced across the road and, after a moment, caught the flicker of movement. My rat companion, following as promised. Relief washed through me, though it didn't in any way ease my hatred of rats, even if this one was on the side of the angels.

Another flicker of movement had my head snapping up; a sharp-faced figure briefly appeared in the top floor window. Then the curtain dropped back into place, stealing him from view.

He was in Gilda's room.

The thought of entering that place again had nausea

rising. I swallowed against its bitterness, then crossed the street and climbed the front steps. A soft scrape had me pausing and looking down. The rat was sitting on his rear haunches, giving me a thumbs-up. I smiled despite the inner tension and rapped loudly on the door. For a couple of seconds, there was no response; then soft steps approached, and the door opened.

The man who appeared was pale of skin with golden hair, blue eyes, and a slight point to his ears. Not a full light elf given his muscular frame, but that bloodline ran through his background somewhere.

Which meant I couldn't magic him. I could only hope that wasn't the case with whoever else might be here, because if things went wrong ...

"Bethany," he said, with false effusiveness, "so lovely of you to be on time. I'm sure Dhār-Val will appreciate it."

"I want to see him," I said flatly. "I want to know he's all right before anything else happens."

"Of course." He stepped back and waved a hand. "Please, do enter my humble abode."

Said the spider to the fly. Though it was interesting that he said "my" abode. That suggested he might be linked to Gilda—maybe a relation or even the building's owner. As a serving class fae, she wouldn't have been able to afford a place in such an upmarket area. Even the rentals were pretty hideously priced around these parts.

I stepped sideways through the door to keep as much distance between us as possible. Another man stood in the doorway to my right, and I could see the shadow of a third man down the far end of the hall, in the brightly lit kitchen. That meant there were at least four here if I included whoever had been peering out the window in Gilda's bedroom. Not great odds if it came down to just me and them. Of course, there was no way Sgott would abandon me, and he had three men ready to hit the place the minute I sighted Mathi. But it would still take them a few seconds to get in. A lot could happen in a few seconds.

Especially when the place stank of magic.

I casually glanced around but couldn't immediately see any spell indicators. My knives weren't reacting, so the magic here was general in tone rather than aimed at me. It didn't feel like barrier spells, either—at least not the sort I was familiar with—but the fact the magic was strong enough that I could sense it was worrying.

"Before we take you anywhere," the pale part-elf was saying, "we do need to ensure you've done as we asked. Please, coat off."

I undid my coat, noting that my hands no longer reflected the inner trembling. That was at least something.

He half smiled, though it was a cold thing bereft of amusement. "All the way off."

I obeyed and hung it up over the nearby coat stand, an action that seemed to amuse the big man near the door. He wasn't elf, and I didn't think he was a shifter, but I suspected he wasn't human, either. He had a weird sort of energy output.

"Garrett," the half elf said, "check her."

The big man pushed away from the door and stepped closer. That strange energy washed over me, and my knives reacted, heating my spine with a flare of heat.

Not because he was trying to magic me. Quite the opposite. He was a fucking seeker. Not a truth seeker, but rather one could magically scan someone's body and uncover hidden anomalies such as weapons.

Garrett stopped and crossed his arms again, his amusement growing. "She's wearing the knives Dhār-Val mentioned. At her spine, I believe."

Meaning he *hadn't* sensed the bug. Relief stirred, but I didn't otherwise react, even though I wanted to do nothing more than knock the bastards down and charge upstairs to see if Mathi was okay. I might not be dating the man, but that didn't mean I wanted anything bad to happen to him.

The part-elf made a "turn around" motion with his finger. I scowled but nevertheless obeyed. The big man tugged up my sweater then something cold touched my skin, slicing through the duct tape either side of the knives. He pulled them free but left the tape where it was.

I tugged my sweater down and tried to ignore the trickle of warmth down my back. "I want them back when we're finished here. They were a gift from my grandmother."

"Oh, you can be sure we'll look after them." Garrett studied the sheathed blades with admiration. "Knives like these are worth quite a bit on the black market."

I didn't say anything, knowing well enough that he was simply baiting me. The only worth my knives had on the black market was whatever value could be placed on their age and the silver in them.

Of course, while anyone else might not be able to use the magic within the blades, that didn't stop anyone from using them to simply gut someone.

Hopefully, that someone would *not* be me.

He placed them on the nearby hallway table and motioned me to raise my arms. I did so, and he stepped forward, quickly and efficiently patting me down. His touch was impersonal and businesslike, but his closeness nevertheless had my skin crawling.

There was something *very* wrong with his energy

output, and I couldn't help but wonder what else might be twisting through it. I'd never crossed paths with a truth seeker before, but everything I knew about them suggested their magic was "clean." Which made sense, given seekers were often used in clandestine situations; they might as well use a claxon to announce their presence if their output had felt like this man's.

He tugged my phone from my pocket, switched it off, and then stepped back with a quick, "She's clear." I had to hold back the sigh of relief. They hadn't found the bug, which meant help remained only a squeak away.

"Right," I said, "I need to see Mathi. Now. Before we discuss or do anything else."

"Oh, I don't think you're in any position to be demanding anything, little lady," the pale elf said, amused. "In case you haven't noticed, you're outnumbered here."

I smiled sweetly at him. "The thing with second sight is that it can't be forced, so feel free to smack me around as much as you want; the more you hurt me, the less likely it is you'll get what you want."

"Oh, we weren't intending to hurt you. We're not that type."

Garrett raised his eyebrows at that statement, suggesting he very much *was* that type.

"Drugging me will have even worse consequences," I replied evenly, "as it completely inhibits the psychic receptors."

In truth, I had no idea if that was the case, but it sounded good, and I had nothing to lose by putting it out there.

The pale elf contemplated me for several seconds through slightly narrowed eyes, obviously debating whether he should believe me or not.

Then he glanced at Garrett and said, "Keep a close watch on the street. Just because we can't see the cops doesn't mean they're not out there." His gaze switched to me. "This way, Ms. Aodhán."

He turned and led the way up the stairs. My fingers itched with the need to reach out and attempt to control him, despite his elf ancestry. But until I knew what waited in the room upstairs, it wasn't worth the risk.

We reached the landing and walked into Gilda's bedroom. Her body parts no longer lay scattered around the room, but the blood splatter and smaller bits of gore certainly did. And the smell ... I wasn't a shifter and didn't have a very sensitive olfactory sense, but even to me, this place stank of blood and death.

Mathi wasn't on the bed; my gaze swept the room a little frantically before I spotted him. He'd been shoved into the corner of the room, between the free-standing wardrobe and the external wall. His hands and his feet had been tightly lashed together with wire, and his face ... I sucked in a breath. His lovely face was a bruised and battered mess.

Standing two feet in front of him was the man I'd briefly seen at the window. If his eyes were anything to go by, he was a cat shifter. Whether large or small didn't matter; either way, when I moved, I'd have to be damn fast.

I moved past the pale elf and over to Mathi. His eyes were closed, and he didn't immediately react to my presence. I squatted in front of him and carefully touched his hands—like his face, they were battered and bleeding, suggesting he had not been captured easily.

"Mathi?" I said softly. "Mathi? Can you hear me? Are you okay?"

Which was a stupid question given his condition but one that had to be asked, if only for the sake of my listeners.

For several seconds, there was no response, then his eyes fluttered open, and confusion flittered across his expression. "Bethany? What are you doing here?"

"Well, it was either come here as ordered or have bits of you hacked off and fed to the rats. And if I'd wanted *that* done, I would have done it myself—and it wouldn't have been fingers or toes as they threatened."

He stared at me for a second and then laughed, though it was a weak sound that ended in a coughing fit.

"Remind me never to parade around naked in front of you again."

It was little more than a hoarse whisper, but relief stirred. If he could make light of the situation, then he wasn't as badly hurt as he looked.

"That's enough sweet nothings between you two," the pale elf said. "Time for you to—"

He stopped abruptly and cocked his head sideways. My breath caught in my throat, but for several seconds, nothing happened. Silence reigned. At least it did if you couldn't hear the song of the wood. The floorboards were echoing with the vibration of a fight.

A heartbeat later, an alarm went off. I didn't wait for the pale elf's reaction; I threw myself backward, crashed into the shifter, and sent him flying. Then I twisted around, clamped a hand onto one leg, and commanded him not to move.

A gargled sound from Mathi had my head snapping around. The pale elf was coming straight at me, his face full of fury. I had no time to get up; I simply twisted around on my back and lashed out with my feet. The pale elf darted to one side but not quite fast enough. My kick hit his right knee hard enough that bone cracked and his leg buckled. He howled in fury and pain, but nevertheless lunged at me. I tucked my knees up to prevent his body fully covering mine, grunting as his weight hit hard enough to drive my knees into my chest. His fists flailed down; I caught one, holding it tight as I twisted my face away from the other. The blow came close enough that the ring on his finger scored my cheek, leaving a stinging, bloody trench in its wake.

Then he was gone, ripped from my knees and tossed across the room like so much rubbish. He hit the wall, leaving a dent in the plaster as he fell to the floor. Two men were on him before he could move—one dragging him up and the other hauling his arms behind his back and cuffing him.

A hand appeared in front of my face, and I looked up to see the thin rat shifter standing in front of me. "You okay?"

"Yeah." I caught his hand and let him haul me up. I might be taller and more muscular than him, but size wasn't an indicator of strength; not when it came to shifters and especially not when, like their animal counterparts, rat shifters could lift more than double their body weight without even trying. "Thanks for the save."

He smiled and offered me my knives and phone. "I was sent in to protect you. The boss would have had my hide if anything more than a scratch had happened to you."

"What set off the alarm?" I drew one of the knives, then returned to Mathi and began to saw at the wire binding him. It might not do the edge on the blade any good, but I couldn't wait for wire cutters. Not when Mathi's fingers were starting to swell and taking on a purplish tinge.

"They must have reinstated an entry alarm after you went in. Didn't sense it until it was too late." He touched his ear, and then added, "Upstairs, main bedroom. Yes, Lord Dhār-Val will need to be taken to hospital."

Mathi hissed as the last bit of wire fell free and began to shake his hands. While I knew it would help circulation, it would also fucking hurt—and the sweat that broke out across his forehead testified to that.

"How the hell did this happen, Mathi?" I asked.

"Don't know. One minute I was walking out of the council meeting to meet the car, the next I was bound and being smacked about."

"What time was this?"

"About eleven—why?"

"Were you the only one attacked?"

"The meeting was ongoing when I left, so I would presume so." His gaze narrowed—or as much as any gaze could narrow given the swollen state of his eyes. "Why?"

"I was supposed to meet Lord Lùtair after the council meeting had finished."

"Seriously? You're going out with that prick?"

A smile tugged at my lips. "Why shouldn't I? I went out with you long enough."

"Yes, but a dark elf, Bethany? That's just—"

"Inconvenient to your own seduction plans?"

"Well, yes, but—"

"There is no 'but' in this situation, Mathi. You played the game and lost the queen. She is free to do as she wishes now."

He made a low sound that was a mix of frustration and annoyance. The game, if what little I could see of his expression through the blood, bruises, and swelling was any indicator, was a long way from over.

But now wasn't the time to discuss that. "Did they beat

you up so badly because you wouldn't answer their questions?"

"No, the pale part elf just smacked me around a few times and then left. The cat shifter came in a few minutes later to keep an eye on me, but that's about it."

Uneasiness stirred. "They didn't question you at all?"

"No." His confusion was evident. "Why?"

"Because they knew about my knives."

"Not from me, they didn't."

"So why did they say you had told them?"

"I have no idea."

"It's more than likely that the information came indirectly, even if they attributed it to Lord Dhār-Val," Sgott said, as he came into the room.

My gaze rose to his. "But how—" I stopped. "Oh, fuck. The council."

Anyone who'd been at that meeting would have seen firsthand the knives were capable of displacing magic.

"It's possible," Sgott agreed heavily. "As is a mole in the IIT itself."

"Surely the latter, if anything," Mathi said, voice still a pained rasp. "The fae council undergoes regular checks."

And those checks *hadn't* uncovered the fact that Gilda had been using Borrachero to get information out of him for *months*. But I didn't say anything. I might trust Mathi, but he trusted the council, and I wasn't about to say anything that could get back to the wrong ears.

And yet I trusted Cynwrig, even though I barely even knew the man in any sense *other* than physical. But that trust didn't blind me to the possibility that he was using sex to get information—to covertly do what the thugs here had tried to do overtly. Dark elves were well known for not taking attacks on their kin lightly, and not only had

Cynwrig's sister been attacked, but two of his cousins had been killed.

I had no doubt he'd take every avenue possible to bring down those behind it all. The attraction between us was fierce and real, but that didn't mean he wasn't using it to further his investigations.

I'd be a fool to think anything else.

Footsteps echoed on the stairs and moved toward Gilda's room. Sgott said, "That's the medics. We'll get proper statements from you both once you're checked out at the hospital."

"I'm fine—"

"Of course you are," he cut in. "But you will nevertheless humor me on this matter. Especially when that wound on your face is still bleeding."

I opened my mouth to protest and then closed it again. I'd known him long enough now to understand when to stand my ground and when to give way.

The two paramedics came in. After doing a quick check on us both, we were escorted down to the waiting ambulance and taken across to the fae hospital's emergency ward.

Unsurprisingly, it was Darby who came into my cubicle to check me over and patch me up. Her gaze swept me and came up relieved.

"What the fuck have you and Mathi been doing to yourselves?"

"It's more a question of what have people been doing to us." My voice was wry. "And haven't you got more urgent cases to look after?"

"It's been a slow night, thankfully, so no, I haven't."

She stopped in front of me, listened to the paramedic's

observations, and then nodded. "Nothing major, at least. Thanks, guys."

As they left, she touched my cheek, her gaze becoming unfocused as she healed the wound. "It might itch for a few days, but it won't leave a scar." She repeated the process with the cut on my leg and then ran her healing energy through the rest of my body, not only checking if there was anything else to be worried about but also healing the small cuts on my back. After a few more minutes, she grunted in satisfaction and then crossed her arms. "So, explanation. Now."

"Hadn't you better check Mathi first?"

"Candice is taking care of him, and she doesn't like distractions while she heals, so stop avoiding and just fill me in."

I did so. She frowned and added, "Have you called Lugh? Because he might be next on their hit list."

"I called him from the ambulance." I glanced at my watch, then sat up and swung my legs off the bed. "He should be here soon to pick Mathi and me up."

"Most excellent news."

I grinned at the anticipation evident in her expression. "Isn't there some sort of rule against attempted seductions while working?"

"Probably. Won't stop me reminding the man that he is mine." She sat on the bed beside me. "I guess the first question in all this is, how did they know your second sight had come online?"

"Mathi told the council." I wrinkled my nose. "He was with me when I found the ruby."

She frowned. "That doesn't explain how these thugs knew it."

"Cynwrig believes there's a leak on the council."

As did the hags, but I didn't mention them. That was just too complicated to go into, especially in a place like this, where there was a distinct possibility of people listening in to our conversation.

Darby's expression was speculative. "You've talked to Cynwrig?"

"Oh, I've done a whole lot more than merely talk." I grinned. "The man *definitely* lives up to his reputation."

Her laugh was a sound of sheer delight. "No more cobwebs?"

"Absolutely none."

"And you're seeing him again?"

"I was supposed to last night, but he didn't show. I left him a message after I got the call about Mathi, but he hasn't responded yet."

"Ah." She wrinkled her nose. "He might have a good excuse."

"Mathi said the meeting was still going after he left, so it's possible it ran very late and he simply went home." I shrugged. "It doesn't matter. It's not like he and I will ever be more than sex buddies."

"Yes, but more than just a night would have been optimal."

With *that*, I agreed. I glanced past her as the curtain parted and Lugh stepped into the room. He gave Darby a nod of greeting and then said, "It's getting to the point where I can't leave you alone."

I snorted. "You will notice I'm absolutely fine."

"Yes, but it might be a case of the third time *not* being the charm. I don't think you should be staying at the tavern alone. It's not safe."

"I'll stay with her," Mathi said from the doorway.

"No, you fucking won't," I replied evenly. "You'll only use it as an excuse to get into my bed."

"Better me in your bed than a man with a knife at your throat," he said.

"There was never a knife at my throat, because the song of the wood warned me before it ever got to that point." My voice was dry. "You're being dramatic. And the answer is still no."

He stared at me through narrowed eyes for several silent beats. "I suppose you'll be asking Lord Lùtair to perform ... bodyguard duties?"

"I'm more than capable of looking after myself, no matter what you think. And just as a reminder, it's none of your damn business who I invite to my bed."

His expression suggested he did *not* agree with that statement, which wasn't really a surprise given his oft-stated intention to get me back into his bed.

And my reply had only made him more determined than ever.

I couldn't help the inner tremble of anticipation. I might never want to go back to a relationship with Mathi, but that didn't in any way erase the delicious prospect of having two very virile men chasing after me.

Lugh cleared his throat. "I've organized Morris to come in and do a complete security update—magic and regular. He'll be there now."

I glanced at him. "You got the poor man out of bed? At this hour of the morning?"

"I've only got one sister. I have no intention of losing her."

"And *that*," Darby said, "is very much why I intend to marry that man."

Lugh wasn't the only one who did a double take. She

gave me a wink and then said, "And yes, I *am* utterly serious, dear Lugh."

Lugh's expression was ... interesting. "Yeah, sure you are."

Darby shrugged. "I have time on my side."

So did Lugh. We pixies might not live quite as long as elves, but we came close.

Several of Sgott's men appeared at that point to take our statements. Darby bid me goodbye and left—but not before taking the opportunity to brush a quick, cheeky kiss on Lugh's cheek. He shook his head at her, but his gaze followed her retreat, and I could almost see the gears in his brain working overtime.

He was definitely tempted. Maybe the only thing holding him back was the fact that she was my friend—even though I'd told him multiple times that I wholeheartedly approved any relationship that might evolve.

Once Mathi and I had given our statements, they removed their bug from my back and told me Sgott would be in contact later in the morning. The doctors cleared us to leave the hospital, and Lugh led us down to the parking area.

"Mathi," he said, as he started the car and headed out. "Do you want to be taken back to the apartment or somewhere else?"

"The apartment will be fine. Thanks." His gaze burned into the back of my head, a silent demand I turn and look at him. I ignored it. "Bethany, do you want to come stay with me? The spare room is available, and I promise no seduction unless invited."

It was a lovely offer, but he and I both knew sex would happen if I did go back. Close proximity and too many pleasurable memories was a dangerous combination—as had already been proven.

"I appreciate the offer, but Lugh and I have something to do first."

Lugh shoved the ticket into the reader to get out and then glanced at me. "Are you sure you don't want to rest up first?"

"I don't think I can afford to." I had a bad feeling the people who'd arranged for the theft of the Eye might well know what the moonstone was—and how to use it to find the crown.

"Well," Mathi said, "the offer stands if in the future you happen to need somewhere safe to stay."

"Thanks. We'll see what happens in the next day or so."

"Which is the polite form of 'when hell freezes over,'" he said, the amusement back in his voice. "But I can bide my time."

I didn't bother replying. I couldn't fight his certainty, not when I wasn't one hundred percent sure he wasn't right. As the saying went, old habits are hard to break.

There wasn't that much traffic on the road at this hour, so it didn't take us long to get to Mathi's. He bid us both goodbye, then opened the door and climbed out. He was reaching for his phone as he walked toward the entrance, and I half wondered when he'd gotten it back. Or maybe, given the thugs hadn't bothered questioning him after they'd called me, they'd simply given it back to him. Trussed up as he had been, it wasn't like he could have used it.

Lugh took off and said, "Do you want to grab some breakfast on the way to the first location? It'll only take us twenty minutes to get over there, but it could be a bit of an uphill hike before we get to the house itself."

"That," I said dryly, "has to be the stupidest question you've ever asked."

He laughed. "Oh, I dare say I've asked dumber."

I grinned. "How'd you go with the search on the standing stone?"

"I managed to input the search criteria, but your call came through before I could check the results." He glanced at me. "Do you believe Mathi's story about the kidnap?"

I wrinkled my nose. "Yes."

"But?"

I glanced at him. "There's a security guard sitting right inside the foyer of the council headquarters; why didn't he give assistance?"

"He might have been paid not to."

"That's a very cynical view."

"These are very cynical times." He flicked on the blinker and turned left. "Did they run full bloodwork on Mathi at the hospital? Check for drugs and the like?"

"I don't know." I got out my phone and sent a text to Darby, asking if she'd check. "The other thing that's bugging me is the fact I sent Ruadhán a message and haven't heard anything back from him yet."

Lugh snorted. "That's hardly surprising. You're the unwanted pixie in Mathi's life."

"The unwanted pixie *formerly* in Mathi's life," I corrected wryly. "But even so, why wouldn't he at least have contacted Sgott?"

"We don't know that he didn't." Lugh shrugged. "Besides, Mathi was talking to someone as we left—it might well have been his father."

That was more than possible ... and yet, a niggle remained. And I had no idea why.

Once we'd gotten food—a breakfast roll and a tea for

me, and two double bacon and egg McMuffins and a coffee for him—we continued on. We eventually reached the outskirts of the Delamere Forest and pulled into the parking area.

I collected the trash, then climbed out and walked over to the bin. The scent of rain ran through the wind, and the threat of a storm hung so heavily in the clouds, it would undoubtedly hit well before we got back to the car. I shivered and hastily did up my coat, thankful I'd picked up one that was fully waterproof.

Lugh pulled out two headlamps, a rope, and a climbing harness from the back of his car, then locked it. After swinging the latter two over his shoulders, he handed me one of the headlamps and said, "This way."

I pulled on the headlamp, adjusted it to fit my smaller head, then switched it on and followed him through the long parking area onto a dirt trail that led into the trees. The track wound its way through old oak and other broadleaf trees that dominated this section of the forest, and I held out my hands, brushing them across the leaves and low hanging branches. The vibration of their song filled me with joy and an odd sort of strength. My branch of pixies had lived in towns for a very long time now, but to be in a forest like this ... it felt like a homecoming.

The track began to climb. I huffed after Lugh, my breath condensing in the chill air. It started to rain a few minutes later, lightly at first but then with increasing intensity, and the path quickly became a gluggy, slippery mess.

I resisted the urge to grab Lugh's belt and let him haul me up, and said, "How much further?"

"Only a few minutes, according to the map."

"You have a map?"

"Of course."

I smiled. "In your head?"

"Where else would it be? Thieves can't steal—"

"What they can't physically see or touch," I finished, with a laugh.

"It's saved many a relic hunt, let me tell you." He stopped. "We're here."

I halted beside him and studied the building dominating the clearing just beyond the line of ferns.

It was a stone double-story building that had partially collapsed down one end, leaving only the large fireplace and chimney standing. The middle section—complete with what looked like Romanesque columns that obviously weren't original but a later addition—was covered in moss and lichen, with shrubs sprouting from the column and the balcony above. The forest, gradually reclaiming its space.

The left side of the house was the most complete. Even the windows seemed intact, though this place had obviously been in a ruinous state for a very long time.

"Is this it?" Lugh asked.

I wrinkled my nose. "Similar enough to be possible."

"I'm not sure I want to be scrambling around a rotting ruin on such a vague assurance."

I snorted. "Since when has that ever stopped you?"

He half smiled. "Shall we take the front entrance or go through the broken bit?"

"Well, we're looking for a cellar and then a cave, so where would the kitchen be located in a place like this?"

"In an original hall house, it'd be in the great hall, but given all the alterations this one has had, I'd have to guess the ruinous end."

"Is there any logic behind that supposition? Or is it really just a guess?"

He smiled again. "Have a look at the fireplace—it's large enough to roast boars in."

"I'll take your word for it."

We moved across the clearing and carefully climbed over the remnants of the building's front wall then stopped again. While the wall was mostly intact, the roof had completely collapsed and this entire section was a mess of stone, roof tiles, and rotting oak beams. It was hard to see the floor, let alone anything that might suggest a staircase down into a cellar.

"Buttery and pantry look to be along the rear wall," Lugh said, after a moment. "It's unlikely they'd have a cellar opening out in the main kitchen, so it's likely to be in one of them."

"Alcohol is your vice, so you can check the buttery."

He snorted but didn't otherwise deny the statement. "If the floor in the pantry is wood, tread carefully. I don't want to be calling an ambulance to you again."

"The song of the wood should tell me whether there's rot present or not."

"That's presuming the song hasn't long faded."

Which was possible, given we had no idea how long ago the roof had collapsed. It might take wood far longer to die from exposure to the elements than humans, but it could still die.

I picked my way through the mess of stone, tiles, and beams then paused at the pantry's entrance, my gaze sweeping the interior. With the roof gone, there was little in the way of shadows, but the increasing heaviness of the rain made it nearly impossible to see clearly past all the rubble that filled the room.

I took a cautious step forward, then bent and pressed my fingers to the old boards. Their song was silent. The only voice to be heard was that of the raindrops dancing across their ancient bones.

I frowned and studied the room again. There was no sign of rot and nothing to suggest the roof caving in had in any way affected the integrity of the floorboards. But given the amount of rubble in the room, there was a very real possibility that dangerous damage just wasn't visible.

I rose and cautiously made my way along the internal wall, watching every step, making sure there was no sponginess or movement that would suggest rot or imminent collapse.

I was halfway around the room when I saw the remnant of a lone newel, complete with a foot or so of handrail sticking out from a mound of debris. I couldn't see whether that debris blocked the stairs themselves, though, as the bulk of the collapsed roof seemed to lie between me and those stairs. If I wanted to check it out, I'd have to risk a shortcut across the center of the room.

"Lugh," I called out, "need the rope and harness in here."

Stone crunched and light danced across the shadows lurking near the doorway as he made his way toward me. "I take it you've found the cellar?"

"Yes, but I won't know if it's accessible until I examine the section more closely, and I don't want to cross the floor without being roped up, just in case."

"Okay, now I'm scared." His bulk filled the small doorway. "My sister is actually being *cautious.*"

I picked up a stone and lobbed it at him. He batted it away with a laugh, then pulled the rope and harness from his shoulders and threw the latter across to me. Once I'd put it on, he tossed me the rope.

"Secure?"

I tested the knot and then nodded. "Right," he said, bracing his body, "proceed carefully."

I drew in a deeper breath and took a cautious step forward. Thunder rumbled overhead, an ominous sound that somehow whispered of danger. I took another step. The boards trembled underfoot, but I couldn't tell if that meant they were about to collapse, thanks to the lack of song and the sheer intensity of the rain drumming into the pantry.

Another step ... the floorboard buckled, throwing my ankle to one side. I froze, my breath caught in my throat. Nothing happened. The board didn't shift any further, despite the fact the crack appeared to be growing.

Two more steps. No sound. No indication that there was any further weakness in the flooring. I risked a glance at the newel and saw the remnants of treads going down. "It's definitely a stairwell going down, but there's a whole lot of rubble covering it."

"Any chance of clearing it to get down into the cellar?"

I wrinkled my nose and scanned the rubbish. "There's some pretty massive beams involved. Let me get a little closer ..."

I took another step.

It was one too many.

CHAPTER
TEN

The floor disappeared, and I dropped like a stone into deeper darkness, only to stop abruptly as the rope snapped taut. I hung from the harness for several seconds, gulping down air as the rain poured into the newly opened space, running in a stream down my face and making vision more difficult.

"Beth?" Lugh shouted. "You okay?"

"Yes. Just a little winded from the sudden stop."

I shielded my eyes from the rain with a hand and looked around. The light coming in through the floor above puddled underneath me but wasn't providing much in the way of illumination for the rest of the area. Thank gods I had the headlamp.

The cellar was long, narrow, and ran a good way past the rear external wall. There were large flagstones on the floor, and wooden shelves that were in surprisingly good condition lining the walls either side of me, but the central space was empty. I looked at the staircase.

"The stairs are blocked by a wall of rubble," I said.

"There's no way we can move it—especially not with bare hands."

"Are you seeing anything from the vision?"

I looked around again, and briefly caught a red reflection. Not rubies. Eyes. I shuddered. "Yeah, fucking rats."

He laughed. "You're too damn big for rats to be bothering you, Beth."

"Says the man who wasn't woken up by several of the bastards running over him when he was a kid." It was an experience I would *never* get over, no matter how old I got.

"You want me to haul you out?"

I sucked in a deeper breath and watched the air condense around the exhalation. "No. Better lower me down. I'm here, so I might as well check the place out."

"Is it safe?"

"Unless you decide to clomp across the floor and bring down more of it, it should be."

He snorted and started lowering me. I hit the flagstones gently; despite the rain, dust puffed around my boots. The red gleams scurried away, and I definitely wasn't sad about that.

"How much rope have I got, Lugh? Because the cellar runs deep into the hillside, from the look of it."

"About twenty feet."

"I'll uncinch then."

"To repeat, be careful."

"I have my knives. They'll not only take care of any physical threat but warn me if there is any magical danger down here."

"They won't fucking warn you about another floor collapse."

"The floor is flagstones. I don't think it's in any danger of collapse."

"Famous last words. Open a line on your phone so I can hear what is going on."

"I might lose signal once I go deeper."

"Until you do, you can give me a running commentary of what you're seeing."

I detached myself from the rope and then rang Lugh and left the line open as I headed left to examine the section underneath the house while providing Lugh with a running commentary of everything I found. There were plenty of shelves here filled with all sorts of bits and pieces, from kitchen stuff to dust-covered wine bottles. There were also a couple of wine barrels and even some terracotta storage pots right at the very back that looked Roman to my admittedly untrained eye. Lugh did get a little excited about them, which suggested he'd have a team back here sooner rather than later.

I retraced my steps and moved into the other end of the long cellar. There was a slight incline once I moved beyond the house's perimeter and a noticeable drop in temperature. The flagstones gave way to compacted dirt, but the walls and arched ceiling remained brick. After a few minutes, the headlamp picked up what appeared to be the remnants of an ancient but beautiful stone wall. No human hand had been involved in building that wall—it was simply too seamless.

I described it to Lugh and then asked, "Is there any record of dark elf activity around here?"

"There're no known elf mounds, if that's what you mean," Lugh said. "Besides, we're closer to light elf territory than dark."

"I know, but given the often-violent history between the two, it wouldn't be surprising if they'd had a series of monitoring mounds buried around here."

I stepped over the lower end of the wall into a circular, high-domed stone room. Rats scattered as I appeared, and I somehow restrained the urge to jump right back over the wall, out of their way. Not that they were coming near me or anything, but still ...

I swept the light around and found the reason for the rats.

A body.

One that had been providing a meal for the rats for some time now.

I swallowed heavily to control the rising tide of horror, and then said, "Lugh, there's a body here."

"Well, fuck."

"Yeah." I ran the light up the stranger's length, spotting golden skin and hair, what was left of one ear, and a symmetrical hole in the center of his forehead. "He's a light elf, and he's been shot."

"Stay there," Lugh was saying, "I'm coming in."

"Don't. Not until you've called the IIT. In fact, it'd probably be best if you head down to the parking area and guide them up. There's a couple of offshoot trails and we don't want them getting lost."

There was a distinct pause, then, "Are you sure you'll be all right down there alone? I mean, there are rats and all."

One of them squeaked as he said that, as if to emphasize the point. I glared its way and said, "If any of the little bastards come within three feet of me, they'll find themselves meeting the pointy end of a knife."

Lugh laughed. "Fine. Just try not to disturb the area too much. The IIT frowns on that sort of thing."

"Personal experience speaking there?"

"No. I just watch a lot of murder mysteries."

I snorted. "In the hour or two of free time you have a week, you mean?"

"They run in the background when I'm working nights," he said. "I'll tie the rope off securely in case you feel the need to come up for fresh air."

He was presuming I had the physical strength to actually haul myself up said rope, and I thought he was being overly optimistic. "Thanks, brother."

He hung up. I swept the light around the room again, looking for some reason for the dead man to have come here. Light elves generally weren't comfortable underground, and, in some respects, I could understand that. While I wasn't in any way claustrophobic, I was nevertheless very aware of the still heaviness of the air and the cloying stench of death.

It was only when I turned the light to the ground that I noticed all the footprints. It very much looked like there'd been a constant flow of foot traffic through here at some point in time, and yet there was no indication as to why ... unless, of course, the reason had been concealed.

I tracked the lines of dusty footprints to the rear wall but couldn't pick up anything untoward from this distance. I hesitated, then carefully walked around the perimeter, keeping as close to the wall as possible to ensure I didn't disturb the prints and any evidence the IIT might be able to glean from them.

It quickly became evident there once *had* been an exit point here at the back of the room—one of the footprints had been cut in half by the now solid stone wall. And the only people who could do that sort of thing were dark elves.

But what were they concealing, and why?

We really wouldn't know until the dead man had been

identified. I half turned but caught the glint of something metallic in the dirt and bent to examine it.

It looked for all the world like a silver chain.

I hesitated, knowing I shouldn't in any way disturb possible evidence, and yet unable to ignore either curiosity or the odd certainty that I needed to see whatever the chain was connected to. I took a photo of its location then carefully snagged the end on one finger and tugged on it lightly.

The chain resisted moving, making me fear it was lodged under the wall. I applied a fraction more strength, wary of breaking it and, after a few tense seconds, it slipped free.

Revealing what looked to be a silver coin so worn by time that its surface was close to smooth.

Disbelief and grief hit so hard and fast that my legs gave way and I landed on my butt.

I knew this coin.

It had once borne the image of Egeria, a goddess of wisdom and good fortune, and it had been handed down through the generations of my family for longer than anyone could remember.

And it had been around my mother's neck the day she'd disappeared.

A sob escaped, but I bit down on my lip to contain the rest of them; if I let my grief go now, I might not be able to stop it. And it *had* to be stopped, at least for the moment, because this was the first clue any of us had found as to where Mom had been the day she'd disappeared. I couldn't waste time or energy crying when there were questions to be answered.

Questions like what had she been doing here and how was she connected to the light elf's murder?

I raised my gaze to the wall. Other than the half cut-off

footprint, there was nothing to indicate there'd ever been an entrance here. The answers, if indeed there were answers to be found here, were likely to be found in whatever lay beyond this wall.

I curled the chain and coin in my hand and closed my fingers around them. Energy stirred, and emotions rose. They weren't mine, but rather distant, fragmented ghosts that lingered on the coin, reflecting the last moments of the woman who'd worn it. Ghosts that echoed with fear, regret, and anger.

Someone had betrayed her.

Someone she'd trusted.

I swallowed heavily and tucked the chain and coin into my coat pocket. There was no way known I was going to hand it over to the IIT. No fucking way at all. Aside from the fact it'd disappear into their archives never to be seen again, I wasn't about to implicate my family in the light elf's murder. The council already suspected Lugh. I couldn't let them smear Mom's name—especially not if those ghosts were right and Mom had been betrayed.

And *that* meant I'd have to destroy some evidence.

I took a deep breath that didn't in any way ease the guilt of what I was about to do, then rose and set about carefully erasing the prints, starting at the wall and working ten feet back. Hopefully, the cloud of dust would have settled by the time the IIT got here, and they wouldn't suspect the destruction was deliberate.

I then proceeded to leave a trail of my own, following the line of the wall around to the body and then retracing my steps all the way back to the half wall. The center prints I left intact; hopefully, they'd believe that they were the result of some sort of fight that had ended with the light elf's murder rather than the foot traffic from a now closed tunnel.

I perched on the half wall and tucked my feet up, keeping them well out of the way of the still roaming rats. The bastards did not, in any way, seem intimidated by my presence. But then, they hadn't been when I was younger, either.

I pulled out my phone again and, until the battery died, scrolled through various social media pages to take my mind off the charm, the body, and the knowledge that I could land myself in very deep trouble if anyone discovered what I had done.

Thankfully, I wasn't left alone with my thoughts and my grief for too long before the bright spots of light appeared down the far end of the tunnel. "That you, Lugh?"

"Yeah. The IIT team is here with me."

They quickly approached, the various flashlights providing enough light for me to see the men with Lugh. Three of the four were strangers; the fourth was Mathi's father, Ruadhán.

He was, in many respects, simply an older version of Mathi and just as good-looking, though age lines creased his forehead and he had what Mom used to call frown furrows near his mouth. His eyes also lacked the cool amusement so often evident in the blue of Mathi's gaze; in fact, Ruadhán was rumored to not have cracked a smile in nearly a century—something his son had refused to confirm or deny.

The question was, though, what the hell was he doing here? While Sgott was very much a hands-on investigator, Ruadhán was the direct opposite. He oversaw the department from the lofty heights of his office and rarely stepped directly into the midst of any investigation.

Why do so now?

It couldn't be for any *good* reason, that was for sure.

"Bethany," he said, in that icily distant way highborn elder statesmen like him had, "you seem to be at the center of all things right now."

"Trust me, I'd rather *not* be at the center of this thing." There was just the slightest edge in my otherwise even voice, and I wasn't sure if it was caused by annoyance or by anxiety.

"Then why *are* you here?"

I shrugged. "A vague vision. A body wasn't what I was expecting to find."

Lugh stopped beside me and lightly placed a hand on my shoulder. It was a warning, and it made me wonder what had been said before they'd arrived here.

Ruadhán motioned his people to proceed, but his attention was on me. "Then what were you expecting to find?"

As I hesitated, Lugh said, "She was helping me locate a possible Roman site. There've been recent reports of finds up this way, and given the council has ordered the suspension of my search for the Claws, I decided to check it out."

Ruadhán raised an eyebrow, his expression skeptical. That skepticism scared me. I did not need him deciding to fully interrogate me; not until I'd had a chance to see what lay beyond that damn wall, anyway.

"There are no forts recorded in this area," Ruadhán said. "Indeed, it is the least likely place for any sort of Roman dwelling to be found."

"And yet there are a number of amphorae at the other end of this cellar, along with other Roman-looking relics," Lugh said

Ruadhán acknowledged that comment with a soft "Ah"

and returned his attention to me. "Does that mean the second sight you claimed not to have has now surfaced?"

"In a fragmented, half-assed manner, yes." I shrugged. "According to my aunt, it sometimes takes the women of our family a century or so before they fall into their true power."

I had no idea if that was true, but I could vaguely remember Gran saying something along those lines, and it's not like they'd bother contacting Riayn to confirm the statement.

Or at least, I hope they wouldn't.

His gaze held mine for a heartbeat or two and then moved away. "I owe you gratitude for saving my son's life."

Which wasn't in any way an *actual* thank-you, I noted a little bitterly. "I could hardly do anything else."

His gaze returned to mine, his expression giving little away. "You owed him nothing."

"I'm not sure how it works in your world, but in mine, friends do not let friends die."

It was said with a little more anger than was wise, and just for a moment, I thought I saw the glint of speculation in his eyes. But it was gone as quickly as it had appeared and might have been nothing more than a trick of the light.

"Have you disturbed the body in any way?"

The bitterness grew brighter. Now that the evil necessity of having to thank the pixie he'd always disliked was out of the way, it was back to business. "No, but I did walk around the perimeter."

"Why did you do that?"

"Because I wanted to see if there was anything else here other than the body."

"Did you find anything else?"

"Other than a few footprints in the middle of the room,

no. But then, it's not like either relic hunting or forensics are my specialties."

"Some would say your lack of specialties *is* your specialty." His gaze was cold and hard. "Ifan will take your statement and then you both may go. If we need any further information, we will be in contact."

I nodded, swung my legs over the wall, and followed Lugh and the older-looking Ifan back down the cellar.

When we were within sight of the hole I'd created when the floor had given way, he stopped and recorded my statement, asking for clarification on several points before telling us we could now leave.

"You're not going to take Lugh's statement?" I asked, surprised.

"Did he go down the tunnel?"

"No, but—"

"Then there is no need, as what he's already told us is backed by the statement you just made. But if we have any questions for either of you, we'll be in contact."

Lugh pressed his hand against my back, silently urging me to move on. I nodded at Ifan and strode on toward the hole. The rain still pelted through, making the old flagstones shine in the dim light, and the deep heart of the storm I'd sensed earlier charged the air, making the hairs at the back of my neck stand on end. It would hit before we reached the car, of that I was certain.

Lugh climbed the rope, then hauled me up. Another IIT officer stood at the pantry door, but she stepped aside with a curt nod as we approached. The weight of her stare as we left the building made my shoulder blades itch.

Neither Lugh nor I said anything. We just got out of the clearing and away from the IIT as fast as we could. The storm unleashed halfway down the hill, and though the forest gave us some protection, the rain was so fierce, the track quickly became treacherous, forcing us to slow right down.

I sighed in relief when we finally reached the car. After shedding my coat and the harness, I jumped inside, boosted the heater, and stuck my sodden feet under the vent in a vague attempt to dry them out.

As Lugh reversed out of the parking area, I said, in an effort to avoid telling him about the coin for as long as possible, "What did Ruadhán say to you?"

"He all but accused me of Nialle's murder."

"*What*? Why the fuck would he think that?"

"I'm presuming he's heard something from the Eldritch."

"If the Eldritch suspected you, you'd be hauled in for questioning. Ruadhán is probably just being a bastard."

"Or perhaps he's just doing his job. It's possible that the council—who have demanded the suspension of all current research projects at the request of the Eldritch—have asked him to mount a secondary investigation into Nialle's murder and any possible links it might have to either the Claws or the hoard."

It would certainly explain his sudden appearance underground. And why Lugh had made the amphorae comment. "If that's true, it would suggest they don't trust their own investigators."

"And with good reason if they *have* been infiltrated."

"But why suspend *all* projects?"

He shrugged. "Perhaps they feel it is safer given they have no idea, even after six months, who stole the hoard or why."

"And did this order come through before or after the moonstone was stolen?"

He glanced at me, a somewhat wan smile tugging at his lips. "Guess."

After, obviously. "To the suspicious type, that would suggest someone on the council was involved in the theft and needs time to uncover the crown."

"My thoughts exactly."

"Which is why we're now moving on to check the next two locations rather than going home?"

"Those bastards are *not* going to get the crown. Not if I have any damn say in it." There was a grimly determined note in his voice. "But things could get ugly from here on in. Are you sure—"

"Things are already ugly, Lugh. You're not leaving me out of this search. You can't afford to; not now."

"Yes, but—"

"I'm armed. You're not."

He grinned. "I'm over six foot six. You're not."

"Even the mightiest of trees can be felled by a small axe, Lugh."

He puffed out a breath; it was a sound of frustration. He knew I was right. "Fine—but we keep each other in the loop movement wise from now on in. No matter what we're doing." He glanced at me. "All right?"

I nodded. It made sense, given we had no real idea who or what exactly we were up against.

"And now it's your turn," he said, his voice taking on that grim note again, "what did you find that upset you so much?"

I glanced at him sharply. "How do you know I found something?"

"You're my sister. I can read you like a book."

"I'm damn glad Ruadhán couldn't. That might have gotten awkward." Though if I wasn't concealing my emotions as well as I thought, it might well explain his skepticism. "There's no easy way to say this—"

"Beth, just spit it out."

"I found Egeria's coin."

The car briefly swerved onto the wrong side of the road before he regained control. His voice was tight as he said, "Mom's?"

"Yes."

"You're sure?"

"Egeria's coin does not fall easily, Lugh. It was deliberately dropped."

"If she was in that fucking room, where is she now?" Grief etched into his face, but there was deep anger in his voice.

"I suspect in the tunnel that's behind the wall."

He took a long, shuddering breath in an obvious attempt to control his emotions, but the grief remained visible. "We have to go back there. Tonight."

"Yes." I scrubbed a hand across my eyes in a vague effort to stop the sting of threatening tears. I really couldn't cry; not until I knew for sure my suspicions were right. "And we can't go alone. Sgott will have to be with us."

"We'll also need the services of a dark elf." Lugh glanced at me. "How much do you trust Lord Lùtair?"

"His sister was attacked the same night you were, and a cousin is missing. He's got as many reasons as us to uncover what the hell is going on."

"Can you contact him, then?"

I half smiled. "I can contact him once the phone is recharged, but whether he'll answer is another matter entirely. He hasn't so far."

"Seriously? Your wiles are obviously slipping, little sister."

"They're just out of practice when it comes to dating after being with Mathi for so long."

He smiled. "Then perhaps it'd be better if Sgott contacts him."

"Might be easier—that way, if he *is* avoiding me, he can avoid an awkward refusal and send someone else to help us out."

"The man can hardly contact you if your phone is dead. Why do women always think the worst even when it's not our fault?"

I grinned. "Because ninety percent of the time it is."

He laughed, though the grief remained, a deep blanket of sorrow that seemed to be echoed in the sudden intensity of the storm. "We won't be able to head back until late—the IIT boys are likely to be there for a while."

"Do you think they'll place a guard there?"

"No idea, but Sgott will be able to tell us." He pointed to the McDonald's up ahead. "A cup of tea to warm you up?"

"And some fries—I'm starving."

We went through the drive-through and, once we'd collected our order, shared the chips as we continued. As it turned out, neither of the other two buildings matched the one I'd seen in the vision, so we headed home.

Lugh stopped the car at the entrance to the rear lane. I grabbed my coat and tugged it on. "Shall we say one? We close at ten during the winter months, so that'd give me plenty of time to do the tills, then grab a shower and a late-night snack."

Lugh nodded. "I'll contact Sgott."

"Use his private number. Don't contact him through the IIT, just in case."

"I hardly think anyone will be eavesdropping on his

calls—and if they are, they're likely to also be monitoring his personal line."

"Yes, but if there are spies in the IIT, it'd be easier for them to do the former than the latter without raising suspicions." Especially given Sgott was aware of the possibility.

"Mom really did instill a fine sense of distrust in you, didn't she?"

"Mom was betrayed by someone she trusted, Lugh."

Grief flared in his eyes again, a river so strong it briefly felt like I was drowning. "Egeria told you that?"

"Wisps of her last moments still clung to the coin."

"Ah, fuck ... not Sgott? Please don't say it was Sgott."

"I wouldn't be asking you to contact him if I thought it was."

"You're sure?"

I nodded. "They were partners for over sixty years, Lugh. If he'd betrayed her, the grief on the coin would have been fierce and black, even after all these months."

He swallowed heavily but looked relieved. "You saw nothing else that would give us a clue as to who *had* betrayed her?"

"No."

"Annoying."

"Yes."

He placed his hand over mine and squeezed lightly. It was a small gesture but said so much. "I'll see you at one."

I nodded, climbed out, and ran for the back door. Once I'd plugged in my phone to recharge, I grabbed a shower, changed into my work outfit, and then headed back down to help the team out, manning the bar while Ingrid and the two waiters—Jonnie and Zoe—ran food and drinks. We were surprisingly busy given the horrendous nature of the storm that still raged outside, and the hours slipped past quickly.

It was nearing closing time when Ingrid—a short, but fierce-looking pixie with curly green hair and deep brown eyes—leaned on the lower section of the bar and said, "A rather delicious-looking man just ordered a double shot of Laphroaig. He also asked if the owner could deliver it. Said something about needing to see the shorts in their natural environment. You want me to oust him?"

Cynwrig. It had to be. A silly grin touched my lips, and I quickly scanned the room. Though the crowd had started to thin out, I couldn't see him, which meant he was probably in one of the booths on the other side of the stairs that ran down to the ground floor. "No, he's a friend. You able to jump behind the bar and look after things until closing?"

"Sure. He's in booth five."

Which was one of the smaller two-person booths over near the door and invisible from the bar. I poured his drink and a single shot for myself, then placed them both on a tray along with a bowl of nuts and walked over.

He was sitting in the booth with his back to me, but nevertheless seemed to sense my approach, because he turned. His dark gaze swept me and came up delighted. "I can see why this place gets so crowded. That outfit reveals a surprising amount of your lush body while providing the illusion of completely covering you."

I placed the drinks and the nuts onto the table, slid into the booth opposite him, and tucked the tray beside the table leg, out of the way. "You didn't notice this the night I rescued you?"

"I was under the influence of a drug and really wasn't certain if I was imagining it." A smile tugged at his luscious lips. "Or you, to be honest. I admit to being very relieved you were every bit as gorgeous as I'd remembered when you appeared at that council meeting."

I couldn't help the wry smile. "And if I hadn't been?"

He shrugged. "With an attraction *this* fierce, it really wouldn't have mattered."

"Right answer."

"Truthful answer." He picked up his glass and clinked it lightly against mine. "Here's to many more nights of heated attraction."

I raised an eyebrow. "And is that why you're here early? I take it Sgott did contact you?"

"He did, but I came here with absolutely no expectations. I really just needed to see you."

Need was such a lovely word when used that way. "If desire is so fierce, what happened last night?"

His smoky eyes glimmered, though it was hard to say whether it was amusement or frustration. "Mathi being kidnapped happened."

My eyebrows rose. "What has that got to do with anything?"

"The meeting was ongoing when Mathi left. Ten minutes later, the IIT crashed the room, and we were all placed into lockdown, forbidden to contact anyone."

"Forbidden by who?"

"The IIT, of course."

Meaning Sgott had reacted *very* swiftly to protect the rest of the council, even if he hadn't known much more than the fact Mathi had been snatched. "How on earth could they prevent anyone calling or messaging out? They haven't that sort of power over the council, do they?"

"When it comes to security, yes, they do, but the council chambers are actually an electronic null zone—it stops the threat of listening devices being deployed and conversations being recorded."

"Meaning you didn't get my message until it was all over?"

"Indeed, and you subsequently failed to answer my call. I was concerned enough to contact Sgott and ensure you were safe."

A statement that made me exceedingly pleased. "My phone died, and I left it upstairs on the charger."

"Ah, that explains it." He took a drink. "What still puzzles me, however, is why on earth would anyone want to kidnap Mathi?"

"Because they wanted me, and I think he was probably the easiest bait to catch and use."

"Makes sense. Your brother certainly wouldn't be such an easy target. Not without the use of drugs, and they've already proven unreliable."

I nodded. "It's also possible the people who took him thought we were still in a relationship."

He took a drink. "Your calm demeanor suggests he's okay."

"He is. But if the meeting ran until after one, why was he leaving the council meeting at eleven?"

Cynwrig shrugged. "He received a note, gave his apologies, and left in a hurry."

"A handwritten note?"

Cynwrig nodded. "None of us saw its contents, of course."

It was interesting that Mathi didn't mention the note when I'd been questioning him—although maybe he didn't see the necessity. Not to me, anyway.

"Is his kidnap the reason for this late-night meeting?" Cynwrig asked.

"Not at all."

He studied me for a second. "And you're not intending to illuminate the matter until later, when Sgott gets here?"

"Saves me repeating myself."

"Does it involve the Claws?"

"No." I paused and wrinkled my nose. "Is this a good time to mention that the moonstone has been stolen?"

He smiled. "Sgott did mention it when I was talking to him."

"Ah, good." I took a drink. "Why did the council order Lugh to stop looking for the Claws?"

"It was a motion Hendrik Fernsbury brought to the council at the request of the Eldritch. They have evidence that another party is after the Claws, and your brother's continued investigations are muddying the waters."

Which basically confirmed what Lugh had been told. "Did they say what the evidence was? Or why they went to the council with the request rather than speak to Lugh directly?"

"The exact question I asked. They believed the order would hold more weight coming from the council. I rather suspect they are wrong."

And he would be right. I smiled. "Did they say who the other party was?"

"No. But that's no surprise—the Eldritch always play their cards close to their chests."

Something in the way he said that had my instincts prickling. "But you have your suspicions?"

Amusement ran through his expression. "Your ability to see what few others do will keep me on my toes for many months to come."

"And hopefully *coming* would be a prominent feature of those months."

His laugh was a low, sexy sound that had anticipation and delight dancing through me. "That definitely is the plan."

"Good." I sipped the whisky, but the fiery liquid paled in comparison to the heat that now burned deep inside. "Are you going to tell me anything about the suspect?"

"All we actually have is a name—Looisearch."

"That's a rather odd name, isn't it?"

"It's certainly far from common, if our searches so far are anything to go by."

"Who gave you the name?"

He grimaced. "An underground contact who has subsequently disappeared."

"Ah."

"Yes. We're attempting to track his movements in the days before he contacted us. As you can imagine, it is difficult."

No doubt, given the whole black market worked on the premise of being untraceable. "How would the Eldritch have gotten his name? They wouldn't have the same depth of contacts you have."

"There is no certainty that our suspicions match theirs. As I said, they play their cards close to their chests."

"And you have no contacts within the Eldritch? Color me surprised."

He laughed again. It was another of those low, warm sounds that had heads turning our way and my hormones bouncing about in hectic anticipation. "The Eldritch are the closest thing to incorruptible as you're ever likely to get in this day and age."

A smile tugged at my lips. "Which means you *have* tried."

"Multiple times over the centuries. We've succeeded

once, and even then, it was a retired officer, not serving."

"Huh." I glanced toward the bar as a bell chimed. It was the ten minutes to closing warning. I drank the rest of my whisky and then pushed to my feet. "I better go help close. Do you want to go upstairs and wait?"

"Will I be in the way if I stay here and enjoy the scenery?"

I smiled, leaned across the table, and kissed him. He tasted of whisky and desire, and all I wanted to do was race him upstairs and have my wicked way with him. But I had a business to look after—one that would hopefully be around for a long time *after* he'd left. The tavern had to be my priority, even if my hormones were a screaming mess of disagreement.

It took just over an hour to sort the till and clean and sanitize everything. By that time, the kitchen staff had left and I was able to lock everything up.

"Would you like another drink?" I said as I came back up from the ground floor.

He smiled and raised his glass. There was still half a shot in it. "I was too busy enjoying the delightful scenery."

Something I'd been well aware of. "I need to grab a shower—don't suppose you'd like to join me, would you?"

"Is there room in your shower for two?" he asked in a lazily amused way that somehow suggested he'd make it work even if there wasn't. "They tend to be either too small or an awkward, over-the-bath style in places as old as this."

"I have a brother over six foot tall. There is a ton of room in the shower, trust me."

"Then I accept your invitation with great pleasure."

"I'm certainly hoping great pleasure ensues."

"I will do my utmost to ensure that it does."

"Excellent. This way then."

I led him up the stairs to my living quarters then, after grabbing fresh towels, into the bathroom. Mom had doubled its size by stealing space from the kitchen area, which was why we now only had a kitchenette up here. As she'd rightly said, we had proper cooking facilities downstairs, so really didn't need anything more than a microwave and a cooktop up here. The council hadn't objected to the change, but only because the wall between the old bathroom and the kitchen was a much later addition rather than original.

The shower—while not as large as the one in Cynwrig's apartment—was certainly big enough for two, and the showerhead one of those gigantic ceiling-mounted rainwater things. There was also a lovely old claw-foot bath— Mom had preferred them—and a bathroom cabinet large enough to hold all Mom's stuff as well as mine.

It *still* held her stuff. Getting rid of it would have been an admission that she wasn't coming back, and I just couldn't do it.

I might have to, after tonight.

I blinked back the threat of tears, dropped the towels on the edge of the bath, then turned and said, "Shall we undress?"

"Each other?"

"That could take too much valuable time, given Sgott or my brother may well turn up early."

Amusement glittered in his eyes, though it was almost lost to the fierce heat of desire. "The bathroom is equipped with a door. We can close it."

"Point." I reached past him to close the door. "But I'd still rather get naked fast and then proceed at a more leisurely pace from there."

"Also a good point."

Once we'd both stripped off, I leaned into the shower and turned on the taps. When the water was hot enough, I caught his hand and tugged him after me. He slid an arm around my waist and pulled me closer. His body was warm and hard, his erection fierce against my belly. My pulse rate was through the roof, and the low-down ache was fierce. All I wanted to do was claim this man, right here and now, but I resisted the urge, instead wrapping a hand around his neck to pull his lips down onto mine. For the longest time, we kissed under the deluge of water. The steam rising from its heat had nothing on the inner steam the kiss and his closeness caused.

Eventually he drew back, grabbed the soap, and began to wash me. It was an exquisite, erotic torture that left me squirming with desire and wanting. When I could stand it no more, I took the soap from him and repeated the process for him. His beautiful body gleamed like black marble, the water reverently caressing every powerful inch. I washed every glorious bit of him until he quivered as fiercely as I had.

With a low rumble that sounded oddly desperate, he slid his hands down my back to my butt and lifted me. I wrapped my legs around his waist and sheathed him slowly, but so very deeply, inside. For several heartbeats neither of us moved. We simply stared into each other's eyes. I wasn't sure what he saw in mine, but beyond the desire so very evident in the velvety, smoky depths of his lay determination. This man was not about to let this go—*me* go—anytime soon.

And that was damn fine by me.

Then I pushed thought aside, kissed him fiercely, and got down to the business of finishing what I'd started with this magnificent man.

As I'd suspected, both Lugh and Sgott arrived early. We didn't hang around; every minute we wasted put us that much further away from uncovering the truth.

In this case, quite literally.

Once we were in Sgott's car and heading back to the hall house, I told the two of them about the vision, our discovery of the body, Egeria's coin, and, for Cynwrig's sake, what that implied.

For several minutes, no one spoke. Cynwrig placed a hand on my thigh, a silent gesture of comfort that I appreciated, but my gaze was on Sgott. His shoulders shook but no tears trickled silently down the side of his face that I could see. I knew they wouldn't; not yet. Not until he knew for sure she lay beyond that wall.

"Have you received any updates from Ruadhán?" Lugh asked quietly.

"He knows better than to withhold information from me on any event that concerns you two." Sgott's voice was perhaps a little gruffer than normal, but otherwise free of the grief that lay in waiting. "There's no guard, but he has placed a request with the guild for the services of a rock mason."

A rock mason being the official term for a dark elf who specialized in the construction or destruction of stone walls. While most Myrkálfar could manipulate the earth or the things that came from the earth to some degree, it took time and training to become proficient enough to manipulate each particular element with any degree of precision. If Ruadhán had requested a rock mason, he obviously suspected there was more to those footprints.

But was that any real surprise? He was the head of the

IIT—I'd been fooling myself to think that he would have been tricked by my stupid cover-up attempt.

"Has the request been approved?" Lugh asked.

"Yes," Cynwrig said, before Sgott could. "Kendra Dálaigh is booked to meet them at 8:00 AM in the parking area. Had I known the reason for the request, I could have delayed—"

"It matters not," Sgott cut in. "We will have our answers before they ever arrive."

I glanced at Cynwrig. "I take it this means you *can* manipulate rock?"

His gaze met mine, eyes obsidian in the darkness. "Amongst other things."

I raised my eyebrows. "Like what?"

"You're not likely to get the answer to *that* question with me in the car, lassie," Sgott said, briefly sounding more like his usual self. "But given his drunken younger brother disappeared from a cell a few months ago, I would suggest metal manipulation is one of his family's skills."

A smile tugged at Cynwrig's lips. "He *was* returned and placed in a more suitable cell."

"Is there something more suitable for someone who can manipulate stone and metal?" I asked, curiously.

"One cloaked in oak," Sgott said. "No good for light elves, shifters, or you pixies, of course, but perfectly suitable for all others—even humans."

As we got closer to our destination, silence fell, but the tension ramped up, becoming so fierce as we reached the parking area that the air crackled.

I climbed out and hastily zipped up my coat. The storm that had raged for most of the night had finally eased, but it remained bitter. Lugh handed us all a headlamp, then led the way. The path was even more treacherous now than it had been earlier. I took my place in line and cautiously watched my footing, but even so, slipped occasionally. Cynwrig, who was last and seemingly unworried by the conditions, always caught and steadied me.

It took us nearly thirty minutes to reach the clearing. In the gloom of the night, the old house looked forlorn; water still ran from the remains of the guttering and trickled from the corners of the windows, making it appear as if the building were crying.

I suspected I might be joining it sooner rather than later.

Once we were in the cellar—using the pulley system Ruadhán's men had obviously set up to make things easier —I led the way down to the mound room.

"I found the coin just here," I said, stepping closer and pointing to the spot.

Cynwrig swept his fingers across the wall, starting at the spot where I'd found Egeria and gradually moving up and around. He didn't say anything, but his gaze had narrowed, and his face was the picture of concentration.

After a moment, he nodded and stepped back. "There *is* a tunnel behind this wall. It has partially collapsed, but I believe I can get us in there."

"Is there any weight other than stone resting on the earth?" Sgott asked quietly.

My breath caught in my throat. A body, he meant.

Cynwrig glanced at me and then said, "There're two, but more than that, I cannot say."

Sgott motioned Cynwrig to continue, and then moved back and wrapped an arm around my shoulders. I leaned against him, finding comfort in his presence, even if I knew he was hurting just as much as either Lugh or me.

Cynwrig pressed both hands against the wall and

closed his eyes. For several seconds, nothing happened. Then a vibration began to run through the earth and up through the walls around us. Dust sprinkled down from the ceiling, and I glanced up worriedly. There was no sign of damage to the dome, but a fissure had appeared on the wall in front of Cynwrig. It moved, slowly at first, and then with greater speed, in a wide arc until an arch had formed. With a grunt of effort, Cynwrig pushed his weight against the center point of that fissured outline. With a deep, grinding scrape, the stone inched inward. Cynwrig took one step, and then two, pushing the slab past the depth of the wall until there was a wide enough gap either side for both Sgott and Lugh to get through.

Then he stopped and stepped back. Sweat dotted his forehead, and his cheeks were hollow. Manipulation of the living—be it earth, trees, or even humanity—on this sort of scale always came at a cost. For most of us, that cost was physical depletion.

"Whoever sealed this tunnel wanted to make damn sure it couldn't be opened in a hurry," Cynwrig said, his normally velvety voice taking on a rasp that spoke of weariness. "It wasn't just fused but anchored at the top and the sides by metal bolts. Kendra would not have been able to break the seal."

Sgott shone his light into the gap. The metal bolts were as thick as my fist. "How many of your people have the capacity to do something like that?"

"My entire family tree, but this doesn't have the feel of our work. The power that lingers feels foreign."

"As in, not from the UK?" I asked, surprised.

"No, simply not from this county." He took a deeper breath that seemed to flush some of the gauntness from his cheeks. "Follow me."

He led us around the slab and into a tunnel that felt still and old. The scent of decay hung on the air, filling every breath and coating my throat. All I wanted to do was run in the opposite direction.

But we'd been searching for Mom for six months now, and the answer was finally within reach.

Even if it was one I didn't want to accept.

The tunnel itself was a wide, domed affair, its walls as smooth as glass, the precision of which suggested this was indeed one of the old elf mound tunnels. Dirt puffed around my ankles with every step, but the heaviness of the air seemed to swallow all sound. I shivered, though I wasn't sure if it was fear of this place or of what lay ahead.

The tunnel began to curve. The walls lost some of their smoothness, and a myriad of cracks shot through the top of the dome. Cynwrig didn't appear worried about them, but they scared the hell out of me. It wouldn't take much to bring the entire roof down.

But maybe they were here because someone *had* brought it down.

The tunnel continued to sweep around, and the ground became a maze of rocks and loose chunks of soil. The stench of decay became stronger, and the churning in my stomach fierce. Breathing through my mouth wasn't helping, but I suspected nothing would. Not now.

The rubble increased to the point where it forced us to slow, and the lights soon picked out the collapse point. It didn't block the whole tunnel—there was a good three-foot gap at the top that could be crawled through—but it nevertheless looked pretty damn solid. Nothing could have survived under that. Not for more than a heartbeat.

"This collapse isn't a natural event," Cynwrig said.

"Did the same hand do this as sealed the tunnel?" Sgott

asked sharply.

His words echoed, and the darkness seemed to stir. My knives sparked to life, and I lunged forward, grabbing his arm to stop him going any further.

"There's magic here." I stepped up beside them both and drew one of my knives. Lightning flickered down her blade, fierce and bright in the shadows. "Black magic."

"Can you defuse it?" Sgott asked.

"I don't know." I drew my other knife and carefully stepped forward. The jagged veins of purplish light grew fiercer, longer, once again forming a mesh-like shield in front of me.

"Fuck, I never knew your knives could do *that*," Lugh said.

"It's not something I can control." My voice was somewhat absent, my gaze on the shadows to the left of the rockfall. Whatever it was I sensed—whatever the knives were reacting to—had its source there. "It just seems to happen when I need it."

"Which would suggest there's a subliminal connection to the knives," Cynwrig said.

"That's possible," Lugh said. "The knives have only ever responded to the females of our line."

The wrongness I'd been sensing surged abruptly and I stopped, my gaze searching the ground. There was nothing untoward, and yet the certainty that something was very wrong here grew. I hesitated and edged forward one more step.

That's when I saw it.

The ring.

On a hand.

A *woman's* hand.

Mom's hand.

CHAPTER
ELEVEN

A sob escaped, and I instinctively stepped back before I could stop myself.

"Beth?" Sgott said, voice sharp. "What's wrong?"

"Nothing. Everything." I took a deep breath and released it. It was a long, quivering sound of pain. "I found her. She's here."

"What—?"

I felt more than saw his approach and swung around, one knife held up in warning. "Don't come any closer. She's bound by dark magic, and I have no idea what its intent is."

It might not have been aimed at us, but there was no way to be certain of that. The spell appeared to be attached to the ring on her finger—a ring I'd never seen before, one that reeked with age as much as dark magic. It could be the reason she'd come here, but it might also have nothing to do with it.

"Are you sure it's her?" Lugh asked softly.

I glanced at him. In the frost green depths, I saw both acceptance and denial. I understood both. "Yes. She's still wearing the Minions Band-Aid I placed over the cut on her finger the day she left us."

"Ah. Damn." He looked away, but not before I'd seen the sheen of tears. I wished I could cry with him, but I couldn't give in to grief just yet. I had to nullify the spell first.

My gaze returned briefly to Sgott, but there was little to see in his expression or his eyes. He was controlling himself very tightly, and probably would continue to do so until the forensics were done and there was absolutely no doubt.

I took a shuddering deep breath and returned my attention to the ring. The knives' jagged net of light continued to hiss and spit, which very much suggested that whatever magic lay on that ring was indeed aimed at intruders even if it was also the reason for Mom's demise.

I cautiously stepped closer. The caress of darkness increased, and dust fell around me, a light rain that boded no good.

"Stop," Cynwrig said sharply. "Magic just tore at the fabric of the roof above your head."

I glanced up. Some of the cracks appeared wider than they had been only a moment ago. "Can you prevent it from collapsing? I need to get closer to nullify the spell."

"I can try." He stepped sideways and pressed a hand against the wall. After a moment, he nodded and said, "Go, but don't be too long. The magic is a cancer that eats at the stone. I can slow its effects by bolstering the stone and earth, but I can't erase it."

I dropped to my knees in front of Mom's hand. The ground now trembled and the fall of dust from the roof increased. Light had sparked to life deep in the black heart of the stone, and I knew the spell had fully awoken. As the shuddering increased, I raised the knife in my right hand high and then plunged its sharp point deep into the heart of the stone. The blade sliced through the stone as easily as butter and continued on through flesh, bone, and the silver band that encircled both, before burying itself deep into the earth.

The dark light died, and the earth's shuddering stopped.

Cynwrig sucked in a deep breath and then said, "Those knives of yours are fucking powerful."

"Yes." I pushed a little unsteadily to my feet. He caught me, his grip gentle and yet firm. I sheathed my knives and then motioned to Mom's hand. "Can you ... will you ...?"

"Yes," he said softly.

He took my place and pressed his palms into the dusty soil. But as the air began to vibrate with the force of his power and the earth and stone slowly rolled back to reveal Mom's broken arm, I realized I couldn't be here. I didn't want to see her like this. Didn't want my last memory of her to be that of a decaying corpse.

A sob escaped. I pressed a hand to my mouth then turned and ran back up the tunnel, weaving my way through the maze of rubble and tripping more than once. I didn't stop until I reached the middle of that domed room —no doubt destroying a multitude of footprints in the process and really not giving a damn. I hugged my arms around my body, still fighting the grief though I wasn't sure why.

I wasn't alone for long.

Lugh appeared, his face grief ravaged. He didn't say anything; he simply tugged me into his big warm body and hugged me tightly, his tears dropping silently onto the top of my head. I finally dropped all my restraints and sobbed into his chest.

I wasn't sure how long we stood there. Long enough to

cry myself out. Long enough that the rats were once again getting braver and drawing closer. Long enough for the chill in the air to creep into my bones and make them ache.

Light eventually touched the edge of the door slab; a few heartbeats later, Sgott appeared. He remained the picture of stoic restraint, but his eyes shone with restrained tears.

"She's been shot." His voice was a ragged whisper. "She wasn't crushed and left to die, which is the best we could have asked for in this situation."

Another sob escaped my lips. I broke away from Lugh and ran into Sgott's arms, hugging him as fiercely as my brother had me.

"I'm sorry," I whispered. "I wish ..."

"As do I, lass," he said gruffly. "As do I."

He kissed the top of my head and then gently but firmly pushed me back. "Lord Lùtair is staying to help us uncover the bodies, but you two should go home. There's nothing more you can do here."

"We all came in the one car, remember?" Lugh said. "And to be honest, I'd rather not. I just ..."

Need to see this through. Need to make sure there is family present when she's finally taken from this place.

He didn't say any of that, but that's what he meant. I wished I could stay here with him. Wished I had that strength.

But I just didn't.

Mom would have understood. I hadn't been able to stay with her and Lugh while they'd waited for the coroner in Gran's room when she'd died peacefully in her sleep, either.

Sgott nodded and glanced at his watch. "I'll accompany you to the car then, Beth. The team I called in should be here by now."

"You have reception down here?" I asked, surprised.

A smile twisted his lips. "No, but I took the precaution of telling my team to meet me down at the parking area at three. It's just gone that now."

"I'll head back in," Lugh said. "And let Cynwrig know what's happening."

Sgott nodded then caught my arm, tucking it into the crook of his as he escorted me back to the pulley system. Though our arms were only lightly linked, I could feel the fury in him. It was much fiercer than the grief, but only, I suspected, because he was using the former to combat the latter. While I completely understood it, worry stirred. Bear shifters were seriously hard to annoy, but damn dangerous when their temper finally did explode. He'd been a part of my life since I was a toddler and the only father I'd ever really known. I didn't want to lose him too, but if he unleashed that anger and became fixated on capturing Mom's killer, I just might. Two other people had died in this place; it suggested the asshole behind the deaths would do whatever they deemed necessary to get what they wanted.

What *we* needed to uncover now was, what had they wanted? Presuming they'd employed Mom, why then kill her before they'd gotten it?

Or, I thought slowly, had she come here to *stop* them. Given the fear in her eyes the last time I'd seen her alive, that was more than possible.

There were five other vehicles waiting in the parking area by the time we got back down, including a dark van I suspected might belong to the coroner. As Sgott's people climbed out of their various cars and began to kit up, Sgott said, "Harry, can you take Beth home? Escort her to the door—do not let her jump out and go down that lane alone, no matter what she says."

Harry was a wiry-looking man with tufts of gray hair and pale-yellow eyes. A wolf shifter, I suspected. "And after?"

"Patrol the area and make sure there're no unsavory types hanging around."

Harry nodded and opened the passenger door for me. I rose onto my toes and kissed Sgott's cheek. "Keep me updated."

The smile that tugged at his lips was a wan echo of its usually robust self. "I will. Don't you be doing anything stupid now, will you?"

"I'm not the one with the legendary temper."

"And I'm not the one with the recently uncovered second sight. Don't go after anything or anyone alone—promise me."

I hesitated. "I promise."

"Good." He touched my cheek and then, with a sharp motion to his men to follow, turned around and headed back toward the path.

I watched until they'd gone and then moved over to the car and climbed in. There was no small talk on the journey home. Shifters were sensitive to emotion, and Harry could no doubt smell the deep well of pain and anger in me.

He escorted me to the door and didn't leave until I'd stepped inside and locked it again. As his retreat echoed lightly through the veranda's wooden flooring, I leaned my forehead against the door and just let the gentle song of the wood wash through my mind. It was a comforting sound even if it didn't ease the inner ache.

Eventually, I headed upstairs, said the ritual thank-you before I tossed more wood onto the fire, and then made myself a pot of tea. It was pointless trying to sleep; not until I heard more from either Lugh or Sgott, anyway.

But after a while, I got up and began to pace. The itch to do something—anything—was growing. I'd promised Sgott not to go anywhere without company, but that didn't preclude me from *searching*.

I swung around, marched into my bedroom, and fished the Eye out of my discarded jeans somewhat warily. My touch didn't draw a response from the stone for a change.

I returned to the living area, tucked my feet up on the chair, and then held the Eye out to the firelight. The flames caressed its dark surface and lent it an odd sort of warmth. But violence remained deep in its heart—though if this stone had been tuned specifically to the women of my line, perhaps it was simply reflecting my own emotions.

I continued to stare at it, but the Eye remained inert. I blew out a frustrated breath, tossed it onto the coffee table, and finished off my pot of tea.

Sometime after that, I fell asleep.

It was the fierce rumble of thunder that woke me. Rain drummed on the slate tiles, a sound that was oddly soothing despite the violence of the storm overhead. The room remained dark, but the promise of dawn rode the air, even if her light and warmth would be muted for hours yet by the storm.

The fire had burned down to embers, so I rose and tossed some more logs onto it. As the flames caught, an odd hum of energy caught my attention. I glanced around and realized it was coming from the Eye.

For several seconds, I didn't move. I simply stared at the thing, watching the lightning flash in time with the storm overhead through its dark heart.

Were the two connected?

Yes, but only through you.

The harsh but familiar whisper rolled through my thoughts. Beira.

"Did you activate the Eye?"

I had no idea if she would hear me or not, but she'd said we could communicate through the Eye, and it was obviously active, so it was worth a shot.

No, we did not. Only you have that power.

"And yet I'm not even touching the thing."

That is extremely interesting.

"In a good way or bad?" I couldn't help asking.

Possibly both.

I waited but once again, she didn't go on. "Why?"

Because it would seem your connection to the stone is different to that of your mother.

I hesitated and then said, "We found her body a few hours ago."

There was a long pause. *I'm sorry to hear that. We had hoped, against reason ....*

So had I. I blinked back tears and explained where she'd been found. "Do you know that place?"

I do not. She paused again. *I take it you're now intent on using the Eye to seek out her murderers?*

"Is that possible?"

Your mother was unable to direct what she saw in the Eye, but her restrictions might not be yours.

"Any suggestions as to how I should go about it?"

I am not a teacher, she said, mental tone cross. *Nor am I here to hold your hand. The best way to learn is to try, young lady.*

A smile tugged my lips. "I'm not sure we have time for me to learn the hard way."

Perhaps not, but there is no easy path. Not when it comes to the sort of forces that move your way. Contact us if you find anything.

The connection died. She might have claimed that she had no control over it at her end, but I rather suspected that was not exactly the truth. I might like her, I might be inclined to trust her, but I also couldn't afford to forget she *was* a hag and undoubtedly had an agenda that might not be what she'd already claimed.

I walked over to the kitchen to make a fresh pot of tea and then sat back down. The Eye continued to hum, though it remained a background noise and one I really didn't want to connect to on a deeper level. Beira's note had warned that using the Eye to find darkness would also attract it, and I really wasn't up to dealing with any more shit tonight.

Maybe I should try scrying again ... it had to be safer, surely.

Famous last words, no doubt.

I placed the Eye on the point where my legs crossed and then began the slow breathing routine. Calm once again descended, and my senses expanded, just as they had before. The energy of the storm that rattled the windows and drummed on the slate roof danced through me, making it feel as if I was one with her and she with me. It was a sensation that was both exhilarating and scary. These forces were not meant to be controlled by someone like me ... and yet, I had the feeling I only needed to reach out mentally to make a firmer connection, and the lightning that split through the skies and echoed through my soul would be mine to unleash.

Was that true? My father was apparently a storm god, after all, so some sort of affinity with storms was a definite possibility. That didn't mean I could—or even *should*—

reach for the power rolling all around me. Using the Eye without instruction was one thing. Reaching into the storm to channel its power? That was likely deadly.

But maybe my long-absent parent would sense my presence in the storms and decide to turn up and tutor me.

And maybe tomorrow, Mathi would ask me to marry him.

It was a thought that made me smile. I glanced down at the Eye, but its surface remained black ink. For a second, I wasn't sure what to do next. Maybe it needed direction. I'd scried the moonstone with the intention of finding the crown, even if I hadn't actively thought about it. Perhaps I needed to provide the Eye with some sort of direction too. I frowned, but nevertheless began thinking about Mom, the tunnel, and the dark ring on her finger.

The ink rippled, and a cold voice said, "Is it done?"

I jumped, quickly looked around, and then realized the question had come from the Eye. I blew out a relieved breath and narrowed my gaze, concentrating on the voice, on the desire to sharpen the Eye's focus so that I could see who was speaking.

To no avail.

"Yes. The tunnel has been sealed and both the witch and the dwarf buried. None will find them." The second voice belonged to a woman and held a husky warmth that in any other circumstances might have been pleasant.

Neither voice was familiar.

There was a long beat of silence, then the man said, "If you're sure. What of the hoard?"

So, it seemed my suspicions had been right. Mom *had* gone into that tunnel to stop the theft of the hoard and had subsequently lost her life.

But who were these people? Being able to hear but not

see them was damnably frustrating—even more so because I had no idea why.

"We're in the process of securing it," the woman said.

"You've not done a full inventory yet?"

"We dare not risk it. Not for months. The slightest vibration along the psychic or magic lines will bring them down on us."

"Ninkil wishes an update."

The rat god? Fuck, had Mom known the Ninkilim were involved when she'd left the tavern that day? Was that why her fear had been so fierce?

Goddammit, why couldn't the stone just *show* me their faces?

"There is nothing to update," the woman said. "One false move and we risk making his triumphant return a tragedy."

"The hoard remains safe?"

"Yes, but Lùtair is now involved, and that warrants caution. We must be patient."

"Ninkil is not known for his patience," the man said. "And neither am I."

The woman laughed, a deep, barking sound. "He has waited centuries for this moment. A few more months will not hurt him—or you."

The black surface rippled, and the first two voices were cut off by a frosty, "How goes progress on the crown?"

"Slowly" came the reply. "Now that Lord Lùtair has become involved, we need to be cautious."

Cynwrig, it seemed, was causing plenty of consternation amongst his fellow thieves.

"What of the pixie's spawn? There's some recent indication she's inherited her mother's skills, is there not? If that is true, we need to keep an eye on her."

Meaning me, obviously. But there was something in the way he said that that made me suspect he knew me, even if I didn't recognize his voice.

"Oh," the second man said, a vague hint of amusement evident in his tone, "We've both eyes *and* ears on her. She might yet prove very useful."

The black surface rippled once more, and yet again the voices faded. Frustration swirled, but the Eye had not finished with me yet. Figures appeared within the ink—two of them, a man and a woman. They were seated in a room lit only by the dancing light of a fire. He sat on a chair facing the fire, his back to me, meaning all I could really see was long, shaggy brown hair. Even so, there was something about him that sparked a memory—was this Cillian, one of the two cat burglars who'd broken into my house and stolen the moonstone? Possibly. Very possibly.

The woman sat to his right, leaning forward on her chair and speaking animatedly. She was dark skinned and sharp featured, with long dark hair that was tied back in a loose ponytail that didn't hide the pointed tips of her ears. Her features were line free but, if her hands were anything to go by, she wasn't young.

They were obviously arguing, and I wished I could hear about what, but the vision had flicked over to being sight only. At one point, the man thrust to his feet; she sat back in her chair and seemed to be inviting him to leave.

He hesitated and then sat back down; a smile tugged briefly at the woman's lips. There were a few more minutes of conversation, and then she nodded and held out her hand. The man placed a stone in her palm.

The vision's focus sharpened. It *was* the moonstone.

Fuck.

The two of them rose and, frustratingly, walked away

from my point of view position rather than toward, leaving me none the wiser as to whether my guess about the man was right. But really, it had to be either him or the spell-caster, and the shifter hadn't given anything to the caster before he'd left and fled in the opposite direction.

Which didn't discount the possibility of them meeting up afterward, of course.

They walked down the stairs, then through a shop filled with the looming shadows of display cases. The woman opened an old wooden door, and the man exited without looking back. The woman glanced down at the moonstone and then turned and headed back up the stairs.

The vision followed her. She went upstairs, placed the stone in the top drawer of a gorgeous old antique desk, and then locked it. She tucked the key into a small vase sitting on the nearby windowsill, and then moved back across the room.

Then the vision shifted again, this time into the street. The shaggy-haired stranger had tucked the collar of his coat up and was striding away. It wasn't him I was now interested in, but rather the street itself.

I knew it. In fact, Darby and I had dined in the pub a few doors down from the mysterious woman's place multiple times over the years. It was the same street Sgott had mentioned when he'd been talking about Kaitlyn, the woman who brokered stolen goods and thieving contracts. It couldn't be coincidence, given she was the one who'd hired the two thieves. It also meant that if I wanted to retrieve the moon-stone, I had better move fast, before Kaitlyn moved it on.

Only, I'd promised Sgott not to go anywhere alone. I swore but grabbed my phone and rang my brother. No answer. Ringing Sgott and Cynwrig produced the same result. They were obviously still underground, though I would've thought they'd have had plenty of time to retrieve Mom's body by now.

Maybe they'd decided to investigate where the tunnel went and how it related to either the theft of the Hoard or the Claws. Just because Lugh and I had theorized it was a part of the dark elf underground watch system didn't mean it was—or that alterations hadn't been made in the time since the dark elves had stopped using it.

It was tempting—so tempting—to confront Kaitlyn alone, but a promise was a promise.

I took a deep breath and called the one other person I could rely on—Mathi. For all his quirks, he was more than capable of protecting us both. He'd proven that a few years ago when a couple of would-be muggers had unwisely chosen us as their target. To say they regretted their decision would be something of an understatement. Even Ruadhán had gently chided his son for his retaliatory attack, which in some ways was a little surprising, given he was well known for his not-so-gentle interrogation techniques.

The phone rang long enough that I thought it would switch over to voicemail, then his sleepy voice said, "Bethany? You don't need to ring me. You can just come right on over and join me in bed anytime you desire."

A smile twitched my lips. If ever there was a perfect example of a one-track mind, he was it. "This isn't a booty call, Mathi."

"No? Color me sad."

My smile grew. "I need to borrow your battle skills, not your bedroom ones."

"Ha." Sheets rustled, and the image of silk sliding away

from taut golden skin rose. I told my hormones to behave themselves. "Why do you need said skills?"

"I found the location of the moonstone—"

"Moonstone?" he cut in. "What moonstone?"

I gave him a quick update and then said, "The woman I saw is a broker. If I don't get there fast, she could pass the stone on to whoever contracted her retrieval services, and I'll lose it totally."

"Do you know her address?"

I quickly gave it to him and then said, "I'll meet you at the pub on the corner in what ... fifteen minutes?"

"You don't want me to pick you up first? The storm is pretty bad—"

"I'll be fine. Don't be late."

"I won't be." He paused, and then added, in an utterly sincere tone, "I'm sorry to hear about your mom, Beth. I know how close the two of you were."

I closed my eyes against another wave of grief. "Who told you?"

"My father rang me a few hours ago. He and Sgott *will* catch whoever did this."

"I know."

He paused, said, "See you soon," and then hung up.

I glanced down at the Eye again. I didn't want to risk taking it with me, and I couldn't keep leaving it into the pocket of my discarded clothes. I also couldn't risk placing it in any of my storage holes, because someone outside of my immediate circle of family and friends obviously knew about them. And given the people behind the theft had to know I was a pixie, entwining it into the fibers of the building's structure or even furniture, was also out of the question. Our branch of the pixie tree wasn't the only one who could manipulate wood, and there were plenty out there who'd have no qualms about taking a contract to search for the Eye.

I looked around and then walked over to the kitchen and dropped the stone into the fourth mug of the seven hanging off hooks from the overhead cupboard. A pixie wouldn't find it there, and the likelihood of a sniffer doing so was remote; magic had to be faintly active for them to do their thing, and the Eye had only ever come to life in the presence of my mother or grandmother. And now me.

And I crossed all mental fingers that *that* remained the case.

I ran into my bedroom to collect my keys, phone, and credit card, and then pulled on fresh boots. Once I'd strapped on my knives, I rang a taxi and headed toward the back door to grab my coat. The storm had eased a little by the time I stepped outside, but the wind was fierce, and it seemed to blow right through me, whispering of darkness and trouble looming.

I shivered, tugged my hood up over my hair, and ran down to the taxi stand and the waiting vehicle. But as I opened the door to get inside, a weird sensation rolled across my skin and I paused, looking quickly around. There was nothing and no one about, and yet the wind whispered of eyes watching.

"You getting in or not?" the cabbie growled. "The seat is getting wet."

"Yeah, sorry."

I jumped in and gave the cabbie the address. The sensation of being watched faded with the wind's touch, but trepidation still rolled across my skin. It made me wish I'd jumped into the front seat; at least then I could have pulled down the vanity mirror and checked if anyone was following us. Although given the approaching dawn hadn't yet made any impact on the darkness and the few cars that were on the street were using their headlights, it would probably have been a pointless exercise.

The lack of traffic on the roads meant it didn't take us long to get across to Falkner Street. He let me out close to the corner of Walker Street, and I once again dragged up the hood of my coat. The rain had finally eased to a drizzle, but the sky still grumbled, and the wind spun with the taste of rain. She still whispered of watchers, too, even if I couldn't see anything.

Perhaps the wind's whispers were nothing more than my own paranoia.

I tucked my hands into my pockets and headed down the street. After a moment, I spotted the figure waiting in the arch over the pub's inset front door. Though the heavy trench coat hid his figure, the nearby streetlight was bright enough to chase the shadows away from his face.

Mathi.

I hadn't doubted he'd be here, but it was nevertheless a relief to see him.

He snagged an arm around my waist once I was close enough, dragged me into his slim, muscular body, and simply held me. It was familiar and comforting, and I wasted too many seconds in his embrace, lost in his strength and his caring.

This was the Mathi who very few saw.

He brushed a kiss across the top of my head and said, "Are you sure you want to do this now? You do not wish more time to grieve?"

"I'll grieve when her killers are found, Mathi."

He nodded and released me. "Lead on, then."

I turned and headed up the street. He quickly fell in step beside me.

"So, what's the plan here? Are we breaking in or announcing our arrival?"

"Announcing." I glanced at him. "I'm thinking a person in her line of business will be well protected against any form of break-in."

"No security system is one hundred percent reliable, be it magical or electronic."

A fact I'd been made aware of recently. "Yes, but neither you nor I have the expertise needed to break in."

"Past magic? No. Anything else? Maybe."

I raised an eyebrow. "You're a blueblood elf—I'd have thought learning such a skill would have been frowned upon."

He smiled. "My father wasn't always an inspector, remember. As a youth, I spent a lot of time haunting his footsteps around IIT's headquarters. It was quite educational."

I'd just bet. We reached Kaitlyn's and stopped under the awning, out of the weather. Like most of the other buildings along this portion of the street, it was a two-story red-brick and, aside from the bright blue color of its wooden front door, rather unremarkable. A full-height window dominated the shop front to our right, though a privacy film had been placed over a portion of it so there was no way to see what lay beyond. A small brass sign in the middle of the door said Kaitlyn's Kurios, and there was a new intercom on the brick wall to the right.

I didn't immediately press the buzzer. Instead, I splayed my fingers across the door and listened to the song of the wood that lay within the building's interior. It was faint, mainly because the building's fabric was mostly brick, but it told me there were three levels—a basement as well as the two visible from the street—and her location. She was in the bathroom, perhaps readying herself for bed.

I pressed the buzzer but kept my hand on the door. After a moment, footsteps bounced through the wood song as she moved out of the bathroom and into the room above.

"Yes?" Even through the intercom, her voice sounded low, warm, and sultry—the exact opposite of what I'd been expecting, given her elf heritage. It was also very different to the voice I'd heard in the Eye.

"This is Bethany Aodhán. We need to talk."

"Oh," she said, amusement obvious, "I don't believe we do."

"You're in receipt of a moonstone that was stolen from me. I wish it back."

"And if I do not wish to give it back?"

"The floor on which you stand is wood. How would you like me to send both it and you crashing down into the basement?"

There was a long pause then a buzzer sounded, and the door clicked open. "Please do come in. The stairs are—"

"I know where the stairs are," I cut in brusquely.

"Indeed? Interesting."

As the light on the intercom went out, Mathi murmured, "Could you have done what you threatened?"

"Yes." Of course, it would have wiped me out, energy wise, and seriously pissed off Sgott or Ruadhán, given one of them would probably have to deal with the resulting paperwork.

Would that have stopped me if she hadn't obligingly opened? No—although there wasn't any real need to wreck an entire building when breaking a board or two would likely prove the point and achieve the same result.

"I'm suddenly very grateful you didn't decide to destroy

the internal structure of my apartment when you walked out on me," Mathi said.

"Truth be told, I didn't think of it."

I pushed the door all the way open. I couldn't see any obvious traps, but I nevertheless drew a knife and held it in front of me. Thankfully, the blade remained inert.

I stepped inside and moved cautiously toward the stairs. There was a multitude of glass cabinets in the room, and many of the items on display were definitely valuable antiquities. They all had to be legally acquired, of course. She might be good at her job, but I doubted even she'd be brazen enough to openly display stolen goods.

Light flickered down the knife's blade as we reached the stairs; there was magic here somewhere, but it wasn't close, and it wasn't aimed at us. Not specifically, at least for the moment.

I ran my free hand along the banister as we climbed, using the faint song of the wood to locate Kaitlyn's position. She was standing near the fire, which was directly opposite the stairs.

Outside, thunder rumbled, and a sense of dread rolled through me. I stopped abruptly. I had no idea what was going on with me and the weather, but something felt very off. And while I couldn't say what, I wasn't about to ignore it.

Mathi paused behind me and placed one hand on my shoulder; I could feel the tension in him through the light touch, and knew he was ready to move.

I briefly squeezed his fingers, then bent and pressed a hand against the floorboards. They confirmed where she was standing. I deepened my connection to the wood and then mentally caught the fibers of the boards on which she stood and, with a silent apology, ripped them up with violent force. The protesting scream of stretched wood fibers made me wince, but the sudden echo of movement told me Kaitlyn had been sent staggering. I thrust upright and raced up the few remaining steps. Saw Kaitlyn fall to her knees and a gun slither away from her grasp. Mathi lunged past me to grab the thing before she could reclaim it.

I healed the fractured and broken fibers of the floorboards and then said, "While I'd prefer to keep negotiations pleasant, if you wish to play rough, I most certainly can oblige."

She picked herself up and, with an elegant sniff, walked over to the chair I'd seen her use in the vision. Mathi returned to my side and kept the gun aimed at her. He seemed completely at ease with it, but perhaps weapon handling and usage was another skill he'd learned in the halls of the IIT. It wouldn't surprise me, given Ruadhán would want to do everything possible to protect his only son.

After sitting down and crossing her legs, Kaitlyn straightened out her skirt and said, in an unfazed manner, "What makes you think I have this moonstone of yours in my possession?"

"Aside from the fact you made no initial denial of the statement, you mean? I saw that scruffy-haired gentleman give it to you less than an hour ago. You were sitting in that same chair, and he was in the red one facing the fire. I believe he was attempting to renegotiate his fee."

The latter was a guess, of course, but it seemed to fit what I'd seen.

She stared at me for several heartbeats and then said, "You have your mother's gift?"

"Yes."

"Interesting." She didn't look interested. She looked bored. But I rather suspected that taking anything she did or said at face value would be a mistake. "But it is of no consequence. Visions cannot be used as evidence in the courts, and I will of course deny any knowledge of said stone should it ever reach that far."

"I'm not here for the stone's location. I already know that. I was merely giving you the opportunity to cooperate."

She raised an eyebrow. "I don't believe you."

And *I* didn't for a second believe *that*. She was just playing for time; perhaps she had help on the way.

Or, more likely, it was nothing more than a means of testing just how far my skills went.

I glanced at Mathi. "Watch her while I retrieve my property."

I strode over to the window, tipped the fake pansies out onto the sill, and picked up the key. But as I moved across to the desk to unlock the drawer, the knife in my free hand flared to life.

There was protecting magic around the desk and a deeper spell on the drawer lock. While she'd obviously have safes and other secure storage facilities on these premises for larger or more precious items, it made sense for the smaller ones—like the moonstone—that would be moved on quickly, a simple protection spell around a desk drawer would do the job.

I laid the blade against the desk; there was a short, sharp explosion, and wisps of smoke and tiny sparks of dead magic briefly littered the air. I repeated the process with the drawer, then shoved the key into the lock, opened it up, and retrieved the moonstone. It was tempting to go through the entire drawer to see what other ill-gotten items might be in there, but caution raised its head. Claiming what I was owed was one thing; sticking my nose into her other business was quite another. I didn't need to make even more of an enemy of this woman.

I walked back to Mathi. "Who took out the contract to retrieve the stone, Kaitlyn?"

She shrugged. "No one. I am both a buyer and a seller. The man you claim to have seen was simply selling that item."

I suspected that was the truth, given the contract had been for the Eye rather than the moonstone. Still ... "Unfortunately for you, Danny O'Conner was stupid enough to get himself caught, and he sang like a bird."

Something flickered through her otherwise calm expression. Annoyance perhaps. "It is his word against mine, and I'm a respectable businesswoman. Who do you think the courts would believe?"

"I don't care what the courts believe. I'm just after the name of the man who placed the contract."

She raised that eyebrow again, expression lazily amused. "Or what? I don't take kindly to threats, young woman."

"My mother and at least one light elf were murdered attempting to stop the theft of the item to which this stone belongs." I somehow kept my voice conversational despite the sharp rise of anguish and anger. "It's very possible the man who placed the contract to snatch the stone from my tavern is behind those murders. That, I would suggest, makes you an accomplice after the fact."

I had no idea if the latter was true or not, but it sounded good. She studied me for a good few seconds and then sighed. "I can give you the contractor's name, but I have no certainty he was, in fact, the originator of the request."

"Is that usual?" Mathi asked.

Her gaze flicked to him. Recognition flared in her eyes. "Yes, young man, it is. As your father could no doubt tell you, if you but ask."

"You deal with my father?"

She shrugged. "It's sometimes beneficial for a woman in my position to pass on certain information to the IIT."

I wondered if that included Sgott's team, but I would ask the man himself rather than this woman. Being economical with the truth was probably built into her DNA.

"Was the spellcaster also the contractor?" It was a guess, but a fairly safe one given what both she and Danny had said.

"Indeed, he was."

"Then give me his name and address, and I'll walk out of here without informing the IIT where I found this stone."

"I have your word on that?"

"Yes."

A smile touched her lips. "I guess I will have to trust you, then."

"Just as much as I have to trust you."

She laughed. "I like you, Bethany Aodhán. Perhaps one day we might work together. His name is Aram. I don't know his last name, but he works out of a place in the port area. Be warned, he is a spellcaster of some power."

"Elsmoot Port?" When she nodded, I added, "And the address?"

She gave it to me and then said, "Now that our business has concluded, please feel free to leave."

"We'll drop this near the door." Mathi raised the weapon. "Just in case."

Amusement touched her cool expression; maybe she'd been thinking—hoping—we'd be foolish enough to leave it within her reach.

We headed back down the stairs. Mathi unloaded the gun and placed it and the bullets on the top of the cabinet closest to the door.

"Aram's place next?" he said, as we left the building.

"Yes, but we'll need to be careful. I wouldn't put it past her to ring and warn him."

"If she does, it's more than likely we won't find him home. Criminals tend to avoid confrontation with the law if possible."

"We're not the law."

"I'm the son of a chief inspector, and you're Sgott's daughter in all but blood." His voice was dry. "In the eyes of the unlawful, that's a little too close for comfort."

"I'm inclined to believe that those behind the thefts of the hoard and the search for the crown aren't too worried about the IIT or anyone else."

"They might not be, but the peripheral players will be."

I hoped he was right. I suspected he wasn't.

We headed around the corner into Walker Street. His car was parked several houses down, and his driver wasn't present.

"You drove yourself?" I reached up to feel his forehead. "Are you all right?"

He caught my hand and dropped a kiss onto my palm before releasing it. "There was no reason for two of us to be up at an ungodly hour."

"And no time for him to get there anyway."

"That might also be true."

I laughed and opened the car door to climb inside. But once again the sensation of being watched rose. I frowned and looked around. Nothing, as before. So why was the wind insisting trouble was brewing? Why was the encroaching storm filled with the threat of darkness?

I shivered and did my best to ignore the growing trepidation. It had to be a result of nerves or shock or maybe even a mix of both, but if I'd had the Eye with me, I could have checked. It did make me wish the family's second sight worked without it.

Of course, second sight wasn't the reason I could hear the storm or the wind. That *had* to come from my father's side of the tree, but why on earth was it emerging now? And what the hell was it, exactly?

I suspected Beira could answer both questions. Whether she would or not was another matter.

Mathi started the car once I got in. I dragged out my phone and sent a text to Sgott and my brother, telling them where I was going and who I was with. At least if something went wrong, they'd know where to start looking for us.

"I'm not going to let anything happen to you," Mathi said, with a glance my way.

"I know, but underestimating the enemy is never a good way to start the day." I shifted in the seat to look at him fully. "I don't suppose your father mentioned anything about the body we found in the tunnel yesterday?"

"It belonged to the bibliothecary who'd been missing. Why?"

"Did he have any suspicions as to why he was there?"

"No, but there are old Myrkálfar tunnels around that area. Your mother and another were found in one."

"I know." And his comment suggested that he didn't know I was the one who'd found them. Had Sgott kept that from his counterpart, or had Ruadhán failed to mention it to his son?

He glanced at me again. "I'm surprised you've not asked Cynwrig about those tunnels."

There was a slight edge in his voice and inner amusement stirred, though I didn't let it show. "I haven't exactly had time to contact him of late, what with your kidnapping and the discovery of Mom's body."

He looked a little contrite but also somewhat relieved as he turned left at a roundabout and drove onto the motorway.

"What's the situation with the men who kidnapped you?" I continued. "Was there any link back to Gilda's murder?"

"No, but questioning is ongoing."

I frowned. "They've denied any involvement in what happened to her?"

"Yes." He glanced at me. "Why?"

"There can't be two parties after the rubies. That's too much of a coincidence."

He shrugged. "We have no idea how many people Gilda might have mentioned the ruby to. She was a lovely woman, but not the brightest spark in the box."

"She was smart enough to fool you," I commented.

His lips twisted. "That was definitely a case of the little head overruling the big."

I laughed. "The story of your life, I fear."

"Indeed."

He glanced at the rearview mirror, and something in his expression had unease stirring. "What's wrong?"

"Nothing." He paused and took another look. "Maybe."

"Meaning?"

"There's a van getting a little too close for comfort."

I flicked down the vanity mirror. The van was a standard white thing used by thousands of companies every day to transport goods. It wasn't yet close enough to see the driver, but that didn't stop the thick rise of fear.

"How long has he been behind us?"

"He pulled in behind us from Greenfield Crescent."

Which was before the motorway entrance and nowhere near Kaitlyn's place. It was probably nothing more than a coincidence, and yet ... Given the whispers of the wind earlier and the continuing rumble of incoming darkness coming from the sky, I wasn't about to ignore it.

I bit my lip and studied the road ahead. There wasn't a whole lot of traffic about, and our options for detours were somewhat limited. "We could turn left up ahead and wander through a few side roads. That'll sort out if he's following us or not."

Mathi nodded and did just that. The van continued through the intersection.

"Nothing more than paranoia," I said, unable to conceal the relief in my voice.

"Not when the driver was concealed, it's not."

His voice was grim, and my gaze shot to his. "It could have been a heavily tinted window."

"It wasn't. Trust me."

I did. A light elf's sight was generally far sharper than either a human's or a pixie's. "Why didn't they follow us then?"

He shrugged. "Maybe they figured we were onto them. Or maybe they know where we're going and have gone ahead to plot an ambush."

I wrinkled my nose. "Do you think they're Kaitlyn's men? She wouldn't appreciate the loss of face my taking the moonstone back would have caused."

"Her reputation is her business, but I doubt she'd risk attacking us. Or, at least, me."

I glanced at him sharply again. "So, you *do* know her?"

"Only through my father. He has had dealings with

her." He shrugged. "To get the required results sometimes means wading through murky waters."

I was pretty damn sure Sgott didn't feel that way, but then, he was a shifter, not a light elf. The latter tended to be a little elastic when it came to right and wrong.

Mathi did a U-turn and headed back to the motorway. It was lovely and wide, with two lanes in either direction and good visibility now that dawn had risen to chase the last shadows of night away.

But as we neared an overpass, any sense of comfort disappeared. A white van was parked on the shoulder underneath the bridge.

"So much for them driving ahead to plot an ambush," I said.

"Yes, and there's nowhere for us to go this time."

Nothing until the Runcorn and Warrington off-ramp, anyway, and that was kilometers away. "They wouldn't try anything on the motorway, though, would they? I know the peak hour hasn't fully hit yet, but there's still a bit of traffic about."

"I wouldn't have thought so, but I also have no idea who we're dealing with or what they might want." He glanced at me. "If it's the same people who arranged my kidnapping, then anything is possible."

Because anyone who was willing to risk Ruadhán's ire by kidnapping his only son either had no understanding of what they had unleashed or were very confident about their ability to escape retribution.

We swept past them. The driver was nothing more than a blur. He was definitely using a concealing spell alongside the heavily tinted windows.

In the rearview mirror, I watched the van pull out and speed up until they were right behind us again.

"Well, they're making no effort to conceal their intentions, are they?"

"If it's only following us, then I'm perfectly fine with that."

"I don't think either of us believe that's their only intention."

A smile tugged briefly at his lips but failed to lift the concern in his eyes. "If they do want to run us off the road, there's a couple of perfect places just ahead."

I glanced out the side window. While there was a metal barrier along this section of the road to prevent cars going off into the trees and fields beyond, I knew it disappeared once we got deeper into the farming district. "Running us off the road at this time of day would be dangerous, surely? I mean, people will stop to help."

"Would they? You have more faith in humanity than I have. Besides, it would depend entirely on how far in advance they've planned this." He glanced at me. Though he didn't say it, he knew, just as I knew, he wasn't the target. "If they have a healer and another car waiting, then injuries don't really matter, do they?"

"Witnesses do."

"Not if they're all using light shields."

"True." I took another look in the rearview mirror. All I could see was the van. The plate number, like the driver, was concealed. I shifted and unbuckled my knives.

"What are you doing?" Mathi said, voice sharp.

"I can't risk losing them."

"Without them, you've no counter for magic."

"The mob who kidnapped you and maybe killed Gilda has shown no inclination to bind anyone's mind with magic, but they certainly *did* show an appreciation of my knives." I opened the glove compartment and placed them inside. "Besides, if they do snatch us, do you really think I'll be allowed to keep them?"

"No." His gaze flicked to the rearview and then widened. "Brace, Bethany! They're about to—"

The rest of his warning was lost as the van hit so hard that it lifted the rear of the car up for several meters and then sent us barreling forward. Mathi fought briefly for control, then hit the accelerator. The big engine roared as we hurtled down the road in a desperate effort to escape.

Another hit. This time, the van clipped the right edge of the car and whipped us sideways for several meters down the road.

Mathi muttered something under his breath but again regained control. I grabbed my phone and tried to ring Sgott; he didn't answer. I quickly sent another text, telling him what was happening and mentioning where I'd left my knives.

I'd barely hit send when a third hit sent the phone tumbling from my grip. I swore and bent to grab it.

It was probably the only thing that saved me.

The van smashed into us again; this time, it sent us hurtling off the road and into the trees and shrubs that lined the verge. Glass shattered as a branch speared through the windshield, scraping across my spine before embedding itself into the back of the seat. I swore again, this time in pain, but the words choked off as the car tipped over and began to tumble through the undergrowth. I screamed, a sound that seemed to echo through the sky and the wind. All I could see were flashes of light in between green and red. Blood red. In the air. In my eyes.

Then my head smacked against something solid, and I knew no more.

Waking was a bitch, though I had to be thankful I was alive *to* wake.

But everything hurt—head, body, even my damn hair, for gods' sake. Pain was a storm that raged through my body, and it made me wish that I could just slip back into the black peace of unconsciousness.

But something held me awake, and it wasn't the pain. It was a voice. A harsh, *unpleasant* voice. A voice as filled with rage as that inner storm.

It took too long for recognition to surface.

Beira.

It was only then that I realized the storm wasn't only raging within, but without. Windows rattled, rain pounded across the roof, and water dripped. Not onto me, but close. The wind tugged at my shoulders and whipped across my body, as if attempting to drag me upright. One of the rattling windows was obviously broken, but try as I might, I couldn't force my eyes open to check. It took a few more minutes to realize why—something glued them shut.

I raised a shaky hand and gently scraped a finger across

them. The muck that caked them flaked away, and suddenly I could see.

The room was small and bare. The walls were brick, and there were bars across the two sash windows, one of which had several broken panes of glass. The poor quality of light made it hard to say if was closer to dawn or dusk, but either way, it was decidedly dark.

There was no furniture in the room other than the metal bed on which I lay, and the floor was stone. I twisted around to see what lay behind me, causing a dozen different aches to spring fiercely to life. A metal door, and one that was obviously old, as it was dented and rusted in a dozen different places. There wasn't a lock or a handle on this side of it, either.

That told me two things—one, that whoever had dumped me in here wasn't taking any chances on me escaping, and two, they'd likely been planning this for at least a couple of days. Rooms that were basically prison cells weren't easy to find at the last minute.

I slowly and carefully pushed upright. My vision spun briefly, and warmth trickled down my spine, but it appeared that nothing had been broken, and that was something to be thankful for, given the seriousness of the rollover.

I wondered if Mathi was okay. Wondered if he'd been left in the mangled mess of the car or snatched right along with me. If the people who'd rammed us were also the same people who'd kidnapped him, then the latter was a distinct possibility.

I glanced around as the wind shrieked in through the broken window and tugged at my hair, as if desperate to gain my attention.

Only it wasn't the wind but rather the woman who could control it.

I reached out with one shaky hand. I had no idea how this was meant to work; it wasn't like anyone had ever trained me.

The wind circled my fingers, but Beira's voice, which had been so clear when I was unconscious, remained muted.

That suggested I might need to be in some sort of meditative state to hear her properly. I pushed back against the wall, winced as rough bricks pressed against the wound on my back, and then began the deep breathing exercises. It took far longer to reach the point of inner calm than it should have, thanks to the multiple rivers of pain that continued to run through me. I might not have broken anything, but I had a bad feeling that underneath my clothes I was a bruised and bloody mess.

Beira's voice sharpened so abruptly I jumped.

It's never polite to scream into the wind without supplying a reason, young lady, she growled. *I'm past my prime, you know. That sort of thing does the heart no good.*

Despite the seriousness of the situation, I couldn't help smiling. *It isn't like I had any fucking idea I was doing something like that. Maybe if someone had bothered to teach me a few basics—*

This is hardly the time for recriminations, she snapped. *You need to get out of there.*

And how do you propose I do that when I'm in a locked room filled with metal and stone?

Use the wind.

How?

Her sigh ran across my senses, the sound one of exasperation. *If you can hear the wind and the storms, you will be able to control them.*

I'm thinking this is another of those situations where I haven't the time to learn.

There was a brief pause, and then she said somewhat crossly, *You could be right. I'll check the situation with the door.*

The strands of wind unwound from my fingers and any sense of Beira went with them. The door rattled several times before the wind surged into the room with greater force. A heartbeat later, there was a soft clunk, and the door swung open.

It was then I heard the footsteps coming down the hall toward my cell.

I swore, twisted around, and lay back down. I had no idea who or what might be approaching, but I couldn't give them any reason to suspect I had anything to do with the door being opened.

The wind curled around my fingers, and Beira said, *Play their game and stay alive. I'll go muster some help.*

Whose game, Beira?

The question fell into the emptiness. She and the wind had already left. I took a deep breath that didn't in any way ease the fear or pain and closed my eyes.

As footsteps drew close—there were two sets, one heavier than the other—there was a soft curse and a scuff of sharper movement. Then the door creaked fully open, and someone exhaled sharply.

"Thank fuck for that." The speaker was male, in a voice that was unusually hoarse. "The boss wouldn't have been pleased if she'd escaped."

"I thought you said you checked the door?"

It was said by a woman, and there was something in her

tone that suggested she didn't like me. Which was odd, given her voice didn't strike any memory chords.

"I did."

"Not very well, obviously."

The woman stepped up to the bed but didn't move or say anything for several seconds. Then she snorted, and the flat of her hand struck my face hard, leaving it stinging.

I swore again and lashed out with a clenched fist, but she laughed and jumped out of the way. "You'll have to be faster than that, young Aodhán."

I opened my eyes and looked up ... and up. She was close to Lugh's height, with a thinnish build, sharp golden eyes, and a pinched face. Her long hair was a pale orange-gold and braided in a manner that made it look as if she wore a crown.

But it was her hair and eye color that told me what she was even if I didn't recognize her—a Tàileach pixie. From which branch, I couldn't say. The three different lines that worked out of Deva and its surrounding areas all had the autumn coloring, but the way she'd said my surname in a sneering manner suggested she might be from the Serpentine area. They certainly had no love for my family after an ancestor had stolen an artifact sacred to the Tàileach in that area.

It might have happened centuries ago, but the Tàileach really did hold grudges.

"Speed isn't going to save you when I get out of here," I said, surprised at how even my voice was.

She laughed. "What makes you think you're going to get out of here?"

"What makes you think you will?" I retorted. "The people you're working for have a bad habit of abandoning or killing their employees."

"Only those who do not do their job as required," the man said. He had rust-colored hair, a thinnish build, and brown eyes ringed with gold. Some sort of hawk shifter, I suspected, which would also explain his hoarse, unpleasantly high tone. "Up, young woman. There is work to be done."

"I'm going nowhere until you tell me where I am and where Mathi Dhār-Val is."

"Do you really think you have any choice in the matter?"

She reached down, obviously intending to grab my arm, but I twisted around and kicked her hard in the gut. I was nowhere near my full strength, but the blow nevertheless sent her staggering backward.

I pushed upright, but before I could take advantage of the situation, there was a soft click. I froze. I might not have had any experience with guns, but I'd watched a lot of crime shows over the years and knew exactly what that sound was.

"That'll be enough, young lady." The shifter's manner was calm, the gun he pointed at my face steady. "Or it won't be you that pays the price but rather that Mathi fellow."

"Harm him, and you'll bring the might of the IIT down on your heads." I kept my gaze on the older pixie as I spoke. Tàileachs were known for their quick-fire temper, and the bitch was not going to catch me unawares a second time.

She clenched her fists but, despite the promise of retribution burning deep in her golden eyes, all she said was, "The IIT has to find us first, and that ain't going to happen."

I gave her a benign smile. "You keep on thinking that if it makes you feel better."

Her gaze narrowed to mere slits, but once again she didn't bite. Instead, she stepped back to her companion's side and motioned for me to rise.

I did so. The aches briefly intensified, and the flow of blood down my spine increased. Despite my best efforts, a hiss escaped.

The amusement washing from the pixie was so damn strong, I could practically taste it.

"To repeat my earlier question," I growled, "where's Mathi?"

"Safe."

"Here? Or elsewhere? I want to see him before I do anything else."

The woman snorted. "You ain't in a position to be dictating terms, young Aodhán. Now get out the door before I give into the desire to kick you out."

I raised an eyebrow, silently challenging her to make the attempt.

She took one step forward before her companion snapped, "Raen, enough. Take the fucking lead before the boss starts wondering what the fuck is going on."

She glowered at me for another second, then spun and stalked out the door. The man stepped back and motioned me to follow.

I hobbled after her.

It wasn't like I had any other choice.

The hall was narrow and filled with shadows, and I couldn't help but wonder if that meant night was settling in or whether it was simply a result of the storm that still rattled the building.

If things went sour—if Beira didn't get back here in time with help—then that storm might be my only way out ... *if* I could figure out how to use it without killing myself in

291

the process. It was all right for her to say I'd inherited the ability to control it, but I was half pixie. I wasn't entirely sure flesh and blood could ever hope to contain or control such a force.

I shook the worry from my mind and tried to concentrate on my surroundings as our footsteps rang through the emptiness. There were at least a dozen doors lining either side of the long hallway. While most were wood, a few metal ones were scattered through them. There was even a couple that looked to be made of—or at least, coated with —silver—which meant they'd been designed with shifters in mind.

It very much appeared to be either a prison or maybe even an old sanatorium. There were plenty of those scattered about the English countryside in various states of disrepair. This one appeared to be in reasonable condition; the ceiling in this section of the building was whole and the wind wasn't whistling past the open doorways, which suggested the windows in those rooms were intact.

One lone door at the far end of the hall was not only closed but locked via a thick old iron bolt. There was no padlock in use, though it wouldn't be necessary if the person inside couldn't manipulate metal.

Mathi certainly couldn't.

Of course, there was no guarantee he was imprisoned within, but I crossed mental fingers and toes that he was. This place felt huge, and the last thing I needed was to be running around aimlessly trying to find him once I managed to escape.

We turned left, strode past what looked to be a guard's station, and then headed down a set of grime-covered wooden stairs to the lower floor. The area we entered looked to be a main lobby, and it was an airy and rather beautiful space, even if the wallpaper hung in sad-looking strips and the stone floor was covered in filth and broken bits of furniture. Large windows lined the external walls to my left and right, though there was nothing to see beyond the glass but darkness. The storm rumbled overhead, and the rain continued to beat across the roof, but neither held anything approaching its earlier fierceness. I couldn't help but wonder if that was because Beira had released her grip on it.

We went through a set of double glass doors that had been wedged open into a wide corridor. There were only three doors here and, given the office-type furniture that remained in the first two rooms, it was a safe guess that this had once been the administration area.

We entered the room at the far end. It was bright and warm thanks to the fire that raged in the grimy Victorian fireplace. Half a dozen comfortable-looking chairs were scattered about, but there was little else in the way of furniture.

There were two people waiting. Neither was an elf, though why I'd been expecting them to be I couldn't say. The man had the aura of a shifter—though something far bigger than the bird shifter behind me—and the silvering in his black hair suggested he was in his twilight years. The woman was around my height, with gray hair, a pinched face, and sallow skin. The barely visible shimmer surrounding her suggested she was either a spellcaster or being protected by magic.

Maybe even both.

The pixie motioned me over to one of the chairs and then moved across to the fire. The bird shifter remained near the door, the gun lowered but not holstered.

I sat, tried to ignore the fresh wave of pain, and crossed one leg over the other in a casual manner.

"So, what's this all about?" My gaze flickered between the big shifter and the spellcaster. "Who the hell are you two?"

The older man smiled, though it held little in the way of humor or warmth. "That is not important, young lady."

"I disagree." My gaze drifted back to the pixie. "I really want to know the names of everyone I need to hunt down once this little adventure is over."

It probably wasn't wise to be mouthing off at a time like this, but the truth was, they were unlikely to hurt me in any major way until they'd gotten whatever the hell it was they wanted out of me.

Besides, my inner bitch really enjoyed needling my fellow pixie.

"There's quite a bit to do before this adventure is over for any of us," the spellcaster said.

Her voice was calm and unemotional, and it made me suspect this was nothing more than a job for her. If that were true, it also meant these two weren't the brains behind this whole thing, even if the hawk guarding the door had called one of them "boss."

"I'm not about to go anywhere with any of you until I know for sure Mathi is safe."

"Refuse to do as we ask, and your Mathi will pay the price," the big man growled.

Bear shifter, I thought, and wondered if Sgott would know him. There weren't that many bear shifters roaming around England, as they tended to keep to the wilder parts of Scotland. I knew most of Sgott's now-adult cubs were up there.

"Hurt him any further, and you lose the one thing that'll make me compliant."

"You're not immune to magic or drugs, young woman," the spellcaster said.

"No," I agreed. "And neither is my second sight, so if it's the reason I'm here, you might want to rethink the use of either."

The woman's gaze narrowed, but after several seconds, she looked at my fellow pixie. "Go up to the elf's cell and FaceTime proof of life."

While I'd been hoping they'd take me there in person so I'd know for sure exactly where he was, the fact that she'd said "up" meant my guess he was in that closed cell might be right.

Raen nodded and disappeared. Neither the shifter nor the spellcaster moved, but they watched me with unnerving intensity. I resisted the urge to fidget and switched my gaze to the fire. It was a shame I couldn't control flames; burning the fuck out of them might have provided one way out of here.

Although knowing the way my luck had been running of late, I'd probably kill myself in the process of setting both them and the building alight.

The minutes ticked by extraordinarily slowly. Then, with a suddenness that made me jump, the spellcaster's phone rang. She took it out of her pocket, swiped sideways, and then turned it around so that I could see the screen.

Mathi lay on a thin mattress that covered a metal bed base. There were cuts all over his face, and his clothes were a torn and bloody mess, but at least some of his wounds *had* been looked after. There was a bandage around his forearm and another around his right thigh, and I hoped that meant none of the rest were too serious.

Raen moved closer to the bed and focused the screen on his chest. I watched its rise and fall for several seconds and then glanced at the woman. "Have you drugged him or spelled him?"

She raised an eyebrow. "What makes you think I'm a spellcaster?"

I waved a hand up and down her length. "That energy shimmer thing you have going."

"Interesting," she said. "But no, I have not spelled him. Why would I, when a drug is more efficient and takes less effort on my part?"

I was glad she hadn't, because I had more hope of getting him out of here if he was drugged rather than magicked. Especially when I didn't have my knives with me.

Hopefully, Sgott had gotten my text and rescued them from the wreck.

"So, you're just going to keep him drugged until I do whatever the hell you brought me here to do?" I asked. "And then what? You kill us both?"

The woman shrugged and pocketed her phone. "That is a decision neither of us will make."

Meaning I was right—they weren't the real power behind this particular throne. "Then who?"

She smiled benignly. "Not something I'm able to divulge."

There was something in the way she said that that made me think she literally *couldn't* tell me. She obviously did know her employers, so did her inability to say mean she'd been spelled? Or had a telepath been messing about in her mind?

I had no idea if either was actually possible.

"Then we've circled back to my initial question—what do you want?"

"We want you to use this"—the shifter pulled the moonstone out of his pocket and placed it on the small coffee table between him and the spellcaster—"to find the crown for us."

"I've already been trying to do that, without much success."

"Yes, we know," the woman said.

I stared at her for a second, an odd sense of dread washing through me. "What is that supposed to mean?"

Her smile was cool and unamused. "Did you not use your inherited talents to see a moonlit cave through which a trickle of water ran? And the crown buried so deeply into the earth wall of that cave that only one point was visible?"

That wash of dread grew stronger. How could she possibly know any of that? It wasn't a description I'd mentioned to anyone except Lugh, and he wouldn't have betrayed me. Not in any way.

"Who told you that?"

But even as I asked the question, a suspicion grew. When I'd scried using the Eye, the second set of people talking in the vision had mentioned keeping an eye *and* ear on me. I hadn't really thought anything about it—which was a stupid mistake on my part—but even if I had, I would have presumed they had a spy somewhere within my inner circle. And while that was still possible, what if they'd also meant an *electronic* ear? Not just in the tavern but also my living quarters. While I kept the stairs locked these days thanks to the spate of thefts after Mom's death, they hadn't always been. What if those thefts had been nothing more than a diversion? A means of stopping me from looking too closely at what else might have been done.

"How we know is irrelevant," the big shifter growled. "What matters is finding the crown."

"If it was that damn easy, we'd have done so by now," I snapped back.

"Unless, of course, you were reading the clues incorrectly."

That was a definite possibility, given how little I knew about the whole second sight and scrying business, but I wasn't about to admit that.

"You obviously were under the impression that the hall house you saw was also the location of that cave," she continued. "However, had you done a little more research, you would have discovered there are no such caves within the vicinity of the houses you and your brother investigated."

Well, *fuck*. That vague feeling of being watched hadn't been imagination or wind-born uneasiness at *all*.

I twisted around to look at the bird shifter. "I take it you're the one who's been following me from on high?"

He merely smiled. I cursed and returned my gaze to the woman. "I'm guessing you believe the cave is under this place?"

"There's actually a network of old tunnels reachable from the cellars. Some of the nearest caves were used as burial chambers for those who died here without kin to claim them."

Meaning we could be picking our way through the bones of the dead. Great.

"Doesn't mean they're the ones we're after."

"No, but we can look," the bear shifter said. "The moonstone will react when it is close to the crown."

My eyebrows rose. "And you know this how?"

"Research," the woman said. "Up, young woman. The night moves on, and so must we."

"Walking around in darkness armed only with a couple of flashlights isn't really advisable—"

"The nearby dark bridge hasn't activated for years," the big shifter growled, "so there really isn't anything to be worried about."

"And maybe it hasn't activated because there's been no one around here for the Annwfyn to hunt."

No one really understood how the bridges in the regional areas worked, but there'd been plenty of bloody examples over the centuries of seemingly abandoned bridges suddenly activating when human settlement had seeped into the surrounding area.

"Even if that happens and they do send out an exploratory vanguard," the spellcaster said, "Both Raen and Linc will be armed and able to counter them."

A comment that made me think neither she nor the big shifter were coming in with us, and that eased a fraction of the inner tension. The hawk and the pixie would be hard enough to overcome; I didn't need the odds against me ratcheting up even further.

"What happens if we do find the crown?" I asked.

The spellcaster raised her eyebrows, her expression suggesting this was an extremely dumb question. And it was, because we all knew it was but one piece of Agrona's puzzle. But the longer I kept them talking, the more time Beira had to find help and get back here.

"We attempt to find the remaining Claws, of course."

"And what about the hoard?"

"I have no idea what the hoard is, so can't specifically answer that question."

Meaning either these two hadn't been fully included in

their boss's overall plans, or whoever was behind the hoard theft had nothing to do with this hunt to find the Claws.

Maybe Cynwrig's suspicions were right.

"Why do you want the Claws? Why would anyone want to control or extend darkness? At least give me one good reason for this madness."

She smiled benignly. "I can give you five good reasons, but that is neither here nor there. Now get up, before I give Raen the pleasure of dragging you upright. We are on something of a tight schedule here."

There was no way known I was going to give the pixie bitch any chance to drag me anywhere, so I pushed hastily to my feet. A dozen different aches jumped to life with renewed vigor, and I couldn't help another slight hiss escaping.

The bitch chuckled.

I glowered at her. It only increased her amusement.

My gaze returned to the spellcaster. "You know, if you really want me to help you long-term, you might consider getting in a healer."

She picked up the moonstone and tossed it to me. "Perhaps we will once you prove your worth."

Which was a polite way of saying I could go suck on some eggs. I wrapped my fingers around the stone, but it didn't give me anything. The deeper pulse of magic within the stone's heart was still, and I had no idea why.

If it remained that way, I could be in deep trouble.

The spellcaster motioned me toward the door. I turned and headed out. The pixie slung a backpack over her shoulder and fell in step behind me. The intensity of her gaze had the skin across my back crawling.

I drew in a deeper breath and tried to relax. I needed to be calm and on the lookout for any possible escape opportunity. Beira might be bringing in help, but I had no idea how long that might take, and if opportunity knocked, I couldn't afford to ignore it.

Of course, if I didn't find a way to channel the wind or the storm, I'd be relying on nothing more than my wits and my strength, and right now I didn't like the chances of either being up to scratch.

Linc led the way back down the short corridor, but rather than going back across the lobby, we turned left and made our way through a series of long, empty corridors. We eventually reached what I presumed was once the main kitchen facility for the sanatorium, though there wasn't much in the way of equipment left—just a few wooden prep tables and a couple of grimy butler sinks.

We walked past an empty pantry, then on through an old-fashioned laundry area before heading down a set of worn stone stairs into a cellar. The air was musty and still, and water dripped slowly somewhere in the distance.

The shifter dug out a flashlight, flicked it on, and continued. I couldn't tell how big the cellar was, because there was nothing but darkness beyond the flashlight's beam. But the soft echoes of our footsteps suggested it was large.

We walked through a brick arch into a tunnel that dove down steeply for several meters and ended at a T-intersection. Linc headed left, moving with an assurance that suggested he knew exactly where he was going. I wondered how long they'd been here, searching for the cave I'd talked about before they'd given up and decided it would be easier to grab the source itself.

The tunnel curved around to the left and gained a slight incline. The sound of dripping water grew stronger, and, ahead in the distance, beyond the reach of the flashlight's glow, there was a faint shimmer.

As we drew closer, I realized what it was—a moonbeam. One that fell on the top of a stone step.

The image I'd seen briefly in the vision.

An odd sense of dread ran through me, and I shivered. Not so much because it proved the accuracy of what I'd seen, but because if a moonbeam could get into this place, so too could the shadow folk.

We entered a circular room, and my gaze was drawn not to the moonbeam but rather what looked to be multiple rectangular cuts in the walls.

Tombs.

Thankfully, the bird shifter didn't sweep his light around the walls to reveal the grim contents that no doubt lay within each one.

I shivered again and said a silent prayer for both the souls of all those who lay there and for any ghosts that might remain. I couldn't help them or even move them on, but the chill in the air lessened.

Could have been my imagination, of course.

We approached the moon-touched steps, and I glanced up. The light filtered in through a hole no bigger than my fist, and the moon wasn't visible from this angle. The wind still howled through the night, however, and wisps of it followed the light down into the room, teasing my hair and playing around my fingers. I couldn't feel Beira's presence, though, and the tension within rose.

Not because I feared she would abandon me, but rather that she wouldn't get back in time.

And I did *not* want to examine the reason behind that fear.

Really, I didn't.

I clenched my left hand in a vague attempt to catch the tenuous, fragile strands of wind and take them with me. A chill swirled lightly around my fingers, though whether that meant I'd been successful or not, I really couldn't say.

We continued down. Water seeped down the walls on either side, and the steps were slick with moisture and slime. I placed every step carefully, because the last thing I needed was to slip and break something.

The bitch behind me would no doubt thoroughly enjoy hauling me upright and forcing me on.

We reached the end of the stairs and moved into what looked and felt like a very old tunnel. Moisture dripped from the rough stone roof and trickled past my boots, heading into the deeper darkness. Linc paused, swinging the beam of light left and then right.

It was utterly black in either direction.

"Which way?" he said with a glance at me.

"How the fuck do I know?"

"The moonstone," the pixie said, in a tone that suggested she was running out of patience. "Use it."

I glanced down at the stone in my right hand, but it remained inert. I swore silently and then, with little other choice, attempted a light scrying. Almost immediately, the stone's inner energy stirred to life, and its secrets whispered through my mind. "We go left, same way as the water."

The shifter nodded and led the way. I followed but glanced down at my left hand and wondered how I could get the air that continued to stir around my fingers to scout ahead. Beira obviously used it that way, so it was possible I could ... the thought had barely crossed my mind when the wind fell away and moved on through the darkness.

I hoped she came back with good news.

Hoped I could understand her even if she didn't.

The pulsing in the moonstone grew as we moved deeper into the narrowing tunnel. The trickle of water was also stronger now, making every step even more treacherous.

Then, from up ahead, came a faint scratch. Linc immediately stopped and raised his gun.

"What?" Raen said.

She'd obviously not heard the sound, but then, she was several meters further back from the shifter and me.

"I don't know." Though his voice was no louder than the pixie's, it seemed to echo. "Could be rats."

"All the way down here, when there's nothing for them to feed on?" The pixie snorted. "Get moving. I don't want to be down here all freaking night."

The shifter hesitated and then obeyed. The scratching wasn't repeated, but the sense of wrongness was growing deep within me. I flexed my fingers and wished I had my knives. Wished I had a gun, even if I didn't know how to use one.

The tunnel began to widen, and the moonstone's pulsing sharpened abruptly.

"We're close," I said.

"How far?" Linc asked.

His tension was now very evident in the set of his shoulders.

"I'm not holding a tape measure," I snapped. "We're close, that's all the information I'm getting."

Aside from the fact that whatever had made that scratching noise was also near, that is.

The shifter cursed, then walked on more cautiously.

After a few more minutes, light appeared ahead. It was little more than a translucent, shimmering beam but I knew immediately what it was.

A moonbeam.

My heart began to beat so fast and loud that it seemed to echo through the darkness.

We were approaching the cave that I'd seen in the dream—the one in which the crown was buried.

I took a deep, somewhat tremulous breath and said, "That's the cave we need up ahead."

Linc stopped close to the tunnel's end and then said, "Raen, flares."

The pixie slipped past me, shrugged off the backpack, and unzipped it. She handed him three and then pulled out a couple more. They removed the caps, lit the flares, and then tossed them strategically into the cave, until the entire place was lit.

Linc stepped back and motioned me forward. I hesitated, and then moved past them both. The cave was oblong in shape but otherwise much the same as what I'd seen in the dream. The moonlight came in through what looked to be a wide, naturally formed fissure long enough that the storm-clad sky wasn't visible.

The whispers in the moonstone grew stronger, and I went left, my gaze scanning the end wall. After a moment, I spotted it.

"It's here," I said, and walked over.

Linc stepped past me and brushed his fingers across the crown's point. "That's definitely metal. You got the pick, Raen?"

She pulled it out of the pack and handed it to him. As he quickly chipped away at the dirt and rubble surrounding the crown, I found myself studying the other end of the cave.

The flickering flare light didn't quite reach that area, and the creeping sense of being watched was growing. The wind still circulated, but as I half raised a hand to call her back and give new directions, the shifter grunted, dragging my attention back to him.

He pulled the crown free and shook the remaining bits of dirt from it. It was surprisingly simple in design, with just the six points and the inset area at the front for the moonstone.

Linc glanced at me and made a give-me motion.

"Obey," Raen said, when I didn't immediately, "or I'll take great delight in taking the thing from your unconscious body."

I shot her a somewhat amused glance. "Which means you'd have the joy of carrying me back."

"Why carry when I can drag? They might want you alive, but don't be fooled into thinking that means healthy."

An illusion that had never crossed my mind. I handed the stone to the shifter and watched as he clicked it into place. Energy flickered across the crown's points, black lightning that indicated the crown was primed and ready to use.

Fuck, fuck, *fuck*.

The soft scratching echoed again. The pixie turned sharply around, her gun raised.

There was nothing visible. Nothing moving, either in the spluttering light of the flares or beyond.

But they were coming.

Not rats, as I'd seen in the dream.

The Annwfyn.

I tried to ignore the thick rise of terror and said, "We need to get out of here, before those flares die."

"I suspect you may be right." She grabbed the crown

from the shifter, shoved it into the backpack, and then slung it over her shoulder. "This way, quickly."

We retreated into the tunnel, moving as fast as the slippery conditions allowed. The flares' light warmed the tunnel wall for several meters, but the darkness soon reasserted itself once we got further in.

Flashlights were flicked on, but the bright puddles of light offered little comfort. Annwfyn were very adept at avoiding puddles.

The wind stirred around my fingers again. I tried to capture her, tried to hear her whispers and warning, to no avail.

Maybe because fear was everything. It was all I felt, all I could think about.

I risked a look behind. The visible flares were sputtering; even as I watched, one blinked out. In the faint light of those that remained, shadows loomed.

"Faster," Linc ground out. "We need to go faster."

He didn't shift shape, didn't fly away from us, even though he could have, and that was at least something. Raen broke into a run, and we followed, our steps echoing across the deep darkness.

The last flare must have gone out, because the air now vibrated with movement.

They were coming.

THIRTEEN

They hit hard and fast, and for several seconds there was nothing but chaos. Gunshots and shouts rang out, sharp sounds that were almost drowned by the screams and howls of the Annwfyn. A shadow hit me side-on and sent me crashing back into the wall. Pain shuddered through my body, and for a moment, I couldn't even breathe properly. Then the wind screamed a warning, and I shoved the pain aside and dropped low. The thick, yellowed claws that would have ripped out my throat whipped over my head and scoured a deep trench in the tunnel wall. I swore, twisted around, and kicked out at the Annwfyn's pale, spindly legs; there was a crack, and a deep snarl that was pain and fury, and the air was whipping down at me again. I had a vision of those wicked, dirt-stained claws descending and threw myself sideways; this time, the blow that would have removed half my face dug into my boot instead, tearing it off my foot and slashing down into skin.

I screamed, and suddenly the wind was there, in front of me, providing a barrier. I raised a hand and pushed it toward the Annwfyn, not sure it would work but out of other options.

The wind responded, lifting the Annwfyn off his feet and flinging him back down the tunnel. I scrambled to my feet, bit down on another scream of pain as warmth flooded across my injured foot, then heard a strange, gurgling sound and twisted around.

The Annwfyn had the shifter surrounded and were attacking him with tooth and claw. He was battering them with the end of his gun, but he might as well be using a feather. His left arm swung uselessly by his side, broken in at least a couple of places, and blood sprayed the air as chunks of his flesh went flying.

I swore, caught the wind, and flung it at the Annwfyn. It picked them up as one, smashed them into walls, and sent them tumbling back down the tunnel. I hobbled across to the shifter, dragged him upright, and tucked an arm under his. He made an incoherent sound that was filled with both agony and fear.

"Run," I said grimly. "You have to run."

His legs began moving, and we ran, as fast as we were able, up the dark tunnel. The pixie was nowhere in sight—even the glow of her flashlight wasn't visible. It was possible the Annwfyn had dragged her down and killed her, but I suspected it was more likely she'd abandoned us.

Which, given the crown was far more important in this situation than either my life or Linc's, was in some ways understandable.

But also unforgiveable.

The air whipped around me, and once again, she vibrated with movement.

I swore, but I couldn't go any faster, and even if I could, I wouldn't abandon the shifter. I couldn't. To do so would mean his death would be on my hands, and that was a curse I didn't want.

Which left me with one option.

I moved across to the wall, propped the shifter against it, and held him in place with one hand.

But as I gathered the air for another assault, a big hairy form appeared out of the darkness and bolted past me.

Sgott.

In bear form.

Tears stung my eyes, but the battle wasn't over yet.

His growl reverberated—fierce and deep and angry—and the Annwfyn shrieked in reply. The two hit, and the Annwfyns' screams of anger became howls of pain as the fury of a bear shifter in full berserker mode hit them.

Another shadow, long and strong, bolted past me. Light sputtered to life, outlining Cynwrig's familiar form as he tossed multiple flares around the melee, forcing the Annwfyn away from Sgott.

Hands grabbed me, turned me.

Lugh.

Relief hit so hard that my knees briefly buckled; it took all my remaining strength to keep them locked.

"We need to get out of here," he said urgently. "The flares will only hold them for so long."

"Take the shifter," I said. "He can barely walk."

Lugh handed me the flashlight and scooped up the shifter. "Go."

I went, as fast as I was able.

The sound of fighting stopped behind me, and footsteps echoed as the two men ran to catch up with us. Cynwrig scooped me up in one quick, easy movement and led the way while Sgott remained in bear form at our rear.

It was tempting—so very tempting—to relax into the

heady security of Cynwrig's arms and just let go, but there was a crown to retrieve, bad guys to catch and question, and until I made my rescuers aware of all that, I had to remain alert.

We wound our way back through the tunnel to the tomb room and then upwards. There was no sign of Raen, and I wondered how she'd managed to avoid the three men. They surely would have stopped her had they seen her, though that would probably have meant one of them staying behind with her. Her branch of pixie was rather adept at escaping.

We finally reached the cellar. Several battery-fed lamps had been set up here, and they were bright enough to deter any Annwfyn who might still have been following us.

Cynwrig slowed and glanced at me. Relief and anger burned in equal amounts in his bright eyes, though the latter was not aimed at me.

"Who did this?"

"That is the question of the evening." I glanced around as Sgott entered the room. He shifted to human form and strode toward me, strides long and fierce. "We need to get upstairs, and fast."

"Why?" Sgott growled, even as we moved on.

"Because we were brought here to find the crown—"

"We?" Sgott cut in. "Mathi's here?"

"He's upstairs being held hostage for my good behavior. We need to grab him, but we also need to track down the crown—"

"You found it?" Lugh said, voice incredulous.

"Yes, and right where my vision said it would be."

"Then where is it now?"

"In the hands of a Tàileach pixie—don't suppose you ran into her when you came down the tunnels?"

"No," Sgott growled, "we didn't."

I swore. "Then we need to find her before she can give it to her employers."

We raced up the steps and through the series of long corridors. Then, just as we reached the old kitchen, a single gunshot rang out.

My heart plummeted.

Fuck, not Mathi, please don't let it be Mathi.

"That came from the right," Sgott said. "Where's Mathi?"

"In the cells on the first floor, to the left."

"Right. Lugh, put the shifter down. You and Beth go get Mathi. Cynwrig and I will chase down that gunshot."

Cynwrig immediately placed me back on my feet, waited until I'd gained my balance, then dropped a quick kiss on the back of my hand and chased after Sgott.

Lugh placed the unconscious Linc on the floor, then swept me up. "How do you want to play this?"

I hesitated. "Do you trust me?"

"Is that a trick question?"

I smiled, despite our desperate situation. "If the cell door is open, scream and race in."

"That could get us both shot."

"It could if the wind doesn't answer me."

"A comment you'll need to explain once this is all over."

Once we all survived, he meant.

We raced swiftly through the lobby and up the stairs toward the long corridor of cells. Mathi's door was open, and my heart stuttered to a halt.

We couldn't be too late. We just couldn't ...

The wind surged in response to my desperate fear. I gathered her force around my fingers and then pushed it out, until Lugh and I were surrounded by a spinning, invisible vortex of incredible power.

As Lugh launched us through the doorway, yelling like a banshee, I unleashed the vortex.

The bear shifter stood in the middle of the room, a gun in his hand as he twisted around to face us. The vortex hit him, swept him up, and then smashed him against the wall so hard his head all but exploded.

The wind died, and my stomach rose. As his body slid to the ground, I punched Lugh's arm in warning, and he immediately released me. I staggered over to the corner of the room and vomited until there was absolutely nothing left.

"Gods," I croaked. "I hadn't intended—"

"You saved Mathi's life and ours." Lugh handed me a handkerchief. "I think that's all that really matters right now."

"But the shifter could have told us—"

Lugh gripped my shoulders and turned me around to face him, and then gently lifted my chin. "Listen here, sister mine, that man was armed, and we weren't. If we'd handled the situation any other way—if you'd done anything different—he would have killed Mathi and probably one of us."

"But I now have blood on my hands—"

"And you saved Mathi and that bird shifter. That more than evens out the blood ledger."

I hoped he was right, because none of us needed a blood curse dogging our steps right now.

I took a deep breath and nodded slowly. "You'd better check Mathi."

Lugh hesitated, his gaze sweeping my face, no doubt checking that I wasn't going to collapse the minute he released me, and then went over to Mathi and knelt beside the bed.

"His pulse is good and breathing is steady," he said after a moment. "I take it he's drugged?"

I nodded. Lugh grunted and hauled him off the bed and over his shoulders. "Let's get out of here."

I turned and led the way. My foot hurt like a bitch, but the bleeding had stopped, which was at least something.

Cynwrig appeared as we reentered the lobby. "The Tàileach is dead."

"And the crown?" I asked.

"Gone," he said grimly, "along with whoever shot the pixie."

I carried a tray of hot drinks over to the table and handed coffee mugs to Lugh, Sgott, and Cynwrig before placing my teapot down and tugging my chair a little closer to Cynwrig. He smiled and slipped his hand across the top of my leg, a caress that was as warm as it was comforting.

Twenty-four hours had now passed, and it was late in the evening, but this was the first time the four of us had been able to catch up. Sgott had been dealing with the fallout of the shooting, and I'd only been released from hospital a few hours ago. Healers could fix all manner of internal and external injuries, but the brain was a different matter entirely, and they'd been worried about concussion.

Mathi remained in hospital. While they'd healed his injuries, he'd had a severe reaction to the drug he'd been given, and they were keeping him in for observation for another twenty-four hours, just to be safe.

I poured myself a cup of tea and then glanced at Sgott. "I take it you've removed all the bugs from the tavern?"

He smiled. "Wouldn't be meeting here if we hadn't. We found three in your living area, one in the bedroom, and five scattered through the two tavern levels."

"I hope they had fun listening to absolutely nothing happening in the bedroom." My voice was wry. "Did your people have any luck following the trail of the spellcaster from the house?"

He grimaced. "We found her body in the woods about half a kilometer away from the sanatorium. Her name was Janice Whitewater, and she was a caster for hire with a string of minor misdemeanors behind her."

"I take it she was shot?"

He nodded. "No sign of the crown or anyone else. The search is ongoing."

I wasn't surprised, and I certainly didn't feel even a trickle of sympathy for their fate. They'd have no doubt done the same to me and Mathi once I'd done what they'd wanted.

"You were able to ID the bear shifter?" Lugh asked.

"The shifter hailed from one of the sleuths that lived in the wilderness areas around Fisherfield Forest, but initial questioning suggests he hasn't been sighted by them for years."

"I take it he hasn't a record, then?" Cynwrig asked.

"No, though he was not unknown to us, as he was employed as a bouncer at The Base and had been involved in a few skirmishes with patrons. Nothing chargeable, of course."

The Base was a nightclub that had something of a wild reputation and was therefore quite popular with the "edgier" portions of Deva's population.

"Did you find any evidence as to who shot the caster?" Lugh asked.

"No, but we did find another set of prints in the office." Sgott's gaze flicked to Cynwrig's. "They belong to Maran Gordan."

"Now there's a name I've not heard in quite a while," Cynwrig said, the warmth in his expression falling away. "Not since she double-crossed us on a deal some twenty years ago, in fact."

"You and quite a few others," Sgott said. "And given there's a warrant out for her arrest, she must be pretty sure her employers will be able to protect her if she's discovered."

"I doubt protection is their game," I said. "No matter how powerful she is, there's no spell that'll stop a bullet."

"Maybe not," Cynwrig said, "But there are certainly a number of them that can provide invisibility, and that's what Maran specializes in."

"Does she also specialize in body morphing spells?" I asked slowly, as the pieces of a puzzle snapped into place.

"Yes," Cynwrig said. "Why?"

The intensity of his gaze on mine made my skin prickle, and I wasn't entirely sure if it was desire or wariness.

"Because the person who broke in here the first time was using a concealment spell, which very conveniently shredded when he moved too fast and revealed his features." I glanced at Sgott. "What if those features were nothing more than a diversion?"

"It's possible," he said. "Did you see anyone when you gave chase?"

"Yeah—a thin woman with curly red hair huddled in an oversized coat." I returned my gaze to Cynwrig. "What does she look like?"

"Thin, bushy red hair, pale skin."

"Well, fuck. She was right there in front of me, and I just let her walk away."

"*That* sort of subterfuge is another of Maran's specialties." He squeezed my thigh lightly and desire stirred. Though, in truth, all I really wanted was to cuddle up in his arms and just let the tumultuous memory of the last few days fade away for a few hours. "Don't worry. I fell into the same trap."

"Why would she be involved in something like this, though?" Sgott asked. "It's not her usual stock in trade."

"What is her usual trade?" Lugh asked. "I take it she's not just a witch for hire?"

"No," Cynwrig said. "She specializes in antiquities. Or rather, the theft of them."

"Suggesting someone has hired her to help steal the Claws," Lugh said. "And that suggests someone knows a lot more about the location of the Claws than we do. Otherwise, they'd be hiring specialist researchers."

"How do we know that they haven't?" I asked.

He glanced at me thoughtfully. "True. There's not many of us, so I'll have a nose around and see what I can find."

"That still doesn't give us a reason why they're going after these Claws," Sgott said.

"You know, Janice said something odd when I asked her that same question." My gaze went to Cynwrig. "She said she could give me *five* good reasons … didn't you say the Annwfyn killed or snatched five women nearly six months ago?"

He stared at me for several seconds and then swore harshly. "Yes. But I can't believe—"

"You believed Jalvi was looking for the Claws to avenge her sister," I cut in. "Is it such a big step to think that the parents of the other victims would also seek a goddess's weapons of darkness to bring destruction down on the Annwfyn?"

"Extending darkness won't hinder the Annwfyn," Sgott said before Cynwrig could reply. "It helps them."

"Unless extending isn't their plan," Lugh said. "If the Claws jointly give the holder ultimate control over darkness —however unlikely that would seem to be—it would not only mean extending it, but also *banishing* it."

"Make it so that it was never dark, and the Annwfyn could never emerge," I whispered. "Fuck."

That had to be it. *Had* to be.

Cynwrig thrust to his feet. "I think we'd better go talk to the victims' families. Now, before this goes any further."

"Now laddie," Sgott said, even as he rose. "Don't you be going off half-cocked. It's not going to help the situation."

Cynwrig's fist clenched, and rage practically oozed from every pore of his skin. "These people attacked my sister. Do not tell me what to feel or how to react, Sgott."

Sgott smiled and gripped Cynwrig's shoulder. Tension rippled through Cynwrig's muscular body, but he otherwise didn't react to the touch.

"I know, laddie, and I'm sorry, but if we go charging in, we'll alert the others. We need to be strategic until we know for sure they're behind this plot."

Cynwrig stared at him for a few seconds and then nodded. "We nevertheless need to discover their whereabouts ASAP."

"On that, we agree." Sgott picked up his coffee and downed the rest of it in one gulp. "Beth, I think it's advisable that you are not alone for the foreseeable future."

Being with Mathi hadn't stopped them from attacking me, but I simply nodded. Sgott knew that as much as I did.

I watched them both walk out and then picked up my tea and took a sip. "So, brother mine, what's the plan?"

He grinned and leaned back in his chair. "What makes you think I've got anything more than protecting your ass planned?"

I gave him the look. The one that said "don't be daft."

He laughed. "You and I need to be doing a little investigative work ourselves."

"You don't believe they'll be able to track down the parents of the five who were killed?"

He raised an eyebrow. "Do you?"

"No, but I can't see how we're going to help that situation any."

"That's because we need to tackle the whole situation from a different angle."

I studied him for a moment, seeing the excitement bubbling in the background of his expression. "By researching?"

"No, dumbass. By breaking and entering."

I just about choked on my tea. "Sgott is *not* going to approve."

"He doesn't have to know. I am an antiquarian, remember, and not all my finds have been legal."

I couldn't help smiling. "That's not what you tell your bosses at the museum."

"My bosses are under no illusion as to how some relics come into my possession."

"So, where are we going to do this breaking and entering?"

"Where else? The very place all this started."

I stared at him for a second. "Nialle's place?"

He nodded. "Nialle uncovered something about the Claws. It sent him to France and got him killed. I haven't found anything at the museum, so that means it has to be at his apartment."

"His apartment was ransacked after he was murdered."

"And they obviously didn't find what they were looking for, because why else would they then come after me, and then you?"

They wouldn't. Not if Nialle had given them whatever information he'd found regarding Agrona's Claws

I took a deep breath and released it slowly. "When do you want to go?"

"Is there a better time than now?"

"I guess not." And at least Sgott and Cynwrig were otherwise occupied.

"I'll need to dash upstairs to grab my knives and phone first." Sgott *had* gotten my message and retrieved both, though the phone was deader than a doornail by the time I got them back at the hospital. "What about the Eldritch, though? They'll still be monitoring Nialle's place."

"Oh, don't you be worrying about them, sister mine. I thought of the perfect way of getting into Nialle's apartment without being seen."

There was something in the way he said that that had all manner of alarms going off.

"Lugh—"

He grinned and clapped a hand on my shoulder. "It'll be fine. Trust me. Have I ever led you astray?"

"Multiple times."

He laughed. "Go get your stuff."

I did so then followed him through the room and out the back door.

I hoped he knew what the hell he was getting us into.

And that it didn't involve tunnels or rats.

Also by Keri Arthur

.

Kingdoms of Earth & Air

Unlit (May 2018)

Cursed (Nov 2018)

Burn (June 2019)

The Outcast series

City of Light (Jan 2016)

Winter Halo (Nov 2016)

The Black Tide (Dec 2017)

Souls of Fire series

Fireborn (July 2014)

Wicked Embers (July 2015)

Flameout (July 2016)

Ashes Reborn (Sept 2017)

Dark Angels series

Darkness Unbound (Sept 27th 2011)

Darkness Rising (Oct 26th 2011)

Darkness Devours (July 5th 2012)

Darkness Hunts (Nov 6th 2012)

Darkness Unmasked (June 4 2013)

Darkness Splintered (Nov 2013)

Darkness Falls (Dec 2014)

.

Riley Jenson Guardian Series
Full Moon Rising (Dec 2006)

Kissing Sin (Jan 2007)

Tempting Evil (Feb 2007)

Dangerous Games (March 2007)

Embraced by Darkness (July 2007)

The Darkest Kiss (April 2008)

Deadly Desire (March 2009)

Bound to Shadows (Oct 2009)

Moon Sworn (May 2010)

Myth and Magic series
Destiny Kills (Oct 2008)

Mercy Burns (March 2011)

Nikki & Micheal series

Dancing with the Devil (March 2001 / Aug 2013)

Hearts in Darkness Dec (2001/ Sept 2013)

Chasing the Shadows Nov (2002/Oct 2013)

Kiss the Night Goodbye (March 2004/Nov 2013)

Damask Circle series
Circle of Fire (Aug 2010 / Feb 2014)

Circle of Death (July 2002/March 2014)

Circle of Desire (July 2003/April 2014)

Ripple Creek series

Beneath a Rising Moon (June 2003/July 2012)

Beneath a Darkening Moon (Dec 2004/Oct 2012)

Spook Squad series

Memory Zero (June 2004/26 Aug 2014)

Generation 18 (Sept 2004/30 Sept 2014)

Penumbra (Nov 2005/29 Oct 2014)

Stand Alone Novels

Who Needs Enemies (E-book only, Sept 1 2013)

Novella

Lifemate Connections (March 2007)

Anthology Short Stories

The Mammoth Book of Vampire Romance (2008)

Wolfbane and Mistletoe--2008

Hotter than Hell--2008

ABOUT THE AUTHOR

Keri Arthur, author of the New York Times bestselling Riley Jenson Guardian series, has now written more than fifty novels. She's won a Romance Writers of Australia RBY Award for Speculative Fiction, and five Australian Romance Writers Awards for Scifi, Fantasy or Futuristic Romance. She's also received a Romantic Times Career Achievement Award for urban fantasy. Keri's something of a wanna-be photographer, so when she's not at her computer writing the next book, she can be found somewhere in the Australian countryside taking random photos.

for more information:
www.keriarthur.com
keriarthurauthor@gmail.com